RADIANCE
A NOVEL

Grace Draven

Grace Draven
Grace.Draven1@gmail.com
http://gracedraven.com

Publisher's Note: This is a work of fiction. Names, characters, places, and incidents are a product of the author's imagination. Locales and public names are sometimes used for atmospheric purposes. Any resemblance to actual people, living or dead, or to businesses, companies, events, institutions, or locales is completely coincidental.

Book Layout ©2013 BookDesignTemplates.com
Cover Illustration © 2014 by Isis Sousa

Radiance/ Grace Draven. – 1st ed.
ISBN 978-1-5061197-1-7

This book is dedicated to those who inspire and those who make it happen:

Mel Sanders, Lora Gasway, Isis Sousa, Emma Ricks, Kim Sayre, Cheryl Schnitzer

Thank you.

CHAPTER ONE

Today was Ildiko's wedding day, and if she managed not to retch on herself or a guest, she'd consider the entire event a resounding success.

Her maids refused to meet her gaze while they laced her into her gown and twitched the train into perfect folds, but she'd caught their looks of pity mixed with horror from the corner of her eye. Ildiko told herself to ignore them. Arranged marriages were the fate of nearly all aristocratic Gauri women, each one made for power, for trade, for good of country. His Majesty, Sangur the Lame, had married off both his daughters to princes of foreign lands as part of the negotiations for access to ports and allies in war. The Gauri king's niece was no exception to the protocol, and Ildiko had always expected a similar fate. The only question was when—not if—it happened.

But you never expected a Kai groom.

The thought scraped across her mind. Saliva flooded her mouth as the nausea roiling in her belly threatened to surge into her throat. Ildiko closed her eyes and swayed where she stood on

1

the tailoring stool. A hand gripped her leg to steady her, and she opened her eyes to stare down at the royal dressmaker.

Worry lines gathered even more wrinkles into the woman's face. She spat the pins clamped between her lips into her free hand. "Are you all right, my lady?"

Ildiko nodded. She wouldn't shame herself or the Gauri court by falling apart before their Kai guests. She breathed deep to quell her fear. The time for tears and sickness had passed. She'd indulged in her terror earlier in the privacy of her bedroom. She might be chattel, but she would remain dignified.

Her future husband faced the same fate. With the gift of privilege came the burden of expectation. As the younger son of the Kai king, his duty was to marry in a way most beneficial to his people. He'd meet Ildiko for the first time as they stood before a flock of bishops and pledged their troth to each other.

A trickle of cold sweat slid down her back beneath the gown. As his wife, she'd have to bed him. No one ever heard of any living children born to a Kai and human couple, but that didn't matter. A consummated marriage acted as the blood seal on a contract, even if she never bore him children. If Sangur the Lame didn't think it might offend his future in-laws, he'd insist on a contingent of witnesses standing in the bridal chamber to verify the consummation and assure everyone the alliance he'd wrought through this arranged marriage was complete. But the Kai were not human, their culture different and mostly unknown to those outside their borders. Ildiko was grateful for their mystery, which prevented such a public humiliation.

The royal dressmaker tugged a few more times on her gown, snapped out orders to her assistant seamstresses to pick up pins, thread and needles and pronounced their work done. She helped Ildiko off the stool. "Come to the mirror and see, my lady. You look beautiful."

Ildiko followed her to the full length mirror standing in one corner of her room. The pale reflection looking back at her did nothing to cheer her, and for a moment she fancied she stared at a stranger.

The gown was a masterful creation of embroidered bronze silk that hugged her breasts, hips and thighs before flowing out into a skirt and train. The fabric followed the line of her shoulders but left her neck and collar bones bare. Long sleeves ended at points over her hands. Her hair was coiffed in an intricate style of braids woven together and fastened with jeweled pins. She wore the rich trappings of a woman of high station and great wealth.

She frowned at her image. "What a waste."

Behind her, the dressmaker blanched. "You don't like the gown, my lady?"

Ildiko reassured the woman she considered the gown perfect. "However, I think all this will be lost on my groom and his Kai entourage."

The other woman's lip curled in disgust. "Ugly bastards. All of them. What would they know of beauty?" She realized the insult in her remark. "I'm sure your groom will be different and appreciate how lovely you are."

The likelihood of that happening was small. Were she marrying someone other than a Kai, the dressmaker might be right. She only hoped she and her intended managed not to bolt in opposite directions when they first sighted each other.

She requested an hour of privacy before she had to present herself at court and sent the group of dressmakers and maids from the room. The scent of spring flowers from the gardens drifted through the chamber's open window, enticing her.

Ildiko would miss very little when she left with her new husband for his home. She was the king's niece, the orphaned child of his younger sister. Her place in the family insured a stately home, regular meals and fine clothes. It insured nothing else, and there was no love lost between her and her living relatives. This new marriage might offer nothing different, except a change in her place in court hierarchy. By marrying the prince, she became a duchess, a Kai *hercegesé*.

The window opened onto a panoramic view of the manicured gardens with their rolling swards of green grass, fanciful topiaries, and colorful borders of flowers. She would miss the gardens. They had been her sanctuary over the years, an escape from her harassing cousins and a means to assuage her loneliness.

If the Kai royal family had gardens, Ildiko suspected they were nothing like these. She imagined all manner of strange, macabre plants twisting and swaying as they grew out of exotic soil by moonlight and bloomed with menacing flowers that hid fangs amongst the petals. One didn't walk amongst such flora without armor. She shivered.

Her thoughts propelled her out of her room and down a short flight of stairs to a back hall leading to the gardens. Warm sunshine caressed her shoulders. Ildiko raised her face to the light and breathed deeply of honeysuckle and jasmine. The dressmaker would have a fit of the vapors when she saw the ruin done to her creation's hem, but the thought didn't stop Ildiko from journeying into the depths of her favorite place in all of Gaur. Besides, no one at the wedding would be looking at her hem. They'd be too busy gawking in horror at either the groom or the bride.

She strolled leisurely along a winding path that meandered past bubbling ponds filled with large goldfish as tame as dogs, regiments of poisonous foxglove in every color and hue, and clusters of orange butterfly vine draped over trellises and swarmed by hummingbirds. Willow trees hugged the shores of the larger ponds, creating canopies of green shade that sheltered ferns and silver-leafed lungwort. Ildiko had spent many a quiet hour as a child hidden behind a willow's drape, reading a pilfered book in the dappled light that spilled through the branches.

Stately oaks dotted the landscape, their great branches of rutted bark thick with leaves. She followed the path leading to one of the giants. She didn't visit this part of the garden often. The queen's roses grew here, and Ildiko avoided those places the queen favored. She felt safe enough visiting today. Fantine was too busy playing hostess to her guests or counting the treasure they'd brought as bride gift. Ildiko could admire the hundreds of rose bushes planted in clusters and lines in solitude.

Or so she thought. She turned a corner and halted. A figure, cloaked and hooded in black, stood motionless next to a dense patch of thorny roses the color of blood. It turned at the sound of Ildiko's steps. She inhaled a harsh breath. A pair of nacreous eyes, without iris or pupil, stared at her from the hood's shadowed depth. A long-fingered hand, gray-skinned as a corpse's and tipped with dark nails, lifted in silent greeting. Ildiko balanced on the balls of her feet, poised to flee. If she didn't know better, she'd believe she stumbled across a demon amidst the roses. This was no demon—despite appearances—but one of the Kai. And it would be the height of rudeness for her to run screaming from a future relative by marriage.

CHAPTER TWO

Brishen braced for an ear-pinning scream from his unexpected visitor or, if he was lucky, a quieter gasp and mad dash through the hedgerow to escape him. The Gauri woman who stared at him wide-eyed with her strange gaze did neither. He'd obviously startled her with his presence in the garden. She flinched away when he raised a hand in cautious greeting, but she didn't run.

"Forgive me, madam," he said softly. "I didn't mean to frighten you."

Most of the Kai party sent to witness the wedding and accompany the bride and groom on their return journey to Haradis had traveled to Pricid, the Gauri kingdom's capital, a fortnight earlier. They'd had time to adjust to the Gauris' appearances. Brishen and his personal escort had arrived only the previous day. Though he and some of his troop dealt with the Beladine humans neighboring his territorial borders, he didn't think he'd ever seen so many repellent-looking people gathered in one place.

Thank the gods he wore a hood that hid his expression; otherwise he might inadvertently give insult to his unintended companion. She was young—that much he could tell. To the human Gauri she might be beautiful or banal; to him she was profoundly homely. His upper lip curled in distaste at the sight of her skin. Pale with pink undertones, it reminded him of the flesh of the bitter mollusk Kai dyers boiled to render amaranthine dye.

Her bound hair burned red in the punishing sunlight, so harsh and so different compared to the Kai women with their silvery locks.

Her eyes bothered him most. Unlike the Kai, hers were layers of opaque white, blue ringed in gray and black pinpoint centers that expanded or contracted with the light. The first time he'd witnessed that reaction in a human, all the hairs on his nape stood straight up. That, and the way the contrasting colors made it easy to see the eyes move in their sockets gave the impression they weren't body parts but entities unto themselves living as parasites inside their hosts' skulls.

He was used to seeing the frantic eye-rolling in a frightened horse but not a person. If the parasite impression didn't repulse him so much, he'd think humans lived in a constant state of hysterical terror.

The woman crossed slender arms. Despite the odd skin and grotesque eyes, she had a lovely shape and regular facial features. Brishen began to bow, eager to take his leave of this awkward situation.

"What do you think of the royal gardens?"

Her question made him pause. She had a pleasant voice—even yet not toneless, low but not hoarse. Brishen cocked his head and studied her another moment before speaking. She'd lost the frightened hare look, and while he still had difficulty correctly reading the more subtle emotions in human faces, he could tell she watched him now with curiosity instead of fear.

Had she asked him what he thought of Sangur's armory, he might have waxed more eloquent. He shrugged. "There are plants and flowers and trees." He paused and offered her a pained smile she surely couldn't see within the depths of his hood. "And a lot of sunshine."

She motioned to him to follow her. He hesitated before falling into step beside her until she led him to a stone bench cast in the shade of an oak's thick branches. She sat and indicated he do the same. It was Brishen's turn to startle. During his short time in Pricid, his Gauri hosts had been civil, accommodating, and almost obsequiously polite. They were never friendly. This woman's affable manner surprised him. He sat, grateful for the relief from the bright summer light.

She turned to face him, her parasitic gaze scrutinizing every part of him from his booted feet to his hands resting on his knees to his eyes he knew glowed back at her from the hood's shadows. "Does the sunlight truly bother your eyes?"

He blinked. He'd expected her to ask his name or offer hers. He liked that she didn't. This brief anonymity offered a certain respite from formality. He was a prince of the blood, and the Gauri stepped lightly amongst Kai royalty. "We are a people of night. We see better in the dark. The moon is the sun to us; we live by her light."

"Yet you walk our gardens in midafternoon."

Brishen chuckled. "A guarantee that no other Kai will be about."

Her serious features relaxed into a wide smile. She possessed the teeth of a tiny horse--white and square except for two pairs of pathetic canines. He'd seen Kai toddlers with milk teeth sharper than those. He tried to focus on her words.

"Nor Gauri either. The royal household is far too occupied at the moment with its guests and the wedding."

The way she said "wedding"—in the same way someone might have said "execution" or "torture session"—made him sputter with laughter. He had no doubt he'd uttered the same word in the exact same tone recently.

She was a challenge to look upon without wincing, but he very much liked her wry humor. Until now, he'd wondered if most Gauri were only capable of speaking in monosyllabic sentences. His kin who'd come here before him had little good to say about them, finding fault in everything from their manner of dress to their food preferences. Brishen had no expectations about his bride, but he hoped she might possess a small amount of the same pleasant demeanor this woman exhibited.

He gave an exaggerated sigh. "A more tiresome affair of state I've yet to attend. Gauri and Kai each wondering who might eat the other first."

His companion's eyebrows rose. Her lips closed over her teeth, and she smiled archly. She pointed to his face and then to his hands. "I think the Kai, with their teeth and claws, have the advantage over the Gauri in that contest."

Brishen snorted. "True, but you can rest assured we don't find humans particularly appealing as a dinner item."

"Well then, that's good to know. I'm sure I taste awful." She lowered her gaze and smoothed the heavily embroidered silk of her gown over her knees. Brishen swore he heard a whisper of true relief in her gentle sarcasm.

She lifted her gaze once more. He twitched. Lover of thorns, but those eyes disconcerted him. "You don't have to answer of course, but do you think the Kai prince will hate his wife?"

She stunned him with the question. Brishen had always considered himself an agreeable man. He didn't envy his older brother's place as heir to the throne, understood his duty to his kingdom and never balked at the fact he was merely a pawn in the endless power machinations between empires. He assumed his future wife had no choice in the matter either. They were duty-bound by their stations.

"I think the prince expected to marry a Kai noblewoman and father children one day. He never imagined an arranged marriage with a human woman to seal a war and trade alliance between Bast-Haradis and Gaur. He might resent the circumstances thrust upon him, but I doubt he'll bear any ill will toward his future wife. She's as much a pawn in this as he is." Brishen frowned. "Unless the bride is a foul-tempered harpy."

He liked her laughter, a throaty chortle as if she found some additional secret mirth in the moment. She braced an elbow on the bench's back and rested her cheek in her palm, the pose striking in its casualness. "I'm sure her mother called her that a time or two, but she tries very hard to be pleasant."

They gazed at each other before she knocked him flat with another question. "You find me ugly, don't you?"

Brishen had faced abominations on the battlefield without flinching, leapt into the thick of the fighting against creatures born from the nightmares of lesser demons. Not once had he been tempted to run away in fear. Now, his leg muscles rippled with the urge to flee. He clenched his teeth instead, prayed he wouldn't start a war with their newest ally and answered honestly.

"Hideous," he said. "A hag of a woman."

Another peal of laughter met his words. Brishen wilted, relieved she took no insult in him so bluntly validating her assumption. He didn't even know her name, but he liked her and didn't wish to hurt her. Assured she wasn't planning to flounce off and send a pack of offended relatives after him, he turned the same question on her.

"And you," he said. "You don't think me a handsome man?"

She shrugged. "I've only seen your hands and eyes. For all I know, you're hiding the face of a sun spirit in that hood."

Brishen scoffed at the idea. "Hardly." He'd never lacked female company, and his people thought him well-favored. Certainly nothing as wretched as a sun spirit. He slid the hood back to his shoulders.

The woman's eyes rounded. She inhaled a harsh breath and clasped one hand to her chest. Her mollusk skin went a far more attractive shade of ash. She remained silent and stared at him until he raised a hand in question. "Well?"

She exhaled slowly. The space between her eyebrows stitched into a single vertical frown line. "Had you crawled out from under my bed when I was a child, I would have bludgeoned you to death with my father's mace."

Brishen rocked back on the bench and howled. When he finished and wiped the tears from his eyes, the woman was staring at him with her horse-toothed smile in place. He cleared his throat. "I don't know whether that's a testament to my looks or to your penchant for violence."

"The first. If you visited me, I'd have to cover all the mirrors in my house or replace a lot of cracked glass. You could put a pack of wolves to shame with those teeth."

He snapped his teeth together in a feral grin. She didn't draw away from him. "At least I have all my teeth, which is more than I can say for a lot of the Gauri men—and women. Besides, I'd rather look like I can bay instead of whinny."

They laughed together then until the woman's features turned somber. "Thank you for not lying about what you thought of my appearance. You might have a face to turn my hair white, but your honesty is handsome."

She charmed and fascinated him, and Brishen wished he had the leisure to know her better. But there was no time. He married at dusk when both human and Kai eyes could see each other clearly and recoil at the sight.

Voices in the distance carried across the green lawn and into the oak's shaded sanctuary. The woman rose and scraped her hands across the imaginary wrinkles in her skirts. "I have to go. I am missed."

Brishen rose as well and captured her hand, surprised at its warmth when he had expected cold, flaccid flesh. She didn't try to break free of his clasp as he lifted her fingers and brushed his lips over her knuckles. "I have enjoyed our chance meeting, madam." He released her and bowed.

She returned a brief curtsey and a last smile. "As have I, sir. You have lessened my worries. We'll meet again." She turned and hurried toward the voices growing ever closer.

He might glimpse her at the wedding, but there would be no chance for a second conversation. Brishen called after her. "What is your name?"

Her voice drifted back on a hot breeze, raising his suspicions and his hope. "Ildiko. I am Ildiko." She disappeared behind a hedgerow.

Brishen stared at the path she'd taken, her figure no longer visible. Surely, his luck did not run this true. His Gauri bride was named Ildiko.

CHAPTER THREE

"You make a passable bride, Ildiko and will adequately fulfill your duty to the kingdom and our family." Queen Fantine sniffed as she cast a critical eye over her niece's appearance. "And don't forget that duty extends to the bedchamber. It doesn't matter that he's practically a hobgoblin. You're not to jeopardize this alliance by denying your new husband."

Ildiko clenched her jaw so hard her temples throbbed. Her aunt had repeated this same admonishment so many times, Ildiko could recite it in her sleep. If she said it one more time, Fantine would find herself chewing on a mouthful of one of Ildiko's beaded slippers.

A soft rap on the receiving room door drew the queen's attention away from her. "Enter," she called out.

The door cracked open, admitting a wide-eyed court page. To Ildiko, he looked as if he'd eaten a dozen lemons whole. He bowed to Fantine. "Your Majesty, His Royal Highness, Brishen Khaskhem of Bast-Haradis wishes to speak with the Lady Ildiko." He paused. "Alone."

Ildiko's annoyance became trepidation. She laced her fingers together to hide their trembling and turned to fully face the door. Beside her, Fantine bristled in outrage.

15

"I think not. It violates all customs and proper conduct. He can speak to her after the marriage is proclaimed official. The wedding is in less than half an hour anyway. He can wait."

A gray hand tipped with pointed nails curled over the page's shoulder. The man gave a yelp and leapt to the side, leaving space for a cloaked figure to stride through the opening. The queen and the attendants gasped as one. All but Fantine dropped into curtsies as the Kai prince bowed respectfully before her.

"Your Majesty, I beg your indulgence. A private moment with my bride, please."

Ildiko wobbled in her curtsey. That voice! She recognized that voice. The cloak was different than the one he'd worn in the garden—still muted tones of black and gray but lavishly embroidered and cut more for ceremonial use than everyday wear. Amongst the vibrant roses, he'd been a shadow. Here in the receiving room, backlit by the western sun's fiery descent, he was a featureless silhouette.

She straightened to stand silent and impassive next to Fantine. The queen scowled, her expression carving meandering rills into the pale mask of her face paint. "This is improper, sir, prince or not. Can't it wait?"

Ildiko slid a surprised glance to her aunt. That Fantine wouldn't just order the Kai prince to leave at once spoke volumes. She might counsel her niece to death on duty and the importance of this alliance, but she was no hypocrite. She wouldn't jeopardize it either and afforded Brishen an unusual leniency with her question.

The prince obviously knew he held the upper hand. "No, Your Majesty; it cannot. I ask only a little of her ladyship's time."

"You will be late for your own wedding," Fantine cautioned.

"I assure you, we will not." Brishen remained exquisitely polite and steadfastly determined.

The queen's eyes narrowed. She shot a warning look at Ildiko who had no trouble interpreting its message. *Watch your tongue.* Ildiko nodded. Fantine motioned to the maids who lined up behind her like infantry. "You have a quarter hour. No more." She swept out of the room on a tide of dignified annoyance. The maid last in line turned, gave Ildiko a pitying glance, and closed the door behind her.

As soon as they were gone, Ildiko broke into a smile. "It's you." She didn't bother hiding the relief in her voice.

The prince closed the distance between them and pulled back his hood, once more revealing lamplight yellow eyes set deep in their sockets, sharp-boned features cast in shades of slate, and a toothy smile that made her lock her knees against the urge to leap away from him. He reached for her hand. Ildiko didn't hesitate and placed her palm in his, still startled by the unexpected warmth of his skin. If she closed her eyes, she could easily imagine his touch as that of a Gauri suitor's. He brushed his lips lightly across her knuckles a second time and released her.

"Are you disappointed?" That lambent gaze gave nothing away other than a hard squint as a shaft of sunlight speared a window and glanced along his profile.

Ildiko led him to a dimmer part of the chamber where candles provided a gentler light. "Relieved, not disappointed." She gestured to a nearby table holding glasses and a decanter of wine. "Can I offer you a drink?"

Brishen shook his head, the tiny braids woven into his long black hair swinging with the movement. He shrugged his cloak off his shoulders so that it draped down his back. The motion revealed ceremonial armor of blued plate over layers of rust and brown silk. A sheathed sword hung at his hip. Like those of his kin who guested in the castle, he was tall and lithe, every movement an exercise in grace and economy.

Ildiko tilted her head to one side. "You knew I was your intended before you came here, didn't you? How?"

His eyebrows arched. "You gave me your name when I asked. Remember?"

"There are several Ildikos living here. It's a common enough name. I could have easily been a servant."

Brishen chuckled and pointed at her. "In that fine gown? Hardly." He flashed his fanged smile. Ildiko didn't lock her knees this time. "I just knew. Call it instinct." He snapped his fingers with a click of nails. "Or Kai magic. We're all born with a touch of it, you know."

She shook her head, her own lightheartedness giving way to worry. "No, I didn't know. I know very little about those who will become my people once we're married."

He stared at her for a silent moment. *Owl's eyes*, she thought. He and his folk had the eyes of nocturnal hunters, but without pupils, just the glowing luminosity that mesmerized her like a mouse.

"I will teach you," he said.

She blinked, startled out of her stupor by his reply and completely forgetting the thread of conversation. "Teach me what?"

He had thin lips with a natural downturn emphasized by diagonal grooves on either side of his mouth. It gave him a grim look, except when he smiled, which he did now. "About the Kai. If you wish to learn, I will teach you. Far better than any wrong-headed Gauri book written about us."

A wash of relief poured through her, along with a kindling of hope. Her bridegroom wasn't Gauri; he wasn't even human. He was, however, congenial and gracious. She had proclaimed his appearance ghastly and his honesty handsome. Ildiko still stood by both opinions. She could have done infinitely worse. More than a few Gauri women had the misfortune to marry human men with handsome faces and ghastly souls.

"That's generous of you. I intend to hold you to your offer," she said. Her curiosity about his visit remained. "I've led you astray from your purpose. What did you wish to speak with me about?"

Brishen clasped his hands behind his back, and Ildiko had the distinct impression he braced himself to approach an uncomfortable subject. "My question is a delicate one, and I mean no insult by its bluntness. Have you thought of the consummation?"

Ildiko's stomach undulated against her ribs. She fought down a mortified blush and sought to disguise it by a disdainful rolling of her eyes. Brishen took a quick step back. "*Everyone* has been thinking of the consummation," she said. "I can hardly escape all the well-meaning advice, sympathetic pats on the arm, and suggestions for various tricks to employ for how to lie back and think of duty to king and country." She gave him a wry smile. "The most popular advice is to make sure the room is so dark I won't be able to see my hand—or yours for that matter—in front of my face."

Brishen's shout of laughter echoed throughout the room before he clamped down on his mirth and settled for a wide grin and luminous eyes that glistened. "I've been told something similar, only we should consummate at noon, when I'll be virtually blind."

Ildiko's muffled her own laughter behind her hand. "May the winged god Bursin save us from so much helpful guidance."

The laughter faded but their smiles remained. Brishen's thinned a little. "What do you want to do, Ildiko?"

He had asked a question Ildiko thought she'd never hear in her lifetime. No one ever asked her what she wanted; they only told her what she was to do and say. For a moment she was struck dumb. He waited patiently as she gathered her thoughts. "May I be honest, Your Highness?"

He snorted. "In private, call me Brishen. It's a decent enough name."

"It's a fine name. Were you actually born during a rainstorm?" Though he didn't seem as volatile or violent as a storm, his name fit him. Ildiko suspected his easy nature cloaked a character as strong as crucible steel.

Brishen nodded. "You're leading me astray again, Ildiko. To answer your first question, yes. I not only desire your honesty, I demand it." He shrugged. "Besides, I think it a little late to tiptoe around each other, don't you? I've called you hideous, and you've expressed your opinion of my looks by declaring them worthy of a skull-crushing. I doubt we'll offend each other's vanity at this point. Speak your mind."

Ildiko placed her faith in his reasoning and said "I like you, Brishen, but can we delay the bedding? It's not even necessary, really. I can't bear you children, and I'm told the Kai royal line is secure. You have how many nephews?" She clasped her hands so tightly together that the beds of her fingernails went white.

"A veritable litter. Six at last count." Brishen bowed. "I accede to your wishes, madam."

Ildiko forgot propriety, dignity and all reserve. She lunged at Brishen and wrapped her arms around his neck in a tight embrace. He went rigid in her hold; she didn't care. "Thank you!" She gave him a quick peck on the cheek and let him go before he could either free himself or hold her to him.

He inclined his head as another small smile curved his mouth. "Believe me when I say it is I who should be thanking you."

Ildiko returned his smile, then followed his gaze as it drifted past her shoulder and caught. She turned and saw the full length mirror standing in the last rays of afternoon sun. Brishen came to stand beside her and the two stared at their reflections amidst a fine shimmer of golden dust—red-haired Gauri woman and glowing-eyed Kai prince.

Brishen addressed their images. "We'll manage well enough together, Ildiko of Gaur."

She briefly touched his shoulder. "I believe you, Brishen of Bast-Haradis."

A hard pounding on the door warned them their private meeting was over. Brishen presented his arm to Ildiko. "Ready to get shackled, madam?"

She rested her hand in the crook of his elbow. "Try not to smile too widely, Your Highness. You'll scare the children in the crowd."

CHAPTER FOUR

B rishen glanced at his new wife who slouched in the saddle as she rode beside him. They traveled with a party of two dozen Kai toward Bast-Haradis's eastern borders and the capital of Haradis. A half moon, scudded by fast-moving clouds, glimmered above them. Ildiko's hair shone gray instead of red in the moonlight, her face wan and drawn from lack of sleep.

He'd tried to coax her into the small wagon that held a pallet and supplies so she could sleep during the journey. She flatly refused. "Your days are to be mine now. I need to adjust as soon as possible." She'd punctuated that declaration with a successive trio of yawns.

Brishen wagered she wouldn't make it to dawn but had a horse readied for her anyway. He, his bride, and his fellow Kai had taken to the road right after the wedding banquet ended.

Of the many weddings Brishen had attended during his lifetime, his had been the most ridiculous. The ceremony itself had been a proclamation of unification. Judging by the crowd's reaction—both Gauri and Kai—it might as well been a declaration of war. Hands had gone to sword pommels on both sides, and each group watched the other, at the ready to hurl themselves across the flower-strewn aisle and cross blades. His kin were easily outnumbered by Gauri court warriors twenty to one.

Numbers alone guaranteed that if such a fight broke out, it would be bloody but also brief.

Considering the Gauri had pursued this alliance with zeal, and the Kai had accepted with enthusiasm, he could only guess that such an acrimonious response to his union with Ildiko had been the gut reaction of two peoples who knew very little of each other and resented giving up one of their own to those they found loathsome.

He might not be able to read expression in her ghoulish eyes, but he had no trouble interpreting the worry lines creasing his bride's brow. He didn't automatically flinch this time when she glanced at him. "Bursin's wings, Brishen. We'll never get through the banquet without the spilling of blood."

She was right, and he wracked his brain for a way to defuse the tense situation. The air thickened to a simmering broth of hostility when the Gauri bishops proclaimed their union blessed and final. Brishen took both of Ildiko's hands, leaned forward and pressed a soft kiss to her cheek. She might have mollusk-pink skin, but she was warm and smelled of temple incense. He stepped back and flashed a quick grin.

Her hands jerked in his grasp before she arched an eyebrow. "Wolf," she said softly.

"Horse," he replied just as quietly.

Ildiko's lips twitched before she finally gave in and let loose a peal of laughter. The sound was magic, more powerful than any sorcerer's spell, more startling than the roll of a Gauri's eyes. Both the Gauri court and the much smaller Kai contingent visibly relaxed. Hands dropped from pommels, stiff shoulders relaxed and nearly everyone stared at the newly wedded couple as if they were mad.

Brishen took her in his arms and squeezed her until she squeaked. "Well done, princess," he whispered in her ear. "Well done."

The threat of a brawl still lingered, despite the obvious mutual acceptance between bride and groom. Brishen shuddered in the saddle as he recalled the banquet.

Until then, he and his fellow Kai had eaten dishes prepared by a Kai cook Brishen's mother insisted they take with them. The Gauri royal family had willingly offered a portion of the sprawling kitchens so the Kai chef could prepare meals for his people. Brishen had thought it a wagonload of pretentious nonsense and the complaints from his people about Gauri food juvenile rants until he caught his first whiff of a Gauri dinner being prepared and almost retched. His cousin, Anhuset, had cast him a self-satisfied smirk. "I told you," she said in a smug voice.

Oh, how right she had been. At the banquet, he'd sat beside Ildiko through interminable and insincere toasts of happiness to the couple. The wine and ale at least had been exceptional. The food was another matter.

There had been a moment prior to the wedding when he'd feared a revolt from his kinsmen and a possible hericide. He'd gathered the members of his entourage in his guest chambers for an impromptu meeting.

"We need to show good faith toward our hosts. We'll eat what they prepare at the dinner following the wedding."

There had been hisses and cries of protest from every Kai. Anhuset's lip curled in disgust. "Have you seen the food these people eat? If it isn't already refuse, the way they prepare it turns it into refuse. I wouldn't feed it to a starved mongrel."

Brishen didn't budge. "Someone rip out your backbones while you waited for me to arrive?" he snapped. That had silenced them all. "It's one meal. You're Kai warriors, war-trained and battle-tested. You can choke down a bowl of their soup and smile."

"The first time I smiled at a Gauri nobleman, I think he pissed himself." Anhuset's comment heralded muffled laughter. She inclined her head toward Brishen. "You are our lord and prince. We follow you."

Brishen had narrowed his eyes at her. A challenge cloaked in obeisance. They followed him. That meant they expected him to be the first to try every dish before they did. As their leader, it was a foregone conclusion. The role of leadership carried the burden of setting an example; he'd never turned away from that expectation.

He heartily regretted the idea the moment a servant placed a steaming plate of brown ooze accompanied by something that reminded him of a small frozen horse dropping. Ildiko sat next to him at the high table. She leaned close to whisper in his ear.

"It's a stew made with the king's own herd of cattle." She pointed to the brown thing. "That is a potato. Watch."

Ildiko split her own potato thing lengthwise, revealing two smoking slabs of pale inner flesh. The smell wafting to his nostrils made him think of wet dirt. She used her fork to eviscerate it into a heap of glistening mush. He was sure he just witnessed the brutal mutilation of a giant cooked larva. Brishen made a low choking sound and gripped the arms of his chair when she forked a small mound into her mouth.

His kinsmen watched him from their places at the lower tables, their plates untouched as they waited for him to follow his own edict. He took several shallow breaths, followed Ildiko's lead, butchered the larva-potato and took a hesitant bite.

Grainy, soft and tasteless, it sat on his tongue, swelling in his mouth until he thought he'd gag. Once more Ildiko leaned close.

"Brishen, there will be a riot if you spit it out."

He clamped his lips tightly closed and swallowed. There wasn't enough wine or ale in the world to kill the revolting smear coating his tongue, but he drained his goblet and Ildiko's before signaling a servant for more. The Kai continued to watch him, and he glared at every one of them until they picked up their own utensils and braved their potatoes.

Their reactions mirrored his. He'd have to sleep with one eye open and his hand wrapped around a dagger for the next fortnight or find one rammed between his shoulders in revenge. A tug on his sleeve made him turn his attention back to Ildiko.

"I'm sorry, Brishen. Is it that bad?" He heard the sympathy in her voice and patted her hand to reassure her. Bad was an understatement, but he shook his head and lied through his fangs. "No. I've dealt with worse."

He'd eat those words as well over the next three torturous hours. The stew had been as vile as the potato, but neither compared to the following courses of perfectly good eels ruined as they curled in a gelatinous mold studded green with herbs, guinea fowl roasted and seasoned with some concoction that convinced him the royal cook wasn't a cook but a necromancer who ground the bones of the dead and mixed them with the pepper. The cheese plate almost did him in, and he had to ask Ildiko twice if the ones speckled a greenish-blue weren't actually bits and pieces of fermented corpse. Her explanation of how the cheese was made had him wishing they'd served fermented corpse instead.

He persevered and choked down some of everything, each bite followed by a generous swallow of wine. His kinsmen did as Anhuset promised and ate their servings, murder in their eyes as they glared at him over the rims of their goblets.

His fervent prayers to every god who might listen were answered when King Sangur declared the banquet finished and made a final toast. There was no dancing to follow. Any other time, and Brishen would have been disappointed. The Kai loved to dance. Every celebration had dancing, and it wasn't at all unusual for the celebrants to dance until they collapsed from exhaustion.

Now he was just thankful he didn't have to do more than rise and escort his new wife out of the room to the bridal chamber prepared for them. His stomach roiled, hating him as much as his fellow Kai did at the moment.

Ildiko squeezed his hand as the Gauri maids waited to divest her of her gown. She waved them off and turned to him. "There's no reason to stay any longer in Pricid, Brishen. I have no quarrel if you wish to leave tonight."

His ugly, great-hearted bride could obviously read his thoughts. He cupped her face with his hands and kissed her forehead. "Are you sure, Ildiko? Don't you wish to tell your family goodbye?"

She plucked at his sleeve, and her mouth curved down. Grief. An old grief. Brishen was learning to read his wife's expressions the way she read his thoughts. "I said goodbye to my family when

I prayed at my parents' tombs. There's no reason for me to linger here."

With that, he left her to have the servants gather those things she'd already packed and load them into the wagon that would accompany them to Haradis. He found the rest of the Kai gathered in a small courtyard, sharing pitchers of wine between them.

They rose together at his entrance and bowed. Anhuset approached him.

"I hate you," she said.

He shrugged. "I'll live."

"After that vile meal we all choked down for you, don't bet on it, cousin."

Brishen hid a smile. Anhuset was closer to him than his sibling had ever been. She was also his lieutenant and second-in-command of his troop. Deadly in combat and fiercely loyal to him, her death threats were empty one. He remained wary though. She'd have no compunction trying to beat him bloody if he annoyed her too much.

"My wife wishes to leave now," he said.

His eyes widened as the courtyard exploded into a frenzy of activity and several enthusiastic toasts to the new *hercegesé*. Ildiko had scored her first victory with her Kai family, and she wasn't even here to witness it.

They were loaded, saddled and on the road as the moon began its descent toward the dawn. Normally he rode at the head of his contingent, but this journey was different. With Ildiko's dower wagon along, they'd have to travel the main road through bandit country. Brishen's first duty was to protect his wife, and he rode beside her, surrounded by two dozen armed Kai. He was armored himself and bristling with weaponry. Ildiko hadn't balked when he helped her buckle on one of Anhuset's breastplates.

"Is it so dangerous then?" She chewed on her lip and stared down at the armor encasing her torso.

Brishen adjusted the buckles and checked the seams at the shoulders to make sure she was comfortable. "It can be. It's a heavily traveled trade road with caravans ripe for the picking." He handed her the traveling cloak her maids had set aside earlier. "Don't worry, Ildiko. They'll think twice about attacking us. We're not tinkers, and we're heavily armed. It's not only the Gauri who know of the Kai fighting skills."

She'd been awkward in the armor and shy around his kinsmen. They had averted their eyes when she first approached them but bowed low and offered their congratulations to her, along with a salute of loyalty.

Owl hoots accompanied the creak of wagon wheels and the clop of horse hooves, along with the rustle of night creatures that hunted in the forest bordering both sides of the trade road. Ildiko's eyes were closed, and she began to cant in the saddle, sliding toward Brishen. He nudged his horse against hers.

"Ildiko, wake up."

She opened her eyes, the ever-changing pupils expanded to swallow the blue irises. "Is it morning?" she asked in a slurred voice.

Brishen slid further back on the saddle pad, slipped his arms around Ildiko and lifted her from her saddle. He plopped her in front of him. "Not morning yet, but you're about to fall off your horse. If you won't sleep in the wagon, you can ride with me."

She nodded and nestled into the cove of his arms, metal armor clanking between them.

The Kai prince held her against him, learning her warmth and her scent. The feel of her was no different from the Kai women he'd embraced. She was just as warm, her oddly colored skin just as smooth, her hair equally soft. With her asleep, he could tilt his head and gaze at her profile without the distraction of her eyes.

He'd observed the noblemen of the Gauri court as their gazes followed Ildiko during the wedding ceremony. While Brishen didn't find her beautiful, it was obvious to him the Gauri men did. Still, he didn't regret this union. Ildiko was unique and witty, and he enjoyed her company. It was a promising start.

Brishen settled her closer to him. He stiffened suddenly in the saddle at a whisper of sound. "Shields!" he bellowed and shoved a startled Ildiko toward his mount's neck.

CHAPTER FIVE

Ildiko woke abruptly to a mouthful of horse's mane and the weight of Brishen's body smashing hers to the saddle. The air around her hung thick and dark, and it took her a moment to realize she sheltered with Brishen beneath the dome of his shield. Something struck the metal with a hammering ring. Brishen rocked sideways, his arm and shoulder flexing against her side as he absorbed the impact of the blow.

Ildiko clutched the pommel as the animal shied and pranced beneath her. Another hammer blow struck the shield. She gasped as she was suddenly swung to the ground and just as quickly encircled by an armored wall of Kai soldiers. Their armor glinted dull and their eyes shone bright in the dying moon's fading light.

She yelped as a hand pushed her to the ground. "Stay down, Your Highness!" a female voice commanded.

Ildiko didn't protest as a chorus of twangs broke from the trees, followed by a volley of black splinters that arced into the lightening sky before falling toward them. She crouched, covering her head with her arms. Metal rang on metal as arrow points struck shield faces.

They were under attack, and what very little she could see from her lowered position behind the barricade of Kai protectors, they were pinned in place, unable to flee or even engage the enemies who sheltered in the trees.

33

That soon changed. Horse's hooves echoed from the forest depths. They were joined by battle cries and screams of pain.

The road where they stood exploded into chaos. Men dressed for secrecy and ambush bolted into the open, pursued by newly arrived Kai cavalry in support of their brothers and sisters. The shield circle around Ildiko broke. She was jerked to her feet and came face to face with one of the Kai women she'd seen at the wedding. Brishen had introduced her as his cousin Anhuset. Those nacreous eyes stared at her unblinking. "Follow me, Highness. Step lively."

Ildiko recognized the voice—and its authority—and sprinted alongside the woman until they reached the supply wagon.

Anhuset tugged her down. "Under the wagon, Highness. Stay out of sight and don't move."

She didn't give Ildiko a chance to argue but bodily shoved her beneath the wagon frame. Ildiko dropped to her stomach. From her flattened vantage point, she saw mostly running feet. The Kai woman stayed close and was soon joined by three more of her compatriots.

Ildiko searched for Brishen in the melee as their party, no longer outnumbered, clashed with their attackers. She glimpsed him fighting back to back with another Kai warrior. They faced a group of bandits. Brishen's partner fought with sword and shield. Brishen, however, fought as no Gauri nobleman ever would.

He wielded a small bearded axe in one hand and a hunting knife in the other. The knife's blunt side was braced against the line of his forearm, the sharpened edge faced out. Brishen moved as all his kind did, quick and nimble as a cat. He slashed and stabbed with the knife, cut and cleaved with the axe, using the beard to hook his opponent off his feet.

Ildiko prayed for his safety, for all their safety. She abruptly lost sight of him as a wave of bandits rushed her guardians. Anhuset answered with an eerie war cry. She and her companions leapt at their attackers. Ildiko huddled behind one of the wagon wheels and peered between the spokes.

She wanted to help, but she knew nothing of combat and was already a hindrance to those who would guard her. Except for her eating knife tucked into her belt pouch, she was weaponless. The best she could do was follow Anhuset's instructions: stay out of sight and out of the way.

Her heart pounded in her ribs, and she tasted the bitter flavor of fear on her tongue. She gasped when something grabbed her ankle and yanked. Ildiko clutched the spokes and stared over her shoulder. She screamed at the sight of a bandit, filthy, bedraggled and splashed with blood, clawing his way up her skirts.

She kicked at him, managing to clip him in the chin. He jerked back with a howl before lunging at her a second time. Ildiko scuttled on her backside and elbows from the wagon's compromised shelter.

She stumbled to her feet and found herself standing in the middle of the battle. Her Kai protectors fought and wrestled with the enemy, unaware Ildiko's hiding spot had been discovered. She lifted her hem, prepared to run, though she had no idea which way she'd go. The bandit who had attacked her made the decision for her when he rounded the wagon and stalked her, waving a knife and sporting a leer that promised a gruesome death.

Ildiko pivoted on her heel to flee in the opposite direction. She never got the chance. A draft of air buffeted the side of her face and fluttered strands of her hair. A dull crack sounded behind her, and she turned to watch her stalker fall to his knees, an axe blade sunk deep in his forehead. His eyes were wide—fixed—as if he didn't quite believe Death had found him so suddenly, before he fell backward and lay still in the dirt.

Ildiko whipped around to find Brishen running toward her. He grabbed her one-armed around the waist and lifted her off her feet, never breaking stride as he ran for safety. "Not the wedding present I intended for you, wife," he said on shortened breaths. "I'll make it up to you later."

CHAPTER SIX

They lost only three in the attack. Brishen considered it three too many, and the sorrow over their deaths weighed heavily on his mind. The first, Kroshag, had been the middle son of the royal family's steward and one of the first to volunteer under Brishen's command. Neima, the second to fall beneath a fatal arrow shot, had obsessed all the way from Haradis to Pricid over the challenge of dowering twin daughters. Her children would marry without their mother's presence now.

Brishen grieved hardest for Talumey. Young, eager to show his worth, loyal to a fault, he'd nearly turned himself inside out with excitement at being chosen as part of the prince's personal escort to the Gauri capital. Brishen promised himself he'd personally deliver Talumey's mortem light to his mother.

He abandoned his melancholy thoughts when Anhuset approached him. The spread of a blinding dawn backlit her form and bathed the dead behind her in citrine light.

Anhuset's mouth was set in a tight line, and she stared at him with narrowed eyes. Brishen leapt back, shocked when she fell to her knees before him. The activity in the road camp ceased. All fell silent.

She bowed her head and offered her sword to him with both hands. "I have failed you, Your Highness. My life is forfeit as is my mortem light." She spoke to the ground in a voice thick with shame.

Brishen gaped at her. "What are you talking about?"

Anhuset's head remained bowed, the sword still offered. "I was tasked to protect the *hercegesé*. I failed. Were it not for you, she'd be dead."

Brishen scowled. His cousin had obviously tapped into the small cask of spirits stowed away on the supply wagon; otherwise he couldn't fathom how she'd arrived at such a ridiculous conclusion. He had been the one who saved Ildiko from her attacker, but through no fault of Anhuset's. She was a fighter of exceptional prowess, respected throughout their military forces for her bravery and her skill, but she was not the goddess of war.

She and the two Kai who guarded Ildiko at the wagon had been overwhelmed by the number of bandits attacking them. They'd fought hard and fought well but were heavily outnumbered. There was no way Anhuset could have spotted the man sneaking under the wagon without turning her back on her opponents and having her head separated from her shoulders for the effort.

He stared down at her, noting the way her silvery hair shimmered with the light of the sun instead of the moon. He turned and found Ildiko a small distance from him, sitting on a tree stump, heavy-eyed and slumped with fatigue. A guard of grim-faced Kai surrounded her, weapons drawn and at the ready.

"Ildiko." She raised her head wearily. "Come here, please," he said in Common tongue.

She rose, dusted off her skirts and joined him in front of the kneeling Anhuset. She frowned as heavily at the sight as he had. "What's wrong?"

He gestured to Anhuset who still refused to look up from the ground. "My lieutenant wishes for me to execute her for failing to protect you."

"What?"

Brishen didn't need to understand all the finer subtleties of Gauri expressions. Ildiko's exclamation was telling enough. She was aghast at the idea. He had no intention of killing his cousin, especially for a nonexistent offense, and his was the final word in the matter. Still, Kai protocol demanded his role in Anhuset's fate be a secondary, albeit final one.

Ildiko sputtered, her peculiar gaze flitting back and forth between him and the silent Anhuset. "That's just sil—" She clamped her lips closed before she completed the word, for which Brishen was thankful. He agreed with his wife that Anhuset's request was silly, but his cousin's pride was great, and he'd seen her shoulders stiffen at Ildiko's shuttered remark.

"Anhuset believes she has failed in her duty to me by not protecting you from the man who found you beneath the wagon." Brishen kept his voice and expression bland. "However, the alleged offense isn't against me. You are the one most affected by her actions. What say you? Do you perceive insult and wish for punishment?"

Ildiko's eyebrows arched, and she tilted her head in such a way that he easily translated her silent *Are you serious about this?* He nodded, and she rolled her eyes. A mass shudder rippled through every Kai witnessing the exchange between them.

Ildiko paused for several moments before speaking. "I find no offense. She did her duty and protected me from those who meant us all harm. There were many bandits; there was only one

Anhuset." She flashed an equine smile. "Who fought better than three Gauri."

Murmurs of approval and agreement rose amongst the Kai. Anhuset stood, her chin raised. Brishen caught the glimmer of growing respect in his cousin's eyes. She nudged her sword toward Ildiko. "I still offer you my sword, Your Highness."

Ildiko waved it away. "I'm honored, but that would be a waste of good steel. You can certainly put it to better use than I could. I'd likely slice off one of my fingers or toes. Keep it for when you have to act my guard again."

Brishen struggled not to grin or pull his wife into her arms. Skilled as any seasoned diplomat with her words but better than one because she spoke them with sincerity. She had just paid Anhuset the highest compliment by offering her trust in her ability to protect her in the future.

Anhuset's haughty features flushed perse-blue with pleasure before she scowled into the distance. She returned the sword to its sheath and bowed low to both Brishen and Ildiko. "I'll coordinate the rest of the camp set-up. By your leave, Highnesses." At Brishen's nod, she strode away, bellowing orders to get to work, remove the dead, raise tents and set up guard perimeters.

Brishen bent his head as Ildiko leaned close and whispered, "How badly did I muck that up?"

He turned to her fully. Exhaustion had painted the skin around her eyes a lovely dusky shade. Whether or not she was beautiful to humans and ugly to the Kai, she had a good mind and a spirit he was growing to admire with every passing second. "I think you missed your calling, wife. You would have made a fine ambassador."

She blinked slowly. "I'm surprised I didn't speak pure gibberish. I'm so sleepy, I can hardly talk."

She gave a half-hearted protest when Brishen caught her at the back and knees and lifted her in his arms. "Be quiet," he admonished her gently. "You've been awake too long. As have I." He deposited her back on her tree stump and ordered a nearby soldier to bring a saddle and blanket. They had a comfortable backrest set up in no time. Ildiko reclined against it with an appreciative sigh. She was sound asleep before Brishen covered her in another light blanket.

He was tired as well. Except for a few minutes here and there, he hadn't slept in Pricid since he arrived three days earlier. Luckily, Mertok's cavalry had arrived—not only to help them vanquish their foes but also to offer relief so Brishen and his entourage could rest for a few hours.

The rising sun half blinded him, and he squinted as the cavalry captain approached, hooded and cloaked against the daylight. Mertok bowed. "Your Highness, I thought we agreed to meet you near this spot tomorrow. We didn't think to find you this far down the road so soon."

Brishen accepted the mild criticism. The trade road was a dangerous one. He had been sure the size of their party would deter any ragtag band of thieves intent on stealing trade goods. The odds grew even higher in the Kai's favor now that Mertok's horsemen had joined them to travel the rest of the journey together, swelling their numbers to a small army.

But Brishen had been eager to leave Pricid, and with Ildiko's encouragement, they'd set out a day earlier than planned. "My wife wanted to see her new home as soon as possible, so we left right after the banquet."

He glanced beyond Mertok's shoulder, watching as the Kai dragged the dead bandits to a spot beyond the camp and piled them into a haphazard heap. Every one of their attackers had been human, but Brishen suspected none had been Gauri. He returned his attention to Mertok. "That was no flock of thieves who attacked us. Too many and too well armed and organized."

Mertok reached into the depths of his cloak. "We started tracking them to the border two days ago. A raiding party with a message." He held out a bauble, its metal flashing in the sun.

Brishen took it and growled. The royal insignia of Belawat. He wasn't surprised; he was infuriated. The kingdom of Gaur had skirmished with the kingdom of Belawat since Brishen had been a child. The Beladine wanted the profitable Gauri seaports, and the Gauri had no intention of giving them up. Full scale war had seemed inevitable, but there was an obstacle—one that made the alliance with the Kai valuable to both sides.

The fastest way to move armies and avoid the treacherous mountains that divided the Gauri from the Beladine was through a narrow passage in Kai territory. Both human kingdoms knew better than to try and annex the heavily defended tract for themselves. The Kai had turned a blind eye at first to the smaller skirmishes between the two combatants. It was no concern of theirs if the humans slaughtered each other as long as they did so on their side of the border.

But Brishen's father had grown alarmed when scouts reported an amassing of Beladine troops and whispered secrets of a large force preparing to invade Gaur, take its ports, and conquer the Bast-Haradis borderlands along the way.

The trade treaty and war alliance between the Kai and the Gauri had destroyed Belawat's plans. They weren't strong enough to fight two kingdoms allied together. The Beladine king had promised retribution for the Kai's interference in human matters. This raiding party had been the first volley fired. Kill the younger Kai prince and his Gauri bride. Send the message that revenge was swift and merciless.

Brishen flipped the insignia in his hand before dropping it into the pouch at his belt. He eyed the mound of the dead. "Burn the bodies and all their gear. Save a jar of the ash. The Kai will send Belawat a response."

Mertok gave a short bow. "Do you wish to perform a consecrative tonight for our dead?"

Brishen nodded. "Find out who'll volunteer to serve as Neima's and Kroshag's mortem vessels. I'll act as Talumey's."

Anhuset joined them, and the three made additional plans for the remainder of the journey, agreeing to double the guards during the day and increase their pace if at all possible so they cut their road time by a third. When they finished, Brishen discovered the tent reserved for him and Ildiko had been erected.

He carried the still sleeping Ildiko inside and laid her down on one of the two prepared pallets. She murmured softly but didn't waken when he removed her shoes and unbuckled her out of Anhuset's extra breastplate. Brishen didn't think she'd appreciate him stripping off her clothes while she slept. He was too tired anyway to figure out the various lacings and knots complex enough to put a pit trap to shame.

She turned on her side away from him and snuggled beneath the blankets he pulled over her shoulder. Unlike her, Brishen couldn't sleep in his clothes. Splattered in both human and Kai blood, he itched to get out of the armor and the gambeson beneath it.

Ildiko didn't move when he stretched out on the pallet next to her. His eyelids felt as if someone had attached weights to them, and he soon fell asleep beside her, lulled into repose by his wife's soft breathing and peaceful form next to him.

He awakened hours later to twilight's dim haze and the touch of fingertips across his cheek. He opened one eye to discover Ildiko's homely face close to his. She traced the bridge of his nose and the line of one cheekbone.

"You know, except for the gray skin, black nails and the one glowing eye looking at me, I could almost mistake you for Gauri." He gave her a sleepy grin. She paled and frowned at him. "And then you smile," she said. "Bursin's wings, but that's a blood-curdling sight to wake up to at any time of the day."

Brishen chuckled between her fingers as she tried to press his lips closed. He grabbed her hand and kissed her knuckles. "You won't exactly be honored as the greatest beauty in all of Bast-Haradis, wife." Her red hair haloed her head in a corona of tangles, and her eyes were even more grotesque—the whites threaded with thread-thin filaments of blood.

Her mouth curved upward. "Thank Bursin for that. I'll happily pass the title onto someone else. Now, if you all want to name me the ugliest woman in the entire Kai kingdom, then I might have to preen a little."

Brishen attempted to tame her hair by patting it down with one hand. "You're considered a beauty by your people. Why weren't you married sooner?"

She shrugged. "You were the most advantageous for a woman of my rank. My mother was Sangur's sister. Had it been my father who was related to him, then I would have been a princess. But since I was born to the female line of the royal family, I was simply a noblewoman—too high-ranking to marry off to just anyone but not important enough to pawn off to an heir."

"So they gave you to a spare." Brishen said it without rancor. He was the younger of two sons, and his brother had insured the royal succession six times over and counting with his heirs. Brishen's importance for carrying the line had long ago been diminished. There wasn't even any requirement that he beget children of his own. His Gauri bride had simply been a good faith exchange between kingdoms—the post script to a document of alliance.

Ildiko continued her exploration of the contours of his face. "There's a lot to be said for a spare." She drew a circle on his chin with her fingertip. "Your skin color reminds me of a dead eel I once saw on the beach."

Brishen arched an eyebrow. "Flattering, I'm sure. I thought yours looked like a mollusk we boil to make amaranthine dye."

She paused in touching him and stared at her hand. "I am very pink compared to you."

"Just so, since I'm not pink at all."

Ildiko's eyebrows drew together. "Do you eat those mollusks?"

"No. They've a bitter taste, and their dye is too valuable to waste them in the kitchens."

Her relieved exhalation caressed his throat. "That's good to know. I'm not sure I'd like to be compared to something you ate for dinner."

Brishen opened his mouth to retort but changed his mind. He hadn't been completely truthful with her when he told her his people weren't interested in eating the Gauri. The Kai were an ancient race; the humans a young one. Long ago, on the edges of ancestral memory, when the Kai were more feral and humans less savage, his kind had once hunted hers for food.

He hurried to change the subject. "Why are your eyes bloodied?"

Ildiko started and pressed her hands to her eyes. When her fingers came away unstained with blood, she frowned, obviously puzzled. Her expression cleared. "I think most humans suffer that when they first wake up. Our eyes feel dry and scratchy. It's temporary."

She cocked her head. "You and your people are bothered most by human eyes, aren't you? I can see it in the way you react to some of our expressions. It's equal to how frightening the Gauri find your teeth."

No one could accuse his new wife of not being observant. Brishen carefully traced the outline of her cheekbone just below her left eye. "It's the white part that makes them ghastly. It's as if they're attached on strings plucked by unseen hands or some kind of strange leeches that live as pairs inside your skulls."

Ildiko's expression pinched in disgust. "That's horrible! No wonder no Kai will meet my gaze for more than a moment."

"I meet it all the time. I'm meeting it now," Brishen countered.

She acceded his point. "True, but I bet it takes the same effort it takes me not to jump every time you smile."

"We're growing used to each other. My kin will grow used to you and you to them as well."

Ildiko sighed. "I hope so. An ugly stranger in a far land with people not of my blood or my kind." She wrapped a strand of his hair around her finger and tugged gently. "I'll need your guidance, husband."

Brishen cupped one side of her face. "You have it, Ildiko. Along with my protection and my patience. I didn't lie when I said we would manage together."

Ildiko pressed her cheek into his palm for a moment. She pulled away, and her smile turned impish. "It'll be hard not to tease your folk sometimes."

Brishen couldn't imagine how she might go about such a thing. He had no idea if the Kai and the Gauri even knew the same jokes or found the same things funny. "What do you mean?"

He almost leapt out of his skin when Ildiko stared at him as both of her eyes drifted slowly down and over until they seemed to meet together, separated only by the elegant bridge of her nose.

"Lover of thorns and holy gods!" he yelped and clapped one hand across her eyes to shut out the sight. "Stop that," he ordered.

Ildiko laughed and pushed his hand away. She laughed even harder when she caught sight of his expression. "Wait," she gasped on a giggle. "I can do better. Want to see me make one eye cross and have the other stay still?"

Brishen reared back. "No!" He grimaced. "Nightmarish. I'll thank you to keep that particular talent to yourself, wife."

She was still chuckling when he helped her rise from her pallet and left the tent to give her privacy to change and ready herself. It was dark, and the moon hung low when he exited the tent and discovered several Kai staring curiously at him from their places around camp fires. No doubt they wondered how he'd found the courage to bed his hideous wife. No doubt bets had been placed and wagers exchanged over whether he took the easy way and bedded her when the sun was high and the light blinding or the more challenging and swived her as the gloaming rose.

They could wonder until they rotted. Brishen had no intention of revealing anything between him and Ildiko. Theirs was an agreement based on the beginnings of friendship, respect and an intuitive understanding of each other that still left him slack-jawed with amazement. He refused to taint that accord by inviting vulgar conjecture.

He made arrangements to have the travel rations packed by a Gauri cook delivered to the tent and met with Anhuset and Mertok to discuss the upcoming consecrative.

Ildiko found him a half hour later. She'd changed her clothes and tamed her hair into a braid. Anhuset's breastplate hung across one arm. "Can you help me buckle this on again?"

He took it from her and set it against a nearby tree. "We're not riding out just yet. We have three of our dead to attend to."

Her features saddened. "I'm sorry for your loss, Brishen."

Brishen squeezed her hand. "As am I. We'll cleanse the bodies during the consecrative and return their mortem lights to their families to store in a sacred house."

"What is a mortem light? And a consecrative?"

He stilled, wondering how best to explain Kai funerary rites or that to properly honor their fallen comrades, he and two other Kai would literally breathe in the memories of the dead to carry them home—hosts themselves to other entities.

With that realization, Brishen no longer saw Ildiko's eyes as before, otherworldly and separate from her. They were human and still strange, but just eyes.

CHAPTER SEVEN

The physical differences between human and Kai were obvious and in some ways, extreme. Ildiko had accepted that fact before she married Brishen. Her acceptance helped her look beyond his startling appearance to the man himself. She'd held tight to that philosophy: see past the surface to the tides below. In her very short time amongst his people, she observed many similarities to hers—a love of family, comradeship, loyalty to each other, grief over lost friends. Ildiko had no doubt there were many more she'd discover as she took her place amongst the Kai as wife to one of their princes.

The Gauri might share several of the same behaviors as the Kai when it came to the living, but in the matter of the dead, the two parted company.

Brishen retrieved a flask of wine and a blanket from their tent and made a place for her to sit at the entrance. He sat down beside her and passed the flask. "With every generation, the Kai lose a little of their magic. We are an Elder race, but we are fading. We hoard the sorcery we still possess until forced to use it. Though I'm as knowledgeable as my father in family spells and protections, his power is greater than mine and my brother's. And my brother's is greater than his children's. However, the Kai are old, with long memories. The spirits of our dead leave this world but gift the living with their memories—what we call mortem

51

lights. We keep those memories alive in a place called Emlek. They are our history, what defines us beyond how we look or the sorcery we're losing."

"Is Emlek a temple?" She passed him the flask after taking a swallow of sweet wine.

Brishen drank as well and let the flask dangle from his fingers. "Not really. It's sacred, but we don't worship there. Those who visit come to gain knowledge of past days or to find comfort in revisiting memories of those they lost."

Ildiko's heart contracted in her chest. Oh, what she would have given to have her parents' memories with her. She refused his second offer of the flask. "I wish the Gauri had something like that."

Brishen wrapped an arm around her shoulder and squeezed. "It's a comfort to the living, especially when death is sudden, as for those who die in battle or childbirth, which I'm told is its own hard-fought war." He kept his arm around her, and Ildiko savored his strength. "A dead Kai's mortem light is a last gift to their loved ones."

She envied this gift with a fervor that made her wish she'd been born Kai, teeth and all. "How do you bring them home? The mortem lights?"

Brishen took another drink from the flask. Ildiko was still learning the flickers of expression on his features, their nuances harder to capture without the ability to read his eyes, but she sensed an odd hesitation. He stiffened a little next to her and removed his arm from her shoulder. She missed its weight.

He paused for so long; Ildiko didn't think he'd answer her. "Tonight we'll perform a consecrative—a ritual to release the spirit and spark the mortem light." He lifted one of her hands and laced his fingers through hers. The contrast of gray skin and black nails against hers emphasized their physical differences, yet sorrow was sorrow. The grief in his voice was the same as any Gauri who'd ever knelt at a grave and mourned. "I can explain the ritual and how we transport the mortem lights, but you'll better understand it when you witness it."

"May I participate?"

Brishen's mouth curved upward. In a gesture growing more familiar to her and one she liked, he kissed her knuckles before rising to his feet and helping her stand. "I wish you could, but a consecrative can only be performed by the Kai. You're welcome to watch; I'd be honored if you did."

They spent the early part of the evening holding ad hoc court in a forest clearing. Ildiko had been too exhausted the dawn before to meet the new members of their entourage. That, and the aftermath of the bloody skirmish between the Kai and Beladine raiders had precluded any social introductions. Securing a safe camp and clearing the dead had taken up everyone's time.

Brishen informed her they wouldn't break camp until the next night. Tonight would be devoted to the funerals of the three Kai who had perished in the attack.

"What of the dead raiders?" Ildiko tried not to look too often at the corpses piled near the road.

His lambent eyes narrowed to slits. "We'll burn them before we leave and return their ashes to Belawat. Message received." His voice was cold, flat.

Ildiko shivered, not because of Brishen's sudden icy demeanor but because they'd both been targets for revenge. Marriage obviously had many more pitfalls to beware of besides sharing a bed and a household with a stranger. She didn't fool herself into thinking the man who tried to drag her from beneath the wagon had only meant to scare her. He would have butchered her on the spot and smiled while he did it. Ildiko was glad he was dead and equally glad it had been Brishen who killed him.

Some might wonder at her lack of fear regarding her new husband. Dreadful in appearance, lethal in combat, Brishen was all that was cordiality and dignified royalty in every interaction with her.

When their camp had settled in, he took the time to introduce her to the Kai cavalry who'd come to their rescue, and his Master of the Horse, Mertok. As she expected, the Kai soldiers were formal, polite and refused to meet her gaze. They had no problem gawking at her when they thought she wasn't looking, and Ildiko had been tempted more than a few times to cross her eyes and watch their reaction.

As perceptive as he was affable, Brishen squeezed her waist in warning and bent to whisper in her ear. "Don't even think about it, wife. You'll notice half of them are sharpening or cleaning their weapons. All I need is for someone to inadvertently slice themselves open because you startled them."

Ildiko stifled a laugh behind her hand. Brishen's answering predator grin made the hairs on her arms stand up in warning, but she patted the hand at her waist and remained unafraid.

The moon glimmered directly above them—a Kai noon—when all their party, except those on guard, gathered in the clearing and formed a circle around the three fallen Kai. They looked no different from when they were alive except for a change in their skin tone. Instead of the slate gray with its undertones of teal and lavender, the flesh had paled to the color of cold ash. Their bodies were laid out side by side, dressed in their armor. They held their arms crossed over their chests, favorite weapons beside them. Ildiko stood outside the circle on a tree stump tall enough that she could see over the mourners' shoulders and into the circle.

Anhuset entered the circle with a small amphora. From it she poured a glistening stream of oil over her fingers and crouched to draw a mysterious symbol on the forehead of each of the dead soldiers. Like the other female Kai, she shone cold and elegant beneath the moon's pale rays, her silver hair shimmering. She opened the consecrative with a chant in the Kai tongue, a singsong cant answered in chorus by the surrounding Kai. Ildiko only knew a smattering of bast-Kai words, but she easily recognized a lamentation when she heard one.

The dirge continued, rising and falling in volume. The Kai swayed with its undulating rhythm, their glowing eyes bright in the woodland darkness. From her vantage point, Ildiko clearly saw Brishen. He stood on the opposite side of the circle from her, his lips moving as he sang with his comrades.

Ildiko's eyes widened, and she gasped when a soft light suddenly suffused the dead Kai, creating a nimbus that washed like spiller waves over their bodies. The light broke, stretching into sinuous threads until they coalesced into three spectral forms, vaguely human—or Kai—in shape.

The living Kai continued the lamentation, the higher female voices melding with the lower male registers. A single bright light, no bigger than a butterfly, ignited within each of the three specters hovering over the bodies. The memory spark. The mortem light.

Brishen and two others broke from the circle and approached the dead. The phantoms swirled around them, seeming to dance in time with the dirge. Tears filled Ildiko's eyes as Brishen and his companions opened their arms and were embraced by the dead whose spirits twirled and swayed before enveloping the living completely, sending tendrils of radiance into their mouths and nostrils.

Ildiko's wonder battled with horror as the spirits of the fallen Kai possessed their willing hosts. Brishen had told her his were a people of night. They avoided the sun when possible and rejected the day for their hours of activity. Yet seeing her princely husband and his two subjects lit from within by the resplendent dead, she couldn't imagine any who embraced light more than the tenebrous Kai.

Brishen burned like a torch within the circle, his glowing eyes sulfurous instead of their usual nacreous shade. The two soldiers standing with him bore the same look. One staggered with the force of the possession, and the mortem lights pulsed under their clothing—candles lit inside living lanterns.

The possession lasted only a moment before the spectral entities abandoned their worldly anchors on a mournful exhalation and faded into the vast night, leaving their mortem lights behind with their hosts. Their physical bodies collapsed inside their armor, desiccating into a fine dust until they melded with the earth beneath them.

The dirge faded as well until the Kai stood silent together, serenaded only by a cool wind. Ildiko leapt off her tree stump and hurried to Brishen. He leaned weakly on Anhuset, his features as colorless as the dead Talumey who'd gifted his life memories to him for safekeeping. His fellow vessels looked just as weary and stood with the help of others, as if holding a mortem light sucked out all their strength. Brishen's eyes were twin suns in his face, and he reached for Ildiko with a hand that trembled.

She clasped it and drew him to her, leaving Anhuset to hover close by. "Anhuset, help me get him to our tent."

The Kai woman nodded and signaled with one hand. Two more soldiers appeared. Brishen sagged between them as they carried him to the tent and laid him carefully on his pallet. Ildiko knelt by her husband's side and curled her hand around his. His eyes were closed, but the mortem light inside him still glowed through his eyelids.

Anhuset settled on the floor on Brishen's other side. "He and the others be like this for a few hours and then suffer mortem fever."

Ildiko's stomach flipped. "Mortem fever? He'd said nothing of a fever."

The other woman pulled a blanket over Brishen's still body. "A light vessel drowns in the memories of the dead until they become accustomed to them. It's temporary but painful while it lasts."

"Bursin's wings! Do all the Kai go through this?" Ildiko was rapidly reconsidering her envy of such a gift. She stroked the back of Brishen's hand with her thumb.

Anhuset shrugged. "Only those who volunteer. Brishen volunteered to act as light vessel for Talumey until we reach Haradis. He'll turn Talumey's mortem light over to his mother once we've arrived. I'll stay here with you until he adjusts and overcomes the fever." She leaned back against one of the tent supports in a pose that lacked any tension.

Ildiko wasn't fooled. She'd observed the interaction between Brishen and his cousin. Anhuset was worried. "I'm harmless, Anhuset. You don't have to protect him from me," she joked gently.

Anhuset stared at her, mouth unsmiling. "Mortem fever can make a Kai go mad. I'm not protecting him from you, Your Highness, but you from him."

CHAPTER EIGHT

There was madness in memory, especially when the memory wasn't yours. Brishen lay on his pallet, eyes closed, and watched the life of young Talumey twist and entwine with recollections of his own life. Beloved faces flickered in his mind's eye, some his, some Talumey's, along with emotions that accompanied them. Father, mother, two sisters.

Brishen raised a hand to touch the older woman's proud, lined features. "My mother," he whispered.

"What of your mother, Brishen?"

The voice was familiar. Anhuset, his commander. Brishen frowned. No, not his commander. He was her commander. His cousin and lieutenant. "My mother," he said. "Love her. Her name is Tarawin."

His commander spoke again. "No, Brishen. Your mother is Secmis, Queen of the Flatlands. Shadow Queen of Bast-Haradis."

Brishen frowned. Another image replaced that of Tarawin, this one of a woman possessing the haughty beauty that had captured a king's interest and hinted at the brittle soul beneath it.

"What is he saying?"

A different voice, this time speaking in the Common tongue with a Gauri's lyrical accent. The prince's ugly wife with the frightening eyes.

Brishen shook his head. "Lovely inside," he argued with himself. "Laughs easily."

Anhuset answered the Gauri woman in Common. "He's confusing his mother Secmis with Talumey's mother, Tarawin. I don't know Tarawin, but I do know Secmis. She rarely laughs."

He wanted to counter her comment, clarify that he'd spoken of Ildiko, not Tarawin, but his tongue felt glued to the top of his mouth. He was hot, broiling—as if someone had staked him out beneath the sun and let it roast him alive. "Water," he rasped.

A cup pressed against his dry lips, and Brishen drained the water in gulps. A hand caressed his brow, cool on his hot skin. He opened his eyes and found Ildiko staring at him with those strange human eyes. He instinctively jerked away and tried to sit up. "Your Highness," he murmured. He was a lowly soldier and broke all protocol, lying down before a member of the royal house.

Ildiko. She was Ildiko to him in private. Two pairs of hands pressed him back to the pallet. Brishen blinked at Anhuset who offered more water. He turned his head away and sought Ildiko once more.

She stroked his arm, and her voice was soft, worried. "Do you know me, Brishen?"

The constantly shifting patterns of combined memories clouded his vision, even with his eyes open, and his stomach roiled in protest. Brishen closed his eyes. "My wife," he said. "My Ildiko."

"Yes, Brishen. Your Ildiko." Like her touch, her voice soothed him. "Anhuset and I will stay with you until the fever is over."

He wanted to thank them for their vigilance—Ildiko, who'd never witnessed a mortem light's possession of a light vessel and Anhuset who was still put out by having to eat the revolting potato thing at the wedding banquet. An image of the steaming maggot on his plate overrode all the jumbled memories trying to cloud his mind. Bile surged into his throat, and saliva flooded his mouth.

"I'm going to be sick," he muttered.

The words had barely passed his lips before he was shoved to his side. Hands held his head and lifted his hair as he emptied his stomach. More memories surged through his mind—a week of illness when he was a child and clutched a carved wooden bowl to his chest as Tarawin crooned to him what a brave boy he was. Another similar memory, only he huddled in a grand bed holding a silver basin while one of the royal nurses stood safely out of range and eyed him with disgust as he retched.

A cool cloth bathed his hot face, and he captured the wrist of the person wielding it. Fragile bones in his grip. Human bones. Easily snapped if he exerted the smallest amount of pressure. Brishen traced the spider network of tiny veins just beneath her skin with his thumb. Though they were thinner than silk thread, he could feel the blood pulse through them in a steady rhythm.

He cracked his eyelids open just enough to find Ildiko holding the cloth. Her other hand carded through his hair. "Battle and vomit, wife. Not what you should witness during your inaugural trip to Haradis." Nothing had gone quite as he planned since the moment they rode out of the Gauri capital city. "Shall I take you home?" He wouldn't blame Ildiko if she said yes.

She flashed him a brief smile of her square teeth. "You are taking me home, Brishen. There's nothing for me in Pricid."

"What of your family?"

Her smile faded. "Blood ties do not always make a family. My family rests in a crypt overlooking the sea. I need to make a new family now." She traced one of his eyebrows with her fingers. "Can you take a little more water? Rinse your mouth?"

Brishen nodded and this time accepted the cup Anhuset offered him. He lay back, inhaling and exhaling slowly, willing his rebellious stomach to calm down, despite his and Talumey's memories pitching his vision so hard, he felt like he'd spent a night emptying a wine barrel, only to have someone shove him into it, seal the lid and toss the thing into a stormy sea. He refused to think of potatoes.

The sounds of cleaning and straightening filled his ears. He wanted to apologize for the mess but didn't dare open his mouth in case he ruined all their hard work.

Somehow he managed to drift into a restless sleep plagued with dreams and cluttered with two sets of memories. He thrashed on the pallet and ripped the blanket off his body. A surprised yelp filtered through his dreams, followed by two voices speaking in Common.

"Did he slash you?"

"Just my sleeve. Bursin's wings, you are fast!"

"Not fast enough."

"It's just my sleeve, Anhuset."

"Lucky it wasn't your face or your throat, Your Highness. You shouldn't be here."

"This is exactly where I should be."

"Then until he's lucid, stay out of his way. I might not be as quick as you need me to be a second time."

Brishen struggled against the somnolent shackles that held him prisoner. He'd kill whoever had tried to hurt his wife, split his skull the way he he'd done with the Beladine raider who attacked her. She was ugly; she was beautiful, and she was his. "My Ildiko," he whispered.

She didn't offer her soothing touch, but her voice calmed him. "I'm here, Brishen. I'm not going anywhere."

He hoped not.

CHAPTER NINE

They were into the fourth day of their journey, and Ildiko was beginning to miss the sun. She fiddled with her horse's mane as she and their entourage rode ever closer to Haradis, capital of Bast-Haradis. The moon had waned to a slivered crescent in the sky, and the night was so dark, she was virtually blind. The black-armored Kai were no more than vague shapes with disembodied eyes that flitted like pairs of fireflies.

She relied on her mount's sense of direction for home as well as its instinct to stay with a herd for protection. Wagon wheels creaked behind her, accompanied by the distant howls of wolf packs and the voices of the Kai who spoke and bantered with each other.

For a moment Ildiko had the oddest sense of being set adrift alone on a vast sea in a small boat. Her horse's rolling gait was the tide that rocked her. Beyond her senses lay a horizon she couldn't see and land she couldn't reach; the shadows of leviathans that swam the deep abyss and swallowed ships whole lurked beneath her.

The resolve she held to embrace this new life and call these people hers fractured a little. She was an outlander with a strange face and strange habits. Ildiko pushed back the sudden swell of terror and homesickness. It would be difficult enough adjusting to a different household among foreign humans with their own

65

peculiar customs. But this was far more than culture shock. The Kai weren't even human. An ancient, insular people who shunned the sun and swallowed the spirits of their dead, they were nothing like the Gauri or any other peoples Ildiko had ever encountered at court. She would be as a babe just learning to walk as she navigated her way amongst the Kai and their royal court. No doubt she'd make mistakes and embarrass herself—and Brishen—on more than one occasion. That thought sent her stomach plummeting to her feet.

Her husband rode ahead of her, deep in conversation with the cavalry commander. Mertok's arrival during their battle with the Beladine raiders had swelled the Kai troop to formidable numbers. Brishen had assured Ildiko that it would take far more than a band of cutthroats to defeat them now. They remained on alert; however, and kept the day watch doubled when they stopped to camp and sleep.

As if he sensed her gaze on him, Brishen glanced over his shoulder and halted his mount. Kai riders eddied around him as he waited for her to catch up to him. He offered her a tired smile, and even in the suffocating darkness, Ildiko saw the weary lines etched into his features. Recovered from the mortem light's possession, he still bore remnants of exhaustion from the fever.

"That is a somber set to your mouth, wife. What grim thoughts plague you?"

She hesitated in telling him. Brishen had been even more solicitous after he'd awakened from the mortem fever and discovered her sitting nearby with Anhuset. Ildiko had exercised her newly acquired rank and extracted a reluctant promise from the Kai woman not to say anything about her slashed sleeve unless Brishen asked directly.

"You're asking me to lie to my cousin and my commander, Your Highness." Anhuset's eyes had narrowed to glowing slits.

Ildiko had stripped out of her torn gown, aware of the Kai's equal measure of disapproval and curiosity. She shrugged into a new gown, haphazardly tying laces. As long as her clothes didn't outright fall off her, she didn't think the Kai soldiers would much care that she looked more bedraggled than a laundress on wash day.

"I'm asking no such thing." She ran her hands over the skirt in a futile attempt to smooth out the wrinkles. "If he asks what happened, tell him, but there's no reason to run tattling to him over something as trivial as a torn sleeve."

Anhuset crossed her arms, mutinous. "It could have been worse."

Ildiko didn't argue that one. It could have been infinitely worse. Her heart had almost leapt from her chest when Brishen suddenly lashed out in delirium, his nails slicing through her sleeve like knives. She didn't have time to cry out before a hard shove from Anhuset sent her flying halfway across the tent.

"Anhuset, what good will it do to tell him other than to make him worry or fill him with guilt? What's done is done, and I've come to no harm."

"You shouldn't keep secrets from him." Anhuset refused to yield.

Ildiko blew a strand of hair out of her eyes and resumed her seat near a feverish Brishen but out of striking range. "It's not a secret; it's just a fact that offers no benefit in being retold." She mimicked Anhuset's posture and crossed her arms. "Do I have your promise? Say nothing unless he asks?"

They engaged in a silent battle until Anhuset exhaled a frustrated sigh. "I give you my promise not to say anything about this to him unless he asks." She scowled. "You've the skill of a Kai courtier, Your Highness. Able to twist reason to suit your purpose."

Ildiko recognized the mild insult within the compliment but took no offense. "Well at least, there is some commonality between our two peoples."

The two women held an uneasy truce between them, and Ildiko's prayers were answered when Brishen regained his lucidity without any recollection of striking out at his wife while in the throes of delirium. There had been more than one moment when Anhuset practically vibrated with the temptation to blurt out something, but she held her tongue and busied herself with organizing the evening travel plans with Mertok.

"Ildiko? Where are you, wife?"

Ildiko blinked, brought back to the present by Brishen waving a hand in front of her face. "I'm sorry. I was daydreaming. Or would that be nightdreaming now?" She smiled, then remembered his first question. "Not grim thoughts. Just a curiosity. When you were sick with the mortem fever, you confused your mother with Talumey's mother. Anhuset said yours doesn't smile often."

She left her question unspoken, giving him an escape if he chose not to expand on Anhuset's remark. Instead, he leaned back in the saddle, his wide shoulders relaxed. "My cousin is right. The queen isn't one to smile. If she does, then you look for the knife wielded from the shadows."

Ildiko gaped at Brishen. He'd described his mother in such a mild voice, as if the murderous tendencies he hinted at were no more interesting or threatening than if she had an obsessive love for orange slippers. "Are you serious?"

"Quite," he said in that same neutral tone. "I doubt my father has slept a full night with both eyes closed since he married her."

Ildiko shuddered inwardly at the prospect of meeting her new mother-in-law. Her aunt had been a force to be reckoned with. Haughty, self-important and devious, Fantine had been a master strategist, manipulating the many Gauri court machinations with a skilled hand. King Sangur; however, trusted his wife wouldn't kill him while he slept. Obviously, the same couldn't be said of the Kai king and his lethal queen.

"I'm not looking forward to meeting your mother, Your Highness." A few soft snorts of laughter sounded from the Kai soldiers riding nearby. Ildiko met Brishen's wry gaze. "Should I wear this breastplate when we're introduced?"

Brishen's teeth were like ivory daggers in the darkness. "I'll protect you. Besides, she won't harm you. She's too enamored with the idea that I've been forced to take a human to wife. If there's one thing Secmis loves more than plotting an assassination, it's watching misery." He nudged his horse closer to hers and leaned in. "Be sure to act completely disgusted with me and bitter at your fate," he said softly. "She'll make sure we're in each other's constant company."

Ildiko's thoughts reeled. One thing was certain—she wouldn't be bored. Staying one step ahead of her malevolent mother-in-law would take all her wits and focus. How a viper of a woman as

Brishen described managed to raise such a jovial, affectionate man flummoxed Ildiko.

"You must take after your father in temperament," she said.

The humorous snorts from earlier turned into outright guffaws. Brishen's grin widened. "Hardly. My mother sleeps with one eye open as well." He reached for her hand and gave it a squeeze. "Don't worry, Ildiko. You'll understand more about my parents when you meet them. I'm counting on you giving me your honest impressions afterwards. I suspect they will be entertaining."

Ildiko didn't return his grin. He might find all this quite funny; she found it terrifying. She stiffened her back and clutched the reins in a tight grip. Her new in-laws may be a deadly pair, but she refused to be intimidated.

"I doubt we're much different from any other royal family out there, human or Kai." Brishen edged his horse closer to hers. "We marry to strengthen our positions, hold our power, acquire more land and provide heirs for the throne. A business arrangement in every way." His features sobered, the grin fading. "If we're lucky, we find an amiable companion in our spouses."

His description applied perfectly to the royal family in which Ildiko was raised. Her parents' love for each other had been an anomaly rarely seen among the Gauri aristocracy and not witnessed at all in Sangur and Fantine's immediate family. Marriage was business and politics. Affection and bedsport were usually reserved for mistresses or the occasional lover.

"And mistresses?" she said. For some reason she chose not to dwell on, a discordant internal note thrummed inside at her at the idea of Brishen having a mistress.

One black eyebrow rose. "What about them?"

"Do you have a dozen or so?" Ildiko raised her chin at the twitch of laughter that played across his mouth. It was a perfectly legitimate question. Her cousins' husbands each had a mistress and a bevy of bastard children. Her uncle, the king, kept a *prima dulce* named Annais, for which Queen Fantine was eternally grateful.

Brishen lost the battle not to smile. "A dozen? I doubt I could deal with one." He shifted into a more comfortable spot on the saddle. "Besides, I have a Gauri wife to comfort me. Why take a mistress?"

His answer puzzled Ildiko. "But that isn't the role of a mistress."

"Isn't it? I think we all seek companionship, wife. Sometimes it's physical; sometimes it's much more." An odd flicker danced in his eyes, and like his grin before, his smile faded. "Loneliness is an empty void. We look for that friend in the light." His glowing eyes squinted a little, deepening the laugh lines at their corners. "Or in the case of humans, in the dark."

Brishen stopped his horse for a second time and tugged Ildiko's reins to halt her mount as well. He must have given an unseen signal because the Kai riding with them widened the space around them to afford more privacy.

"What is it?" she said. "What's wrong?"

His gaze pressed down on Ildiko. Not the smothering weight of a too-heavy blanket in summer but more like an embrace that invited affection. Not for the first time, she desperately wished she could read his eyes, see past the luminescence to the equally bright soul behind it.

"Will you be that for me, Ildiko," he said. "That beacon in the void?"

Ildiko's heart cracked. Loneliness had been her most constant companion, the silent shadow that hovered over her for years. If there was one thing she understood, it was the emptiness of the internal void. Her reply might not make sense to him now, but she'd explain later when they were alone.

She reached out, fingers tracing the herringbone pattern of his chainmail sleeve. "The void is vast, like the sea at night and no land in sight. I'll be the beacon, Brishen."

He captured her hand and kissed her palm. His lips were cool on her skin. "My parents will loathe you, wife." Ildiko felt all the blood drain from her face. Brishen's smile returned. "Don't be afraid. That's a good thing. They've hated me since birth. They only like those they can crush."

He looked as if he'd say more but was interrupted by sharp cries and excited yips from the other Kai. Ildiko tried to understand the rapid stream of unfamiliar words flowing between the soldiers, but all she could catch was "Haradis," and "gate." She turned to Brishen. "What are they saying?" His reply birthed a legion of butterflies in her belly.

"Beyond that slope is Bast-Haradis and the capital. Welcome to my kingdom, Ildiko of the Kai."

CHAPTER TEN

Brishen escorted Ildiko down the long corridor that lead to the throne room. She held onto his arm, her fingers digging furrows into his skin, even through his vambrace. It was the only sign of her anxiety, besides her ashen pallor. She wore a serene expression, and her steps were sure and steady in the hallway's darkness.

Ildiko had grown quieter the closer they got to Haradis and gone completely silent when they topped the ridge that looked down on the dimly lit city nestled in a small valley ringed by gently rolling hills. She'd answered his questions with nods or shakes of her head, and every once in a while a short yes or no. He could smell the fear rolling off her.

"You're not alone in this, Ildiko," he reassured her for the dozenth time. Before their trek to the throne room, she simply nodded. This time she turned to him, her face wiped clean of expression.

"This is the kingdom of Bast-Haradis, Brishen. I'm human. Here, I am alone."

He halted and she with him. Brishen gazed at his human wife, touching on the colorful hair and strange eyes, the pale skin with its ever-changing shades that were subject to her moods. His soldiers' reactions to her would be nothing compared to those of the Kai court. Insular for so long, most of the nobility had rarely seen a human. Those who had, barely remembered. They'd stare and whisper amongst themselves and do so, so much worse than that.

Brishen wanted to protect her, shield her from the inevitable trial of meeting not only the vipers amongst the court but those who ruled them—his parents. He was powerless to do so. She'd have to face them all, one human amongst a people who once considered all her kind food. But she wouldn't do it alone.

He reached for her free hand. "You are also a princess of the blood through marriage, a member of the royal family. My wife. Every Kai in that room owes you their allegiance and respect. I will cut out any tongue that would try and besmirch you, Ildiko." He pressed his lips to her palm.

The tiniest crack appeared in her serene composure. Her mouth twitched with the hint of a smile. "Or bury an axe blade in their heads?"

His guilt over his inability to rescue her from his own family eased a little at her humor. "I'm adept with spear and sword as well. Just name who you want me to skewer for you."

Ildiko's smile widened. "Not the best approach I think to winning supporters." She inhaled a long breath before slowly letting it out. "I can do this, but you must promise not to let go of my hand, even if I'm breaking your fingers."

Brishen gently pulled her into his embrace. She felt fragile in his arms—barely more than shadow wrapped around slender bones and clothed in Gauri silks. "I promise."

"I will not shame you with my fear, Brishen," she whispered against his neck.

He sighed into her hair. "But I might shame you with mine, wife." He stroked her back and offered a last bit of advice before they made their introductions to the court. "They are only serpents, Ildiko. Crush them beneath your heel."

He led her the rest of the way to the ornately carved double doors guarded by a pair of soldiers. The sentinels bowed, their faces as closed and expressionless as Ildiko's was now. The doors swung open, revealing a cavernous chamber with tall ceilings, walls decorated in tapestry and weaponry and lined by statues of ancient Kai kings and queens—all lit by wavering torchlight.

Brishen barely registered its grandeur. He'd grown up in this palace. The hall had looked like this since before his grandfather was born and probably long before that. Instead, he focused on the pair of figures watching them from the thrones elevated on a platform reached by a set of nine steps.

The silence greeting him and Ildiko gave way to a rising din of voices, a steady buzzing that grew in volume like the approach of a locust swarm. There were shocked gasps, comments about the Gauri woman's terrifying eyes and strange face, expressions of pity for him.

Ildiko might not understand most of what was said, but it didn't take a fluency in the Kai language to know her appearance was causing a stir. Like him, she kept her gaze trained on the king and queen. Her fingers were icicles on his.

"Steady," he said under his breath.

They stopped at the first step leading to the thrones. Brishen tugged lightly on Ildiko's hand and they both genuflected.

Brishen addressed the floor. "Your Majesties, I am your humble servant. I present my bride, Ildiko, niece of the king of Gaur, Sangur the Lame. Now *hercegesé* to me."

The throne room had grown silent once more, pulsing with anticipation as Brishen and Ildiko waited on their knees.

"You may rise." King Djedor's sepulchral voice echoed throughout the chamber. His eyes were nearly white with advanced age, and the gray skin hung on his facial bones like sodden garments clipped to strung line. "I'm told the powers in Belawat tried to have you killed to show their disapproval of this marriage."

Brishen knew his father well enough to know that as soon as this introduction was concluded, he'd be summoned to his father's council chamber for a full accounting of the attack. He shrugged. "We killed them all but lost three of our own. Our companions fought bravely. I carry the mortem light of one."

Another murmuring buzz passed through the crowd of courtiers lining either side of the throne room. Brishen had done the family of the fallen soldier a great honor. The king's expression didn't alter at the revelation. Brishen had expected nothing more. His father had never expressed either approval or disapproval of his younger son's actions. They had no bearing on the throne or line of succession; therefore they were of no importance.

He did turn a curious gaze to Ildiko. "I remember the first time I saw a human. A man. The women are even uglier."

A titter of laughter passed through the crowd and just as quickly died when Brishen turned to note who laughed. Ildiko's fingers twitched in his grasp.

Djedor's wrinkled lips stretched into a grin, revealing teeth gone as black with age as his eyes had gone white. Brishen braced his shoulder against Ildiko's to keep her from lurching backwards. The king turned to his silent wife. "What think you of your new daughter, Secmis?"

The queen, beautiful and as youthful as the day she married her husband, stared first at her son and then at her Gauri daughter. Unlike her husband, she spoke the Common tongue so Ildiko would understand everything she said. "Welcome to Haradis, Ildiko *Hercegesé*. I hope you can find your place here. My son has sacrificed a great deal to marry a human woman and seal our alliance with the Gauri."

Her lip had curled as she spoke, and though her voice was even, Secmis didn't bother hiding her contempt for Brishen's wife.

Brishen fancied he heard Ildiko's back crack as she stiffened next to him. She yanked her fingers out of his grasp and advanced to the second step, shoulders back, chin raised in a haughty manner that challenged the queen's own arrogance. A collective gasp rose among the watching nobility.

Brishen dropped his hand to his sword pommel. Gods forbid he'd have to slash his way out of the throne room to prevent his mother from killing his wife, but he'd do so if necessary. He balanced on the balls of his feet, ready to grab Ildiko and run.

Her own voice was calm, lacking disdain but sure and uncowed. "What sacrifices would those be, Your Majesty? I see only a groom returned home with a bride after an admittedly dangerous trip. He bears no wounds, no scars, and possesses all his limbs. I haven't yet had the time to henpeck him to death."

This time the crowd's laughter was disguised by splutters and bouts of coughing. Brishen didn't know whether to groan or applaud. Ildiko's wit would gain her either respect or a writ of execution.

Secmis's golden eyes narrowed. "You mock me?"

"No, Your Majesty. That would be rude." Ildiko gave a brief bow. "I wish merely to understand my husband's sacrifice. He will live among his own people. I cannot bear him children, but the line of succession is secured many times over. He cannot marry a Kai woman, but if the Kai court is anything like the Gauri court, his union with me won't prevent him from having a mistress. Several if he wishes. If he can't bear the sight of me, we can talk in the daylight when he doesn't see so well. Then I can argue the sacrifice is mine, not his."

Secmis's skin, the color of unpolished steel, darkened even more. Her eyes blazed brighter than all the torches in the throne room combined. She half rose from her seat, long fingers curled. Had Ildiko stood in front of her, she would have been disemboweled.

Brishen had partially drawn his sword from its sheath when the king let out a bellowing laugh. Secmis turned a glare on him hot enough to set his robes alight. He ignored her and slapped his hand on the arm of his chair. "She's ugly, my boy, but fearless too. You could have done worse." He motioned to the doors. "Get her out of here before your mother orders her beheading." He flashed black fangs at Ildiko. "You'll manage well enough, Gauri woman. I look forward to our next meeting."

The return trek to the doors seemed a thousand miles and as many years away. Brishen strangled the urge to sprint for safety with Ildiko in his arms and kept them both to a stately walk. Once the doors closed behind them, they maintained their pace until they were out of sight and earshot of the guards.

Brishen pivoted to stand in front of Ildiko. Even the ashen color to her skin had bled away, leaving her pale as bleached bone. Her eyes were wide and black with terror. She took a step toward him before her knees gave out. He caught her in his arms and held her close.

"Well done, *Hercegesé*! You've faced down my mother and pleased my father. Not a Kai in that room will cross you now."

She shuddered against him, her body as icy as her fingers had been. He heard the rapid chatter of her teeth before she clenched her jaw and drew steady breaths. Once she calmed, she leaned far enough away from him to meet his gaze.

"I've made an enemy of your mother," she said in a mournful voice.

"Everyone is Secmis's enemy, wife. You've just made yourself a worthy one in her eyes."

"I'm going to die, aren't I?"

He kissed her forehead. "No, you're going to eat. We still have a formal dinner to suffer through in a few hours."

"Gods help me," she muttered.

"You'll need it," he cheerfully replied.

CHAPTER ELEVEN

If she disregarded their physical appearances, Ildiko determined that the Kai courtiers were much like the Gauri ones—ambitious, gossip-mongering, and highly skilled at surviving the savage intrigues of court life.

She'd known the moment the doors to the throne room opened and she and Brishen crossed the threshold, they'd pass through a gauntlet of curious hounds eager for the scent of new blood. Anhuset's armored breastplate would offer Ildiko no protection on that battleground.

Familiarity with court etiquette and strategy offered some comfort as she knelt at the lowest step before her new husband's parents. King Djedor was a man stitched of nightmares, a lich not yet completely rotted to bones. Brishen's body against her back had been the only thing that kept her from bolting out of the throne room when the king flashed his black-fanged smile at her.

Her fluency in the Kai speech was adequate enough that she understood a portion of his remarks regarding the ugliness of human women. His insults had done a fine job of eroding her fear and replacing it with indignation. That indignation bubbled into a seething anger when Secmis addressed her in the Common tongue.

The queen had stared at her with eyes that gleamed red at the rims and a mouth that curled into a sneer. She sat on the throne, slender and garbed in a heavily embroidered gown that cascaded over the chair and pooled at her feet. Her silver hair was coiffed and decorated with jewels that winked dully in the low light.

In her rebuttal of the queen's comments, Ildiko had been tempted to ask if Secmis might find it more comfortable if she were coiled around her throne instead of perched upon it. The horrified gasps from the Kai nobles and Brishen's hand on his sword as she challenged Secmis's contempt alerted Ildiko that she already antagonized his malevolent mother to a dangerous point without insults to enflame the confrontation.

Only after they'd escaped the throne room had her courage, fueled by anger, deserted her. Ildiko had collapsed in Brishen's arm, lightheaded at her recklessness.

He'd held her close, his praise of her bravery the only thing that kept her upright as he led her up a flight of stairs and down two corridors to a door decorated with fanciful strap hinges. He opened the door, revealing a spacious chamber, lavishly furnished with a large bed, wardrobe, chests and a table and chairs set near a hearth in which a low-burning fire flickered.

Brishen led her to one of the chairs. Ildiko dropped into it gratefully. She was truly part of the family now. Just like the rest, she'd have to sleep with one eye open, in fear of Secmis.

"Do you want a dram of wine?" Brishen held a goblet in one hand and a pitcher in the other.

"I'll take two," she replied and offered a feeble smile at his chuckle. She took the goblet from him with shaking hands and searched for the right words that wouldn't excoriate Secmis too badly. She was Brishen's parent after all. "Your mother is..."

"A soulless creature with a thirst for murder and an intellect greater than any other in the kingdom." Brishen poured wine for himself in another goblet. "It makes her a ruler unmatched in both malice and strategy. My father would have been overthrown decades ago without her by his side."

Ildiko blinked at him. Her husband continued to flummox her with his matter-of-fact acceptance of his parents' less than admirable traits as well as his own good nature. She could only surmise that like the children of most royal households, he'd been raised by a troop of nannies, tutors and mentors, at least some possessing a compassionate character.

She wanted to ask him more, but talking about the Kai king and queen soured the wine in her stomach. Instead, she focused on her surroundings. "Where are we?"

He took the chair next to her. "Your bedchamber. At least during your stay here in the palace. What do you think?"

Distracted by his second remark, Ildiko gave her surroundings no more than a quick glance. "It's very nice. What do you mean my stay in the palace?" A second knot of apprehension twisted in her gut, taking up residence next to the one slowly unwinding itself from her encounter with Secmis.

It wasn't at all unusual among the Gauri for noblemen to sequester their wives on distant estates, isolated from court life, while their husbands lived separate existences with a few conjugal visits each year to assure the hereditary line continued.

While Ildiko liked the idea of putting as much distance as possible between herself and Secmis, she didn't relish a future in which she withered away in some forgotten castle, kept company only by Kai servants as resentful of their exile as she was.

Brishen brushed her knee with a gray hand. One black nail caught on the fabric of her skirt, creating a pleat. "Don't worry,

Ildiko. I'll be exiled with you. I have a house on the far western borders of the kingdom. We'll stay here for a few weeks so you can become familiar with the Kai court and then journey home."

Brishen said "home" in such a voice that he might as well have said "sanctuary" instead. It was obvious to Ildiko that while he tolerated the Kai court, his heart resided elsewhere.

She recalled a map spread across a table in King Sangur's study—a cartographical masterpiece of the many kingdoms that shared the great expanse of lands this side of the Apteran Ocean. She frowned. "Your estate nestles against Beladine lands."

He nodded, his yellow eyes flaring brighter for a moment. "It does. But I'm not defenseless, and I suspect our human neighbors will either wait before trying another stunt like the one on the trade road or consider another way to foil this alliance."

Ildiko hoped those neighbors would choose the second option or just accept the reality of trade and alliance between the Kai and the Gauri. While she'd enjoy self-imposed banishment with Brishen at her side, she didn't fancy doing so while under siege by the Beladine kingdom.

She finished her wine and rose to set the empty goblet on the table. "Will Anhuset accompany us?" She smiled at his nod. "Good. I very much like her."

A knock at the door halted any further conversation. Brishen bade their visitor enter. A Kai man dressed in livery, hovered just inside the doorway, shadowed by two women. All three bowed, and the man spoke.

"Your Highness, His Majesty wishes for you to meet him in the council chamber." He said more, but Ildiko's understanding of the Kai language was not extensive enough to parse out everything.

Brishen nodded and stood. "Speaking of Belawat, my father will want to know more about the attack on the trade road." He reached for her hand and kissed her fingertips, his touch cool and soft on her skin.

The king's messenger stood to the side so the women behind him could enter the room. Ildiko rose from her chair to stand by Brishen. The women were also dressed in the garb of palace servants. One looked older than the other by a decade, and both were young. While the elder one tried not to gawk at Ildiko, the younger servant ignored her, her lamplight eyes trained solely on Brishen who returned her stare with a like intensity.

"I've seen you in memory," he said gently in the Common tongue. "Are you Talumey's kin?"

The girl's still features crumpled. She fell to her knees before Brishen who frowned. "His sister, Your Highness. Kirgipa. Sha-Anhuset sent word of the fallen. You have honored our family. That a prince would carry Talumey's mortem light..."

Brishen interrupted her with a hand on her arm. "Stand up, Kirgipa." He coaxed her to her feet. His frown had eased but not the sorrow in the downturn of his mouth. "It would have been a better thing had I returned him to your mother alive and unharmed. It's he who honors your family. He was a good soldier and fought bravely."

Kirgipa's chin quivered and Ildiko wondered if the Kai shed tears as humans did when they mourned. The servant bowed to Brishen and then to her before returning to her place next to the older woman.

Brishen turned to the king's messenger waiting patiently by the door. "Send another message to Kirgipa's mother. I'll arrive tomorrow with her son's mortem light." He turned to Ildiko. "Do you wish to accompany me? We'd go tonight, but there's no escaping the celebration feast without unleashing the queen's wrath on everyone involved in our absence."

Ildiko gave an involuntary shiver at the thought of Secmis's retribution. She glanced at Kirgipa before easing closer to Brishen so only he could hear her. "Are you certain? I'm an outlander here, Brishen, and this is Kai business in both flesh and spirit."

His black eyebrows snapped together in a scowl, surprising Ildiko. "You are first and foremost of the royal house of Khaskhem. There is no place barred to you except by the will of Djedor and Secmis."

Were they alone, she might have smoothed the line bisecting the space between his eyebrows. Instead, Ildiko limited her touch to a brief caress of his arm. She didn't miss the watchful stares of the nearby servants or the looks exchanged between them.

"This isn't a matter of rank and access, Brishen, but of discretion. Would a woman mourning the loss of her son welcome a stranger to witness it, especially one who'd draw the attention I will?"

Brishen still scowled, and his eyes glowed a little brighter. "What would you do in her place?"

She shrugged. "When I lost my parents, I found no comfort in the sympathies of strangers, but each person is different. And I am neither Kai nor a mother—two roles in which I have no experience."

He eyed her for a moment. "Will you go for my sake?"

"Yes," she said without hesitation.

Obviously pleased with her answer, Brishen bowed and turned back to the messenger. "Let's get this over with so I may return to my wife." He paused and turned back to Ildiko before stepping into the hallway. "The chamber next door is mine. You're welcome to explore it." He winked at her. "Much to my family's disgust, I'm a man of few secrets."

He disappeared into the corridor, closing the door behind him and leaving Ildiko alone with the two Kai women.

The silence grew awkward as Ildiko considered what to say. "I am still learning your language," she said. Both women shifted in place, and Ildiko congratulated herself on learning how to better read her adopted people's expressions. She'd definitely seen surprise cross the servants' features at her uttering Kai words.

"From what I can tell, your Common is better than my bast-Kai, so why don't we start with Common, and you can teach me words in your tongue as we converse."

They nodded in unison, and the three began a stilted dialogue between them as they helped Ildiko unpack some of her trunks and instructed other servants for where to place the tub brought in for a bath. Ildiko already knew Kirgipa's name and learned the other woman was Sinhue.

During her journey from Pricid to Haradis, Ildiko had grown used to the stares of the Kai, sometimes curious, other times revolted. Sinhue's and Kirgipa's didn't bother her, and they would be nothing compared to what she'd face at the welcoming celebration later—where she'd likely feel anything but welcomed.

Except for a few smothered exclamations when Ildiko disrobed and stepped into her bath, the two servants were circumspect, civil and helpful. Ildiko fancied she even heard a note of approval in Sinhue's voice when she agreed that wearing Kai garb instead of Gauri to the celebration feast was a good idea.

During her preparations, she heard movement and rustlings next door. Brishen must have returned from council with his father and, like her, prepared for the upcoming festivities. He confirmed that assumption when he knocked on her door and entered at her bidding.

No longer dressed in riding leathers and light armor, Brishen had changed into garb even more formal than he'd worn at their wedding in Pricid.

A wide-sleeved tunic with a high collar covered most of a tight fitting shirt and trousers, all in varying shades of black and forest green embroidered silk. Tiny beads threaded through twin braids were woven into his black hair. Except for the braids, he wore his hair loose, and it spilled over his shoulders, dark as a crow's wing.

Being in each other's constant company during the journey to Haradis had changed the way Ildiko saw him—tempered her perception of his otherness. His toothy smile still startled her as much as her eyes unnerved him, but she began to understand why Kai women found her husband attractive.

He hadn't abandoned his martial adornment entirely. A wide belt of thick leather decorated with brass studs cinched the tunic close to his narrow waist. Anyone interested in sliding a knife under his ribs would find it a difficult task getting through the leather for a lethal thrust. The belt sported a large ring sewn to the leather, and from that Brishen had tied his court sword. It rested against his hip, companion to the daggers tucked into the tops of his boots. Ildiko guessed he probably bristled with weaponry; these were just the ones she could see.

"Are we going to war or to a feast?" she teased.

"This is Djedor's court, *hercegesé*," he said. "They're often one and the same."

While Ildiko knew he teased her in return, his remark sent her stomach into a nervous tumble. She wasn't one to partake heavily of wine or ale, but she hoped both ran freely during this meal, otherwise her hands might shake so badly she'd stab herself with her own eating dagger.

She quickly discovered her husband was learning to read her expressions just as she was learning to read his. He stepped closer and bent to whisper in her ear. "Peace, Ildiko. It won't be so bad. And I'll paint the walls with Kai blood if any dare threaten you."

Brishen meant his declaration as an assurance, but Ildiko shuddered. He was fiercely protective of her, and for that she was grateful. Still, she hoped they could get through this dinner without a decapitation or dismemberment.

He stepped away and scrutinized her with a glowing gaze. "I hadn't expected this," he said.

While Brishen met in council with the king, Ildiko had readied for the feast. When her new servants laid out the gowns she'd brought from home across her bed, she'd given a disapproving cluck. "I should have had the forethought to have clothing made that a Kai woman would wear." A new gown or headdress wouldn't make her any more Kai or any less Gauri, but adopting their fashion might demonstrate her willingness to embrace Kai culture.

At her complaint, Sinhue had bowed and fled the room, startling both Ildiko and Kirgipa. The servant returned with two Kai men who dragged a large chest through the door and shoved it against one wall. When they left, Sinhue lifted the chest lid and motioned for Ildiko to come closer.

Ildiko gasped at the sight of lush fabrics stacked on top of each other—muted greens and golds mingled with bronzes and blacks as deep as serpent blood. Splashes of jewel-toned amaranthine and cobalt shone amidst the darker colors.

She knelt beside Sinhue and plunged her hands into the treasure trove, pulling out scarves and silky trousers, embroidered tunics heavy with gold thread and jeweled girdles woven and draped with gold chains more delicate than spider webs. "It's all so beautiful."

Sinhue's wide grin spiked the fine hairs on Ildiko's nape. "His Highness ordered them before he left for your homeland, *Hercegesé*. They're for you. We were instructed to leave them packed until you chose a time to wear them."

Ildiko sputtered, still awestruck by the chest's contents. They were finer than anything even Queen Fantine wore during feasts held for affairs of state. Her own wedding apparel had been beggars' rags compared to these clothes. "Now is a good time," she said.

Two hours and the enthusiastic efforts of her maids to lace her, cinch her, and tame her hair, and Ildiko stood before Brishen dressed as Kai royalty. Of the many times she wished she could easily read Kai expressions, she had never wished more fervently for that skill than now.

She was dressed similar to Brishen—long tunic with wide sleeves over a tighter fitting shirt. Her tunic was longer than his and cut so that it gave the illusions of a skirt but with far greater freedom of movement than a skirt allowed. She wore trousers as well beneath the tunic, their ankle cuffs tucked into laced boots that reached to her calves. The girdle encircling her waist was as wide as his belt but made of fabric in which rubies no bigger than peppercorns had been stitched and gleamed like small demon eyes in the dim light.

Despite Sinhue's and Kirgipa's polite but insistent suggestions that another color might suit her better, Ildiko had chosen to dress all in black. Everything she wore tonight, down to the combs in her hair, had to send a silent message. Wearing the fashions favored by the Kai signaled her willingness to accept her adopted people. Dressing in a color that starkly emphasized her skin and hair signaled she was still Gauri human and unashamed of the fact.

"What do you think," she asked Brishen and pivoted in a slow circle. "Will this do?"

He stood before her, silent for several long moments. Ildiko's palms grew damp, and behind Brishen the servant women crushed their skirts in their hands, apprehension plain in their pale-knuckled grips.

Brishen reached for her hand and tugged until she stood close enough to feel his body heat. His hand rested lightly on her back, fingertips tracing the upper line of her girdle. "You're very clever, wife and have a talent for saying much while saying little." The lines at the corners of his eyes deepened, and the corners of his mouth turned up. "This will more than do."

Something flared between them, a sense of camaraderie, of belonging. For a brief moment, Ildiko felt as if she and Brishen stood alone in this chamber, bound together not only by vows but by similarities far greater than their obvious differences. Brishen of House Khaskhem was as fine a man as any born, whether he was human, Kai or any of the other Elder races that populated these lands, and Ildiko's affection for him grew by leaps with every moment she came to know him better.

"You make a very handsome dead eel, my husband," she said and winked. Sinhue and Kirgipa both gasped.

"For a boiled mollusk, you wear black quite well, my wife," Brishen shot back, and his smile stretched a little wider.

More gasps, and Ildiko caught sight of the two maids gaping at them slack-jawed at the exchange of insults.

The sudden knock at the door made both women jump. Kirgipa was the first to answer and held the door open as a procession of servants carrying a small table and covered trays entered. They set the table near the hearth and placed their burdens on its surface. Plates, knives and linen sanaps were set on the smaller table between the two chairs facing the hearth, and one poured more wine into the goblets she and Brishen had drank from earlier.

The servants filed out as quickly and quietly as they entered, leaving Ildiko glancing first at the trays from which savory smells wafted into the room and then at Brishen who dismissed Sinhue and Kirgipa with a nod.

Ildiko peered at the various trays. "What is this? I thought we were to attend the feast?" She rather liked the idea of skipping that trial and eating in here with just Brishen for company, even if they were terribly overdressed for a quiet dinner between them.

Brishen gestured to one of the chairs. "Take a seat. This is a practice try beforehand." He spread one of the linen sanaps in her lap when she sat. "You'll have the weight of every stare on you at the feast, Ildiko, and you'll be served things you've never eaten before. I'd rather you weren't surprised by what's put on your plate."

Ildiko flinched a little with guilt. Brishen had bravely eaten everything served to him at the Gauri banquet following their wedding. She'd been unable to determine his expressions as he spooned his food into his mouth and chewed, but the tension quivering throughout his body had told her enough to know that dinner had been its own particular torture.

"I'm sorry about the potato, Brishen," she said.

His lips thinned and he took a swallow of wine from his goblet before taking a seat next to her. "No need to apologize, though I'll never understand how the Gauri willingly eat such foul, disgusting food."

Ildiko feared she'd soon echo that sentiment.

Brishen slid the first tray onto the table and removed the lid. The dish was a medley of fresh fruit and herbs drizzled in a sweet sauce. Brishen cautioned her to take only a small portion so she wouldn't be too full to eat later.

Ildiko liked the dish and recognized some of the fruits used in the dish. While prepared a little differently than what she was used to, it tasted good, and she looked forward to the next dish with less trepidation.

By the fourth dish--slivers of guinea fowl roasted and then stewed in spicy gravy—she was thoroughly confused. From what she could tell so far, the Kai royal chefs were superior cooks and the food outstanding. She could grow fat on such tasty meals.

The fifth and final tray proved how terribly wrong her assumptions were. Brishen lifted the lid with a flourish, revealing a dinner pie large enough to feed two people. The savory smoke rising from its top teased Ildiko's nose with the scents of herbs and pepper. The crust was perfectly golden and buttery with a braided edge and fanciful dough cut-outs that revealed the cook was as much artist as baker. Her mouth watered in anticipation of cutting into it.

And then the pie breathed.

Ildiko gasped and half rose from her seat, her sanap tumbling to the floor. "My gods, did you see that?"

Brishen's stoic expression didn't change, and he motioned for her to sit down. "You can't run from this one, Ildiko. It's served at every high feast and celebration. A delicacy among the Kai. It's a surety we'll be served one later. Newly married couples share it as a symbol of fortune and prosperity in the marriage."

Ildiko did as he bid and sat but scooted her chair a little further away from the table. "What is in that pie?" Whatever it was, it was still alive. Fortune and prosperity be damned. Her throat closed up in protest at the thought of having to swallow something alive and still wriggling.

Brishen picked up his dagger. "Watch closely because at some point, you'll have to do this yourself." He stared at the pie, as focused as a hawk on a branch watching a mouse in the field below it. The pie's crust rippled, creating cracks across its smooth surface. A black spine poked through the crust, and Brishen pounced.

He slammed the knifepoint into the pie hard enough to make the plates bounce on the table and splash wine from the goblets. An insectile screech pierced the quiet. Brishen twisted the knife. It made a cracking noise, and the pie abruptly ruptured, sending pieces of crust splattered in a black slime across the table.

This time Ildiko leapt over her chair to crouch behind it, wide-eyed and horrified as Brishen pried his knife out of the destroyed pie. It came free with a sucking sound, revealing a twitching scarpatine impaled on the knife's point. Ildiko clapped a hand over her mouth and prayed she wouldn't be sick.

Brishen placed the scarpatine on his plate, careful to avoid the venomous barb on the end of its lashing tail. The knife had pierced the creature's hard shell to hold it in place. Brishen lifted a second knife and made short work of chopping off the lethal tail and then the head with its multiple eye stalks and curved fangs. What remained were the claws and the thick body of the carcass.

Brishen cracked the rest of the shell in the same way Ildiko had watched sailors split the shells of lobsters. He peeled back the segments, exposing gray flesh. He sliced that away from the main body, leaving a layer of thick, yellow fat and a mottled black vein that ran down its center. Below that, another layer of the gray flesh.

Ildiko slowly stood and watched as Brishen placed the first layer of scarpatine meat on her plate and spooned some of the oily dark liquid over it. He scraped away the fat layer and the vein and carved out the rest of the flesh from the shell to put on his plate.

He started and completed the process without once looking at her. Brishen's focus shifted to Ildiko finally, and his voice held both sympathy and a kind of dark humor. "I'm glad you wore black, wife. No one will see the stains."

She stared at him, sitting calmly amongst the ruin of exploded pie and the remains of dead and gutted scarpatine. Her serving of the Kai delicacy sat on her plate, a pale gray slab glossy with a black ooze that dribbled down the sides. It twitched once.

Ildiko's stomach went into open revolt, and she bolted for the basin on the table at her bedside. A strong arm slid around her waist, supporting her as she retched into the bowl. Brishen's hand smoothed her hair. He held her until she emptied her stomach and offered her a glass of water to rinse her mouth.

Afterwards, she gazed at Brishen, bleary-eyed but resolved. Ildiko had faced down a woman far more venomous than a scarpatine. She would not be defeated by dinner. "At least tell me it tastes like chicken."

CHAPTER TWELVE

Though his mother might be planning Ildiko's murder for her unforgiveable refusal to be cowed, Brishen couldn't fault the queen for the feast she ordered prepared to officially welcome him and his wife home.

The dining hall was lavishly decorated. Flowers from the royal gardens hung in garlands over the windows and spilled in lush bouquets on the tables, their opalescent petals glowing beneath the flickering light of candles and hanging lamps. The tables were covered in cloths of finely woven linen and silk, the benches upon which the nobility sat, lined with velvet cushions.

The high table was even more appointed, set to emphasize the royal house's wealth and power. An army of liveried servants lined the walls behind the tables, ready to serve.

It was all grand, even majestic—fit for a royal *herceges* and his *hercegesé*. Brishen wished fiercely he could grab Ildiko's hand and escape back to her chamber—or his—and share a meal in relative solitude. If not there, then with the soldiers under his command. Even road rations tasted delectable when shared with good company. Ildiko could avoid another serving of scarpatine and he, his parents' poisonous interactions. As it was, escape was not an option, and he prayed for a quick end to the celebration.

He approached the high table, Ildiko by his side and the recipient of countless curious stares from the nobles gathered in the hall. She bore their scrutiny proudly. Attired in her crow-black finery, she was the picture of serenity and confidence— shoulders and back straight, chin raised at a haughty angle—equal to any member of the Kai royal household.

She wore her mask well, but Brishen sensed her fear. Her hand rested in the crook of his elbow, fingers buried in the folds of his sleeve. Were she Kai instead of human and possessed the same sharp nails, she would have sliced through the fabric and scored his forearm bloody. Luckily, her tight grip only managed to slow the flow of blood to his fingers.

Ildiko might not reciprocate the feeling, but Brishen considered himself fortunate to have such a wife. She was shrewd and insightful. Raised amidst another royal court, she understood its machinations and manipulations; its subtle messages conveyed in something as innocuous as the cut of a tunic or its color. He'd shield her as much as possible from the criticisms of the Kai, which would focus on her homely appearance and spread from there, but he suspected she'd manage to hold her own with even the most acerbic Kai aristocrat. They'd witnessed Ildiko stand against Secmis's barbed comments and the implied threat in her pointed questions. Only a few dimwitted Kai would still assume that she was cowardly because she was human.

The nobles bowed as he and Ildiko passed them. Brishen ignored their stares as he always did and leaned closer to Ildiko. "How is your stomach?"

She stared straight ahead, but her fingers flexed on his arm. "It's there," she said softly.

He smothered a smile at her noncommittal answer. The idea to introduce her to the delicacy of baked scarpatine before the dinner had been a strategic one. Even some of the Kai found the dish revolting, and it represented a much more challenging entree to serve as well as eat than the passive, foul-tasting potato.

Her reaction hadn't surprised him. Her determination to eat the gray flesh still squirming on her plate did. Ildiko had rinsed her mouth with wine and water while he set the basin outside her door. "Are you sure you don't want to keep this in here for now?" Guilt rode him hard at the memory of holding her while she emptied her belly of its contents.

She shook her head. "I'm sure."

"What if you're sick again?" It was entirely possible. Cutting the pie and butchering the scarpatine wasn't the worst part.

Ildiko's chin rose, and she marched back to her chair. "I won't be." Before Brishen said anything else, she sat down, grabbed her dagger, sliced off a piece of scarpatine and popped it in her mouth.

Brishen's eyebrows rose. He hovered by the door, ready to snatch the basin back and race to his wife's side. Ildiko chewed slowly, her brow furrowed in concentration. She swallowed and drank her wine.

"Well?" he said.

She glanced at him from the corner of her eye before slicing off another piece. The gray mass twitched between her fingers, and she slapped it against the edge of her plate to subdue it. "It doesn't taste like chicken." She bit and chewed again.

Brishen laughed, delighted and relieved. "No, it doesn't." Assured he wouldn't have to grab the basin, he joined her at the table. His portion of scarpatine had grown cold; he suspected hers had as well. "What does it taste like to you?" he asked between bites.

Ildiko studied the small portion impaled on her dagger's tip. "A little muddy. A little briny. Mostly like someone took a fish, packed it in dirt and let it cook inside a sweaty boot."

He winced at the vivid, albeit accurate, description. "You'd reduce the royal cook to fits of melancholy if he heard you say that."

She shrugged. "He's reduced me to retching with his repulsive pie. I suffer no guilt." She lowered her dagger with the scarpatine still on it and pushed her plate away, a shudder wracking her slim frame. "I won't lie, Brishen. It's beyond foul, but I'm glad we did this now. I would have humiliated us both at the feast."

Brishen shoved his half-eaten portion aside as well and reached for Ildiko's hand. Her fingers notched with his, the skin of her hand so pale, he could trace the filigree of blue veins that ran beneath it with his thumb. "I don't think that's possible, wife."

Her cheeks flushed an unsightly red. Three days earlier her response would have alarmed him into thinking she was ill. He'd since learned such coloration was similar to a Kai's own darkening blush—an expression of anger, embarrassment or pleasure. The tightening of her hand on his assured him hers was one of pleasure at his words.

"You've a stronger stomach than I credited you with if you could eat the scarpatine without gagging." It still surprised him. She'd been violently ill after watching him carve up the creature; he'd had no hope of her being able to eat it without growing sick a second time.

Ildiko untangled her fingers from his and patted his hand. "I doubt the Gauri court is that much different from the Kai one. If the nobility aren't spying on each other, they're maligning each other. Everything is fodder for gossip and ridicule. Unless you want to be the topic of conversation among bored lords and ladies waiting to sink their claws into you, you eat what's served to you and act as if it pleases you. I learned early to hold my breath when I chewed and breathe through my nose when I swallowed. And I always made sure my goblet was full."

She winked at him and lifted her dagger to poke at the now still slab of scarpatine. "This is one of the most horrendous things I've ever eaten, but it's nothing compared to King Sangur's favorite dish—a pea soup I will swear until I'm dead was made of and prepared by packs of rotting demons. The kitchens served it to us once a week without fail, though I don't ever recall anyone having to battle a vicious pod of attacking peas just to gulp down the soup."

With her words, the lingering concerns Brishen had about her ability to withstand another round of Kai food vanished completely, along with any doubts he harbored about her adjusting to this new life. She stood beside him now in the dining hall, frightened but resolved. Not only would this Gauri woman survive in the Kai world, she'd thrive.

A herald announced the king and queen's arrival. The chatter in the hall ceased abruptly, and as one, the guests bowed. Ildiko pressed against Brishen's side. "I hope the queen doesn't decide to roast me for a pie." Amusement colored her voice, but Brishen heard the thread of fear as well.

He pressed her hand to his side with his elbow. "I'll skewer her if she tries, wife."

A soft giggle teased his ear. "You can't skewer her. She's your mother, Brishen."

"And a deadlier adversary I have yet to face," he replied.

They straightened as the monarchs passed, and Brishen's skin prickled under the weight of Secmis's stare as she leveled a narrow look on him and then Ildiko before taking her place next to her husband at the high table. Brishen's brother Harkuf and his wife Tiye followed, taking their places to the right of the king.

Brishen nudged Ildiko into step behind the heir apparent. "We sit on the queen's side," he said.

Ildiko's grip tightened on his arm. "Lovely," she muttered.

The feast began as most feasts like it did—bloated with ritual and artifice. The nobility maneuvered amongst themselves for the choicest seats, arguing over whose rank and family ties entitled them to a spot closest to the high table. Brishen sighed and fiddled with his eating dagger. This happened at every state dinner and celebration and was one of the things he didn't miss when he escaped court to his isolated estate.

Ildiko sat on one side of him, rigid and silent, staring straight ahead. Secmis sat on his other side, her claws drumming a beat on the tabletop as everyone waited for Djedor to start the feast with an official welcome of Brishen's wife.

This time Djedor omitted any insults regarding Ildiko's appearance, and kept his formal acceptance of her into the Kai royal family mercifully brief. Brishen guessed his father was hungry and didn't want to waste any more time on the niceties when there was hot food waiting to be served.

His formal declaration of recognition, however abbreviated, bequeathed power to Ildiko she didn't previously possess. She might be Gauri human in appearance, but she'd just become Kai where it truly counted—court ranking. She was officially a *hercegesé* now, a true duchess. Brishen relaxed in his seat, relieved. Now they just had to get through the interminable dinner and whatever nastiness Secmis decided to throw at them.

They didn't have to wait long. The queen fired her first volley just as the servants set down bowls of soup. "You humans are very pale," she said in Common. "Only our diseased sport that shade."

Those sitting closest to the high table to hear the remark tittered amongst themselves and passed the comment down to those seated out of earshot. Brishen opened his mouth to snarl at his mother. Ildiko's hand on his leg under the table stopped him.

She sipped soup from her spoon, offering no indication that either the soup's taste or Secmis's comment bothered her. She dabbed at her lips with her sanap before answering. "You're right, your Majesty; we are quite pale by comparison. The Kai are very gray. Only our dead are that color."

Secmis's lips thinned until they drew back, exposing the tips of her fangs. More whispers and a few muffled snorts of amusement drifted up from the lower tables. The queen's hand curled around her eating dagger. Brishen shifted sideways in his chair toward her, prepared to act as shield for Ildiko in case Secmis decided to attack.

The glow of her eyes flared hot. She changed tactics. "Your bast-Kai is very clumsy," she said in the same tongue.

"My Common is far more proficient," Ildiko agreed in smooth, flawless bast-Kai.

Brishen hid a smile and started on his own soup. He was intuitive enough to know any interference on his part would not be welcomed by either woman. He suffered the sudden, uncomfortable sensation of sitting between two large cats, both protracting and retracting their claws as they faced off against each other.

The queen continued with her barrage of acerbic observations that touched on everything from the way Ildiko wore her hair to how she held her spoon. She was restricted on what insults she threw out. Ildiko's lineage was off-limits since Brishen's parents considered it acceptable enough for their younger son, but she didn't spare her contempt in other matters. Ildiko remained polite and utterly indomitable in the face of Secmis's obvious disdain.

Brishen leaned forward for a quick glimpse of his brother at the other end of the table. Harkuf either didn't hear the exchange between the queen and Ildiko or he didn't care. His attention remained solely on the food in front of him, with occasional glances at his latest mistress seated at one of the lower tables. His wife Tiye was a different story. Too distracted by the interactions between Secmis and Ildiko, she picked at her food, her expression wavering between fascination and horror as she listened to their conversation.

Brishen imagined whatever bits and pieces she heard shocked her. Secmis terrified Tiye as much as she terrified Ildiko. Unlike Ildiko, Tiye never stood against her formidable mother-in-law in either word or action. He remained undecided if she was weaker than Ildiko or simply possessed a better sense of self-preservation.

The exchange between the Kai queen and her newly acquired Gauri daughter-in-law continued through most of the meal, with the dinner guests perched on their seats to catch every word and expression. Their scrutiny intensified when the last course was delivered—scarpatine pies with their golden crusts and the contents writhing inside them.

Brishen leaned closer to Ildiko. "Are you ready?"

She surprised him with a soft exhalation of relief. "Yes," she whispered. "If this is what it takes to silence your mother, I'll eat this vile pie all day long."

A howl of laughter threatened to escape his throat. Ildiko jumped in her seat when Brishen turned and pressed his cheek to hers so that his face was turned away from the audience, and his lips brushed her ear. It was a stunning display of public affection—one he knew his mother would fume over for days and the court would gossip about for weeks.

He allowed himself a small chuckle then. "I will conquer kingdoms for you if you but ask it of me, Ildiko."

She pulled away enough to meet his smiling gaze, her own mouth turning up. "Just defeat the pie without either of us getting stung, husband. I'll be satisfied."

While Ildiko didn't join in the numerous oohs and aahs over the delicacy served, she didn't flinch when Brishen repeated the process of cutting into the pie and butchering the scarpatine. He could almost feel the wave of disappointment from the guests roll over him as she ate her portion without hesitation or fanfare. Only he heard the measured rhythm of her breathing—when she held her breath, when she exhaled—and made sure her goblet remained filled.

Beside him, Secmis fairly quivered with frustration. She'd been given a pie of her own and vented her wrath on the scarpatine by puncturing the shell and slicing out the flesh with her claws instead of her knife. Oily black blood oozed off her claw tips as she smirked at Ildiko who steadfastly ignored her and Brishen who glared.

When the feast finally concluded and the king and queen quit the hall—Secmis gifting Ildiko with a final scowl—Brishen felt as if he'd just walked off a battlefield. Ildiko stood next to him, her hand once more resting in the crook of his elbow as the two faced the horde of nobles who descended on them to offer their congratulations and satisfy their curiosity.

It was more of an interrogation than a social gathering, and like the feast before it, Ildiko suffered through it with stoic aplomb. It was Brishen who called a halt and refused offers of more drink and food in the various palace chambers occupied by the more powerful aristocrats.

He and Ildiko bowed and made their escape into the hallway. "How fast can you walk?" he said.

For the first time that evening, she offered him a wide smile, flashing her small square teeth. "I can run if you want me to."

"Excellent." He grabbed her hand and they dashed together through the corridors and up a flight of stairs until they stood outside the doors to his chamber and hers.

"How did I do, husband?" Ildiko said when she caught her breath.

Brishen reached for her hand and brought it to his mouth for a kiss, then bowed before her. "You make a magnificent *hercegesé*, my wife."

She trailed her fingertips down his arm. "I think we both caught the message the queen delivered when she gutted that scarpatine, Brishen. Your mother hates me. I'm sorry."

He stepped closer and wrapped an arm around her narrow waist. "If Secmis is smart, and she is, she'll find a way to overcome her dislike and make an ally of you." He kissed her forehead "I've had enough of playing the puppet on display. I crave good company and good wine. Will you join me?"

Ildiko nodded and slid her hands up his arms to his shoulders. "May we invite your cousin? I didn't see Anhuset at the feast, and I imagine she'd enjoy your retelling of the event."

Brishen nodded. "Despite her family's disapproval, Anhuset isn't one for these gatherings and avoids them at all costs."

Ildiko worried at a thread on his sleeve with her fingers. "I envy her."

"So do I," he said. "I'll send a message to have her meet us in my chamber. She'll match my story of this feat with her retelling of our wedding celebration in Pricid. She's still threatening to split my gullet over having to eat one of those noxious potatoes."

CHAPTER THIRTEEN

A week after their arrival in Haradis, Ildiko sat on one of the benches in the palace gardens. Eyes closed and face turned up to the sun, she soaked in the late morning light that spilled into the palace garden. Sunbeams lanced through the spaces left open by climbing vines on lattice work and transformed the various fish ponds dotting the landscape into pools of reflective glass.

Except for the hooded guardsman a discreet distance away, she was alone in the gardens. The palace denizens slept, including her husband who'd wished her a peaceful sleep and left her to find his bed.

Ildiko thought she'd fall into oblivion the moment she pulled the covers over her shoulders. She was wrong. She'd lain awake in the graying dark, listening to Kirgipa's restless sleep and Sinhue's gentle snores. They slept on pallets on the floor at the foot of her bed. As her personal servants, both women spent a lot of time with her, helping her dress in the evening, undress at morning and change for the various gatherings the monarchs, the heir apparent, or the higher status nobles held each night. Besides Brishen and Anhuset, they were Ildiko's greatest source of information regarding the Kai court and its many customs.

She was grateful to them and for their quick adjustment to her appearance—something that still elicited numerous fixed stares and not-so subtle whispers each time she made an appearance at one of the endless social functions she had attended with Brishen since their arrival in the capital city.

Ildiko was well-versed in the rhythm and madness of court life in general. No function was held simply for chit-chat or the pleasure of another's company. Whether they were Kai or Gauri, the nobility used such meetings to plan, to strategize, to negotiate, and to curry favor. Sometimes there were threats; other times there were bribes, all executed in the politest terms. Outright hostility was saved for the literal battlefields where the warfare was bloodier but more honest.

She pretended not to see the sympathetic back pats and shoulder squeezes the Kai men gave Brishen or hear the low-voiced offers of a Kai mistress for the evening. Taking offense made no sense to her. In Pricid, she'd been hailed as a beauty—too pretty for the likes of a repulsive, gray-skinned, fanged Kai prince. The Gauri and the Kai were two peoples with far more similarities than differences, but the differences stood out most, and each found the other hard on the eyes, whether they were glowing or not.

While the Kai men were civil and guarded with her, the women fell into three camps. A few were friendly and curious, asking Ildiko questions about her life in Pricid and what she thought of the Kai palace and its court. Most were as reserved as the men, offering polite congratulations on her marriage and nothing more. The last few practically vibrated resentment and jealousy, and Ildiko surmised these women had been Brishen's lovers at some point.

Her marriage was too young and too odd for her to suffer pangs of jealousy, but she was mildly curious. What about these particular women had attracted Brishen? Had it merely been their beauty or something more elusive and subtle in their character? Her husband was a good-natured man with an easy humor. Ildiko couldn't explain why she'd been so drawn to him since their first meeting. An intuitive sense of the vibrant soul and great heart that lay behind the ugly exterior? She didn't know, but she was grateful for his reciprocal regard. Though she was human and as yet unable to appreciate the beauty in Kai physicality, she understood why a Kai woman he'd once favored might be jealous of her for more than just her elevated rank as Brishen's wife.

Ildiko had chastised herself repeatedly for antagonizing the queen. So far, Secmis had done nothing more than hurl insults at her, but Ildiko trusted Brishen's warnings regarding his mother, and she remained wary. Facing these Kai women who likely considered each other rivals until her appearance at court made her glad she'd publically faced down the formidable Secmis. They might glare and scowl at her, but they hesitated to engage her in an unfriendly verbal exchange.

A solid week of this kind of combat had left her exhausted, but she couldn't sleep. Ildiko lay on her back and stared at the ceiling of her bed hangings. Sinhue and Kirgipa didn't waken when she slid out of bed, pulled on a robe and slippers and sneaked out of her chambers. A Kai guard bowed as she passed him in the corridor. He said nothing but fell into step behind her and followed her as she made her way to the palace gardens.

She found a bench in an alcove sheltered by a half dome of tree branches and now sat to face a sunrise she hadn't seen since she left Pricid.

The gardens, like the Kai, had fallen asleep with the coming of day. Brishen had shown her the gardens shortly after his return of Talumey's mortem light to his family. Ildiko had gasped and clapped her hands at its beauty. Pale flowers bloomed in lush profusion, glowing softly under the moon's light in shades of iridescent pearl and ivory. The leaves on the trees were plated silver, and the entire garden shimmered in the black night like the surface landscape of a fallen star.

This was the first time she had viewed them in daylight, and it was a far bleaker sight. The flowers had closed up behind dark, protective husks, and the leaves crackled black and spiny in the cool breeze. Morning had transformed the garden into an otherworldly space straight out of a nightmare. Sitting beneath the skeletal branches of the angular trees, Ildiko had never felt so alone or out of place.

Tears stung her eyes. She blinked them away. They welled again, stubbornly refusing to dry up even as the rising sun made her squint before its brilliant rays. She breathed slowly—in, out— and refused to succumb to the suffocating tightness in her chest or the sobs rising in her throat.

"I'm tired," she whispered to herself. "Just tired." There was no good reason to cry. Her husband would never win any Gauri beauty contests, but he was an exceptional man. Ildiko liked him very much. Many wives were not so lucky with the mates chosen for them or even ones they chose themselves.

His people, with the exception of his mother, had been civil and welcoming to her in the reserved way of the Kai. While they may never see her as Kai or accept her on her own merit, their respect for Brishen ensured they would always give the respect due to her as his wife. She expected nothing more.

Still, she eagerly awaited Brishen's announcement that they'd leave Haradis and travel to his estate. It might hug the borders with hostile Belawat, but it was solely Brishen's domain, one she hoped she could make hers as well.

She recalled their visit to Talumey's mother, Tarawin. The evening after that first dire court feast , they'd ridden through Haradis's narrow streets on horseback instead of in a carriage. Brishen had offered a choice.

"We can ride in a carriage, or you can ride pillion with me. You'll have more privacy in the carriage if you wish, but you'll be able to see Haradis better from horseback."

Ildiko had chosen horseback and was glad she did. The capital city was a bustling place in the middle of the night, and she had to remind herself that for the Kai, this was the middle of their day. Except for the darkness and the heavy foot traffic of slate-skinned people with firefly eyes, Haradis might have been like any other city—alive with vendors hawking their wares, children chasing dogs and chickens through the narrow alleyways, mothers shouting at them to return or be careful, and pickpockets slinking about to relieve the unwary of their coin. Prostitutes peddled their bodies next to merchants selling wine and various foods roasted on spits or steamed in pots.

The crowds parted as she rode with Brishen through the streets, accompanied by a small contingent of palace guards. Some pointed; others waved, and many stretched their necks for a glimpse of the prince's new wife. The deep hood she wore concealed her for the most part. Brishen had not initially approved.

"You shouldn't have to cover yourself. I'm not ashamed of my bride, Ildiko."

She patted his hand. "It's a matter of convenience, not shame, Brishen. If I go out there bareheaded and barefaced, we'll never get to Tarawin's home before dawn. And when we do, we'll have a mob behind us, all wanting to gawk at me. In her place, I'd find our arrival unpleasant at best."

He'd reluctantly agreed with her reasoning, and they arrived at Tarawin's house with only a small crowd of curious neighbors watching from their doorways. As soon as the woman opened the door and ushered them inside, the palace guard closed ranks outside, a solid barrier between them and any would-be visitors.

Like all the Kai women Ildiko had met so far, Talumey's mother was a tall, lithe creature with silvery hair. She lacked Anhuset's muscular athleticism and Secmis's haughty grace, but Ildiko thought her lovely in the Kai fashion. There was a softness to her features as well as a deep sadness that bracketed her mouth.

She knelt before Brishen. "You honor my house with your presence, *Herceges*. You and your wife."

Brishen helped her rise and held her hand. "I wish I brought a more joyful offering than this."

Tarawin brought their clasped hands to her forehead. "It is still treasured. My son would have never dreamed of such a privilege. I'm thankful you brought him home to us." She glanced at the silent Ildiko, and the lines at the corners of her eyes deepened with her faint smile. "A blessing on your marriage, *Hercegesé*. Welcome to Haradis. Welcome to my humble home."

It was a humble home, spotlessly clean, inviting to any who entered. A young girl hovered behind her mother, and Ildiko immediately caught the resemblance between her and Kirgipa. Tarawin introduced her as Kirgipa's younger sister, Atalan.

Brishen had offered to bring Kirgipa with them when he returned Talumey's mortem light. The servant had refused. "I'll be with my mother when she brings his mortem light to Emlek and comfort her there. I don't think I can bear to see my brother reduced to just light and memory."

They'd taken tea but refused the food Tarawin offered, for which Ildiko was glad. Her stomach was in knots. This was a house in mourning and carried within it a hushed waiting, as if the very walls and floor held a breath as it waited for Talumey's return.

When they finished their tea, Brishen pushed his cup aside. "Are you ready, Mistress Tarawin?"

She inhaled a slow breath, nodded, and rose from the table to retrieve a small crystal globe resting on a three-pronged stand on the mantel above the hearth. Brishen joined her in the middle of the room and gestured for Ildiko to remain in her seat.

Tarawin hesitated. "Are you certain you wish to do this, Your Highness? I can summon a priestess who will take the light and bring it to me."

Brishen shook his head and sank to his knees in front of her. "This is audience enough, mistress. Your son fought and died in my service. It's my honor to do this."

The globe wobbled in Tarawin's shaking hands at his answer. She held it out to Brishen who curved his hands over hers, slender fingers and black claws covering the pale orb.

The skin on Ildiko's arms pebbled at the first line of the chant the two recited in unison. She recognized its cant and rhythm— the lamentation the Kai had used when the mortem lights had first filled their willing vessels.

She gasped and leapt to her feet as black lines like thorny vines sprouted under the skin of Brishen's neck, speeding over his cheeks and across his forehead where they disappeared into his hairline. His closed eyelids twitched, cobwebbed with the same hideous lines, and his lips thinned back against his teeth.

Ildiko had never dabbled in magery, but she knew enough about spellwork to understand the dangers and lethality of interrupting it. This was powerful magic, painful magic, and all she could do was stand aside and wring her hands as her husband clutched the orb and convulsed on his knees, his speech stuttered and clumsy.

A dot of light illuminated the center of his chest, growing until it threatened to consume him and Tarawin whole. Ildiko turned her face away and shielded her eyes as a burst of blinding light filled the room. When she could see again, Brishen had slumped before Tarawin like a puppet with its strings cut.

Tarawin held the orb gingerly, its interior lit with the transferred mortem light until it resembled a small, glowing sun in her hands. She handed it to Atalan who took the globe, kissed it reverently and wrapped it in a silk cloth before setting it in a small chest set on the table where they'd taken their tea.

Assured the transfer of the mortem light was finished, Ildiko rushed to Brishen's side. The jagged black tracery under his skin had disappeared, but he still needed help to stand. She and Tarawin led him to the chair he'd vacated earlier. After several more cups of tea and assurances to a worried Tarawin and equally concerned Ildiko, Brishen announced he was ready to leave.

He was a paler shade of gray when they left the house and leaned against his patient mount for support.

"Brishen?" Ildiko clasped his elbow, frightened by the dullness of his eyes and the way his shoulders drooped.

"I'm fine, Ildiko. Just give me a moment. Giving up a mortem light leaves an emptiness at first." Brishen swiped a hand across his brow and offered Ildiko a feeble smile. "I grew used to Talumey's memories. Did you know his mother often admonished him when he was little for constantly picking his nose?"

Ildiko's nose twitched at the idea. With the set of claws the Kai sported on the ends of their fingers, it was a wonder Talumey still had his nose as an adult if he indulged in such a habit. "You did a fine thing bringing his mortem light back to her, though I'd imagine your parents would thrash you for kneeling before a merchant's wife."

As proud as any human prince of a royal house, her new husband was also amiable and seemingly unaware of his status. No prince, duke, or baron she ever met would ever bend a knee to someone below them, even if it was a mandatory part of a religious ritual.

Brishen snorted. "When I met with my father last evening to discuss the Beladine attack, he opened the conversation by pinning my ears back for lowering myself and shaming my house's name."

Having been a recipient of similar diatribes from her aunt, Ildiko sympathized. "I'm guessing you lost no sleep over his displeasure?"

He shrugged. "None whatsoever. If a simple genuflection of gratitude compromises my character and shames my house, then we are both less than shadow. There is more to royalty than blood and birthright, wife."

They rode back to the palace, Ildiko's grip tight around Brishen's waist. He was too heavy for her to stop him from falling off his horse if he fainted, but at least she could slow the fall. He patted her hands occasionally as if to reassure her. She wished she'd chosen the carriage.

A small army of servants had greeted him in his chambers. Brishen hugged Ildiko, promised he'd check in on her later, collapsed across his bed and promptly fell asleep. She instructed the servants to leave him dressed and tossed a blanket over him. His personal servant assured her he'd keep watch and let Ildiko know if any problem arose.

Ildiko had kept to her room the remainder of the evening and stayed awake until almost dawn, her ears straining to hear any sound from the chamber next door. She fell asleep to the silence and awakened the next evening to Brishen at her door, none the worse for wear and with the offer to show her the royal gardens. They toured the paths. He knew nothing of flowers and plants, and she'd teased him that if they'd toured the armory, he'd be far more informative.

"That's true," he said. "But you please me more surrounded by things of beauty than things of war."

He continued to amaze her, this Kai prince with his wolf smile and radiant soul. With that bit of praise, he'd made the garden her favorite place to visit in Haradis, even now when it slept, brittle and black under the sunlight.

"I have a fine husband indeed," she said aloud to herself as she soaked up the morning rays.

"I wholeheartedly agree," the subject of her thoughts replied.

Ildiko jumped as a heavily cloaked and hooded Brishen sat down beside her. He turned a shoulder against the sun so that his hood protected his face from direct light.

"What are you doing up?" she asked. Only the guards on duty were awake at this hour, and the one who stood sentinel nearby kept watch from the deep shadows cast by leafy limbs of a tree.

Brishen's eyes were yellow slits in his dark face. "I might ask the same of you."

"I miss the sun," she said. She didn't resent changing her sleep schedule to mimic the Kai's, but her body craved a bit of daylight. "And I couldn't sleep anyway, so I thought I'd come out here. It's peaceful."

"With no one around?" His smile had taken on a wry quality.

Ildiko shrugged. "Yes. While the Gauri court was just as crowded and busy, I was often left to my own devices and not so closely..."

"Scrutinized?" Brishen sighed at her nod. "It can be suffocating if you're not used to it."

"Are you used to it?"

"Not anymore."

Ildiko wondered what had changed for him. He answered her unspoken question.

"Since I spend most of my time on my estate, the palace feels like an overcrowded nest of angry wasps." He traced a line down her arm. "What think you if we quit this place and travel home? I'm eager to show you what I call sanctuary."

Ildiko captured his hand and kissed his knuckles. She laughed when he only flinched a little. "Do I have to bid your mother goodbye?"

"If you feel up to a little self torture, certainly. I avoid her whenever possible. When do you want to leave?"

"Now?"

He leaned forward to press a kiss to her forehead. "I'll bargain for tonight. You need sleep and so do I. And I need out of this hideous sun before I go completely blind."

CHAPTER FOURTEEN

"What's the fastest we can load supplies and assemble troops for the journey home?" Brishen glanced over his shoulder as he brushed down his favorite horse. Anhuset leaned against the stall door, her arms draped casually over the top bar. She straightened abruptly at Brishen's question, the perpetual frown line between her pale eyebrows smoothing.

"As fast as you want them. I'll see to it." She rubbed her palms together. "Does this mean you've grown tired of trotting yourself and the *hercegesé* out before the royal court like prized horseflesh?"

Brishen tossed the brush into a nearby bucket and patted the mare's shoulder. "I was sick of it before we even got here. Ildiko has been more patient about the whole thing than I have, but she's done as well."

Anhuset swung the stall door open to let him out and closed it behind him. "She adapts easily."

"One of her many strengths."

She followed him to the pump by the well where he levered water into his hands for washing. Stable hands and soldiers milled around them. They bowed or saluted as they passed Brishen and his trusted lieutenant on their way to or from the royal stables.

Anhuset handed him a towel from a nearby rack. "Did you tell her Saggara is more fortress than palace?"

Brishen motioned for her to follow him as they made their way back to the private palace gates used by the royal family. "She knows we perch near the border with Belawat. I don't think I'll need to explain why that requires a garrison close by."

"She's palace-born and bred, Commander. Saggara lacks the comforts of Haradis and from what I saw at your wedding, it most definitely lacks the finer things of Pricid."

He shrugged and strode to the gates, acknowledging the bowing guards with a quick nod. "As you say, she adapts easily."

It was true that Ildiko had a particular talent for adjusting quickly not only to new surroundings but to circumstance and situation as well. She'd never uttered a word of complaint about sleeping on the ground in a tent or spending hours on horseback when they traveled from Pricid to Haradis. She'd changed her sleeping habits to match those of the Kai and choked down food even some of the Kai found challenging. He had every faith she would take yet another change of scenery with the same equanimity she'd shown so far.

Still, he wanted Ildiko to like Saggara, not simply adjust to it. The estate had been his since the king had given it to him more than a decade earlier on the promise Brishen would hold it in the role of margrave and defend Kai borders against an increasingly hostile Belawat. A five-night ride from Haradis, Saggara was his refuge from court intrigue and the queen's malevolent presence.

Secmis had declared her disapproval of his move to Saggara by calling the old estate a filthy midden not fit for beggars and declared she'd never grace him with her presence while he resided there. It was only one of three times Brishen could recall in his life where he'd been even remotely tempted to embrace his mother.

He and Anhuset discussed their plans for moving supplies and additional troops to Saggara as they passed through the palace's maze of hallways. They'd reached the floor where his and Ildiko's chamber were located when a scream split the air and bounced off the stone walls. Another followed after it. Brishen felt the bottom drop out from his stomach as he recognized Ildiko's voice.

"What in the gods' names..." Anhuset said before they both sprinted down the hall, swords drawn.

Brishen shoved aside a guard who'd joined in the chase, frantic to reach his wife. He rounded the corner and halted abruptly. Anhuset narrowly missed careening into him, her curses salting the air. He ignored her.

Ildiko stood in the hall, motioning frantically to her maid. "Hurry, Sinhue. It's getting away!"

The maid yanked a small axe from the weapons fan that decorated a patch of wall near Ildiko's door. She raced to her mistress and handed her the weapon. Neither woman noticed their would-be rescuers.

"Do you see it?"

"It's gone up the wall. If it gets too high, I won't be able to reach it."

Anhuset thumped Brishen on the shoulder. "What is 'it'?"

He wasn't waiting to find out and chased after the two women as they disappeared around another curve in the hallway. His heart wedged into his throat at the sight that greeted him.

Ildiko and Sinhue jumped about as if they walked barefoot on hot coals, their gazes frozen on the wall in front of them. Ildiko held the axe in front of her, swatting at a large shadow clinging to the stones.

The "it" was a scarpatine—a big female with venom sacs swollen to the size of plums beneath her arching tail. The stinger glistened in the half-light, droplets of yellow venom splashing across her armored back onto the floor where they sizzled and birthed tendrils of black smoke.

Before Brishen could yell at Ildiko to back away, the scarpatine scuttled toward her, its many legs flexing as it prepared to leap on its victim and sink the venomous barb into flesh. Sinhue shrieked, as did Ildiko before she swung the axe. The flat of the blade caught the insect broadside, and Brishen heard bells as metal slammed against stone. The ringing sound was muted by the wet crack of crushed insect shell and innards.

Brishen caught the axe just as it fell from Ildiko's fingers. He handed the weapon to Anhuset and spun Ildiko one way and then the other. Her hair, half out of its braid, flew into her face, and she scraped it away to stare at him wide-eyed.

"Did you get any of the venom on you, Ildiko?" He ran his hands over her face, her neck, across hers shoulders and breasts, hunting for any tell-tale patches of burnt cloth or the reactive sting on his own skin if he brushed against venom splatters. The wall displayed a mural of dead, smeared scarpatine smoking black in the dim light, and the hall reeked with the smell of rotten fish.

Ildiko pushed his hands away. "I'm fine, Brishen." She scowled. "I can't believe the Kai eat those disgusting creatures. I can't believe I ate one."

Anhuset spoke up, and Brishen didn't imagine the amusement in her voice. "We eat the males. The females are too venomous."

She glanced at Brishen and spoke in a pidgin dialect of bast-Kai Ildiko wouldn't understand. "She's handy with a blade. Should you no longer want her as a wife, give her to me. With enough training, she'd make a decent shield mate."

Brishen saw nothing humorous in the situation. He glanced at the remains of the scarpatine as bits and pieces oozed down the wall. He signaled to one of the guards standing nearby. "Send someone to clean this up." He turned to Sinhue who hovered close to Ildiko. "I need you to tend to your mistress."

The maid nodded and bowed. Brishen ushered Ildiko to her chamber, peppering her and Sinhue with questions the entire way.

Ildiko made straight for her wash basin, unlaced the sleeves of her tunic and set to scrubbing her hands and arms. "I don't know how it got in here, Brishen. Sinhue was helping me dress for dinner. Thank the gods she had the foresight to fold down the bedding early." She smiled at her servant who handed her a towel to dry her arms. The smile faded. "The thing was hiding under the covers. It jumped at Sinhue before squeezing under the door to escape."

Brishen and Anhuset inspected the chamber, shaking curtains, crawling under the bed and flipping the mattress off the ropes to check for another hidden menace.

Satisfied that the room was safe and no other scarpatine hid in the wardrobes or chests, Brishen scraped a hand over his face. "You should have let it go, wife. The females are aggressive and their venom strong enough to kill a horse."

Ildiko gave him a look that spoke of her doubt regarding his intelligence. "And let it lurk in the shadows waiting to ambush some poor unsuspecting soul? You perhaps? Or Anhuset? And what if no one managed to catch it?" She shuddered. "I'd never sleep knowing that thing was creeping about somewhere in the palace."

He growled low in his throat. "You aren't a warrior, Ildiko."

She scowled at him. "No, but I can certainly kill an insect."

"You sure can," Anhuset said from her place by the door.

Brishen snapped his teeth at his cousin. "Not another word." His mind raced. Scarpatines liked warm, dark places, but they disliked the smell of Kai and tended to avoid areas where they gathered such as houses. They were more a danger to hunters and trackers who might stumble across them in the wild or stable hands who learned to be handy with pitchforks when they discovered scarpatines hiding in straw piles.

The scarpatine that found a haven in Ildiko's bed had been put there purposefully. A cold knot settled under Brishen's ribs, spreading until he was sure ice water, not blood, flowed in his veins. He reached for Ildiko, tugging on her hand until she stood within the circle of his arms. He could smell the fear pouring off her in waves. The ice water coursed ever colder through his body.

"I need to do something but will return soon," he said softly. "I'll leave Anhuset here with you and your servant. She'll guard you until I return."

Ildiko went rigid in his arms, and her mouth turned down. Her eyes narrowed. "That is a waste of your lieutenant's time, Brishen. I don't need a nursemaid; I can step on my own bug." He made to argue but stopped at the feel of her finger pressed against his lips. She flashed her square teeth in a smile. "Just leave the axe before you go."

Brishen kissed her fingertip, relenting. "The room's clear but keep a sharp eye."

"No worries there," she assured him. Her gaze flickered to every corner of the room before settling on him once more. "I think I'll wear all black again tonight," she said. He gave her a deep bow. "It suits you." He signaled to Anhuset who opened the door. "I'll return in time to escort you to the hall."

The door had barely clicked behind him before Brishen hurtled down the long corridor toward the staircase leading up to the queen's suite of chambers, Anhuset in pursuit.

"Brishen, stop!"

He ignored her, sprinting ever faster toward his quarry where she waited in the center of her web. He grunted as a heavy weight slammed into his back, driving him to the floor. He tumbled with his attacker in a tangle of arms and legs until they crashed against the wall. In seconds he was crouched with Anhuset between his knees, his forearm pressed against her throat until she wheezed.

He eased the pressure, and she gasped for a mouthful of air. "Be glad of my affection for you, sha-Anhuset." He bit out each syllable between hard breaths. His arm lowered, and his hand slid over her collarbones to rest between her breasts. "Or I would have ripped your heart out by now and fed it back to you."

Anhuset grasped Brishen's wrist. "You're my commander and my cousin, Highness. I'd be no friend to you if I didn't try and stop you from running to your own beheading."

"That viper deserves death." Brishen's rage threatened to choke him.

"Maybe, but you don't, and her power is greater than yours. Greater than your father's." White sparks flared in Anhuset's eyes, and faint humor softened her mouth. "Have faith in your *hercegesé*. She did a fine job with the axe. She can hold her own. If you must die to defend her, don't do it over something this petty."

He almost snapped Anhuset's neck in that moment. "Petty?" Her nostrils flared, and her eyes blazed. The gray of her skin had leached out to a mottled ivory, yet she persevered. "Yes. Petty. This is Secmis we speak of, Brishen. She probably cuddles with scarpatine when she grows lonely, then eats them whole when she grows hungry. This little stunt is a joke to her."

Anhuset's words didn't lessen the killing urge roaring through Brishen at the moment, but the sensible voice inside him grew louder and agreed with her. He stood and helped her up. "Do what's needed to prepare. We leave tonight, even if that means only a handful of us goes, and Ildiko travels in her sleeping gown."

Anhuset saluted him but hesitated. "Promise me, cousin, you won't make off for the queen's chambers the second my back is turned."

Brishen shook his head. "I make no such promises." He chuckled at her scowl, the rage inside him subsiding a little. "You've always been faster than all of us. You'd catch me again."

Her frown didn't ease. "Yes I would." She didn't give ground until he turned away from the staircase and strode back to Ildiko's chamber.

He found her in the midst of dressing for dinner. She peeked around the concealing screen in one corner of the room. "That was quick."

Brishen chose not to reveal that his more rational cousin had thwarted his plans to spit his mother on the point of his sword like the scarpatine she was. He glanced at the black silk tunic and trousers laid across the bed—utterly unsuitable for hard riding.

"What do you think," he said, "if we take supper on the road?"

Her eyebrows lifted. "Brishen, you worry too much. I'm quite recovered from my scare with the scarpatine."

"Humor me, Ildiko." She might be fine; he was not and itched to quit the palace, the city and most definitely his dangerous family for the relative peace and safety of Saggara.

She stared at him for a moment. "As you wish," she said. "I'll have Sinhue pull out my riding leathers."

He nodded and instructed the servant to pack as many of Ildiko's things as she could and have the chests delivered to the stables.

This time when he stormed through the palace corridors, he sought out his father in the council chambers. The king sat at the head of the council table, a conclave of ministers on either side of him as they reviewed and discussed the sea of documents spread across the table surface.

Brishen genuflected. "Your Majesty, may I have a moment of your time?"

Djedor waved his son to his feet and eyed him with a milky gaze. "Make it quick."

"I request permission to leave Haradis and return to Saggara in the next hour."

The king scowled. "Have you heard something about Belawat that I haven't?"

Brishen shook his head. "No, but I wish to return to my estate as soon as possible." He offered no more explanation. Djedor might be old, but he was crafty and always informed about the goings-on in his castle. The palace was stuffed to the rafter with spies who reported back to him on every detail.

"You don't wish to bid your mother good-bye?"

They played this game every time Brishen approached his father. Djedor usually came away disappointed by his younger son's lack of reaction to his needling about Secmis. This time, still lightheaded with the urge to commit matricide, Brishen didn't bother hiding his anger.

"Unless I can skewer her with impunity, I don't want anywhere near the bitch," he stated shortly. As one, the ministers gasped, but the king only laughed. "She tried to kill my wife."

Djedor twirled a writing quill between his clawed fingers. "Is the Gauri girl still alive?"

"Yes."

"Then Secmis didn't try very hard." He waved the quill at Brishen, his interest in his son's actions quickly waning. "Go if you want. I'll send a messenger with copies of the final shipping agreements. Thanks to your marriage, we've secured three ships dedicated to the transport of amaranthine to several kingdoms, not including Gaur. Try to keep your ugly wife alive long enough for us to obtain the last document sealing the agreement. After that, she's welcome to drop dead any time."

Seething at his father's indifference though he expected nothing more, Brishen bowed and left the council chamber. In all honesty, he was grateful for his father's willing permission. He could have denied Brishen's request and kept him and Ildiko trapped in Haradis indefinitely from sheer perversity. He wasn't above such behavior.

By the time Anhuset secured arrangements for horses, wagons, and a contingent of guards, midnight had waxed and waned. Brishen found Ildiko outside the stable gates next to the saddled mount she'd ridden from Pricid to Haradis. Anhuset stood next to her, alongside Sinhue also dressed for travel.

Brishen bowed over Ildiko's hand. "One handmaiden only?"

She nodded toward Sinhue. "She wanted to come, and I only need one. Besides, Kirgipa's mother needs her more than I do, especially now that Talumey is gone."

"Have you eaten?"

This time he caught the slyness in her smile. "I did. A potato. It was delicious. We didn't save you one."

Her teasing lightened his heart. Though she wasn't easy on the eyes, she was easy on his soul. He kissed her forehead. "You're a good wife, Ildiko."

"Yes I am," she agreed. Her eyes slid toward their inner corners in a cross-eyed stare.

He flinched and heard both Anhuset and Sinhue gasp. "Ildiko..."

She uncrossed her eyes and winked. "Sorry. I couldn't resist."

Their party was a league out of the city before a messenger tracked them down. Brishen recognized his mother's coat of arms on the rider's livery. The messenger passed a scroll to Anhuset who delivered it to Brishen.

Brishen barely glanced at it. He was familiar with his mother's handwriting as well as her demands he return to Haradis at once. Ink blots marred the writing, and there were holes in the parchment where she'd obviously jabbed the quill tip through the paper as she wrote.

He fished a document of his own out of one of the packs tied to his saddle. His father had only mumbled his irritation at Brishen's insistence on written authorization of departure from court, stamped with the royal seal—in anticipation of Secmis doing exactly what he expected.

"Give this to Her Majesty," he instructed the messenger. "Then make yourself scarce afterwards if you want to live." He watched the rider spur his horse in the direction of Haradis.

"What did her message say?"

Brishen glanced at Ildiko next to him. The moonlight had a way of changing her. It didn't make her pretty by Kai standards, but the shadows it cast across her features hollowed her cheeks, bled the pink from her skin and the red from her hair. He liked the colors of night on her.

"She commanded I return home."

Her puzzled expression grew easier to read each time she revealed it. "But why? I have a hard time believing she misses you."

Nearby, Anhuset snorted. Brishen turned to stare at the rider's diminishing figure. "Hardly. That wasn't a display of affection but of outrage. I didn't ask her leave to depart Haradis." He motioned to Anhuset. "Keep moving. Milling about in the middle of the road won't get us to Saggara any faster."

They traveled for five nights after that without incident, riding across a wide plain covered in a sea of dropseed grass. Tall as a horse's flanks, the grass stems swayed and caressed as they passed, whispering ghostly endearments in the darkness. In the distance, tussocks rose like static swales on the dropseed ocean, and Brishen pointed out a tor crowned by slender menhirs gleaming white in the moonlight.

"Raised by one of the Elder races—the Gullperi, or so the legend goes. The last clan vanished from these lands five hundred years ago."

"You told me the Kai are one of the Elder races." Ildiko's blue eyes were silver in the darkness.

"Yes, though our magic is but a fraction of what the Gullperi's was. I've been to the crown on the tor. Power still breathes there."

He'd gone only once and returned home with the scent of magery heavy in his nostrils and strong on his skin. Anhuset swore he glowed in the dark for a fortnight following that foray.

Brishen's excitement grew as the miles flew behind them, and they drew closer to Saggara. A gentle slope on the plain rose, and the estate came into view. Fronted by young Solaris oaks planted by Kai gardeners decades earlier and flanked by a wild orchard of sour oranges, the sprawling fortress shone as pale under the moon as the menhirs on the tor. Once his grandfather's summer palace, Saggara had passed to Brishen by Djedor's edict, and he'd embraced it as his own.

A pair of crows fluttered skyward out of the orchard, cawing their protests at being woken by the sound of horse's hooves.

Their party paused on the highest point of the low rise. Brishen turned to Ildiko whose gaze remained on the fortress. "Welcome to Saggara, wife; my home. And now yours."

CHAPTER FIFTEEN

A fter two months of not seeing a single human face except the one in her mirror, Ildiko almost fell down the stairs from the shock of spotting a human traverse the halls of Saggara.

From her place on the steps, she watch as a man dressed in livery blazoned with an osprey clutching a fish was led past the stairwell and down the hallway where he disappeared beneath the ornately carved arch of a tympanum.

Ildiko flew down the stairs, thankful she'd adopted the Kai dress of tunic and trousers that allowed her quick movement without the tangle of long skirts. A servant met her as she followed the visitor and his escort.

The Kai bowed low. "Your Highness, I've been asked to fetch you."

Ildiko motioned for the servant to follow as she strode by, keeping her quarry in sight as they headed to the manor's great hall. "Who's our visitor?"

"A messenger from High Salure."

She paused to stare at the servant. In the time she'd resided with Brishen at Saggara, Ildiko had taken pains to expand her knowledge not only of her adopted culture but of its geography.

Brishen's estate consisted of a summer palace turned fortress and a garrison town that supported the fortress with a body of Kai troops and their families. Saggara perched on a strip of the plains that bordered Beladine territory and protected a small population of Kai who farmed fresh-water mussels from a nearby lake and produced the highly prized amaranthine dye coveted by both the Gauri and the Beladine.

After the attack on the trade road by Beladine mercenaries, Ildiko had shuddered at the idea of being so close and this vulnerable to any of Belawat's borders. Brishen had been quick to reassure her.

"We're quite safe, wife. Despite Belawat's attempt to break our alliance, there are factions friendly to us within its ranks. Serovek of House Pangion is one of those. His lands border mine, and his people benefit richly from us selling amaranthine to him for a good price. They resell it for a tidy profit to the aristocrats residing in the capital."

Ildiko still wasn't quite convinced of their safety. "What's to stop them from just invading and seizing control of the lake?"

Brishen's gold-coin eyes had glittered in the solar's semi-darkness. "Because the loss of life and spilling of Beladine blood would be a lot more expensive than just buying the dye from us. That, and we'd poison the lake if necessary. I admire Serovek. He was a Master of the Horse to a Beladine general before he inherited his father's lands. He understands strategy on both the battlefield and in trade negotiations. He won't jeopardize his holdings unless forced to by a declaration of war from his king on mine."

"Your Highness, the *herceges* awaits."

The servant's remark interrupted Ildiko's recollection of that conversation, and this time it was she who followed him to the great hall where Brishen waited with the messenger from High Salure.

She found him standing by the enormous hearth, holding an unrolled scroll. Candlelight lent a glossy blue sheen to his dark hair and highlighted the teal and coral undertones in his gray skin. He glanced up from reading and smiled as Ildiko drew near. Ildiko hid her own smile at the messenger's wide-eyed stare as Brishen grasped her hand and pressed a kiss to her knuckles.

"I'm glad you're here, Ildiko," he said. "We've received an invitation from Lord Serovek to take supper with him tomorrow night at High Salure. Would you like to go?"

Coming from any other man and the question would be rhetorical. In the game of diplomacy, which this invitation was, her wishes were not a consideration. Protocol demanded her presence. But Brishen was like no man Ildiko had ever know— Gauri or Kai. His question was meant sincerely, and he'd accept her answer, even if she chose to decline.

"I'd love to go," she said. It would be the first time since her marriage to Brishen that she'd actually had supper instead of breakfast or lunch at night or eaten with another person who wasn't Kai. She hoped they might serve dishes familiar to her. She'd grown used to most of the Kai cuisine she tried, but she missed those dishes she'd grown up with in the Gauri court.

Brishen took the scroll to a nearby writing table covered in maps and books. He signed the scroll and returned it to the High Salure messenger. "Tell his lordship we will see him shortly after twilight."

The messenger bowed, glanced briefly at Ildiko a second time and followed the Kai servants out of the hall.

"I'll wager this isn't just a night to be spent between comrades catching up on the latest events." Ildiko joined Brishen at the table and accepted the goblet of wine he poured for her.

"I think it is partly." Brishen tapped his goblet against hers in a toast. "Believe it or not, there has been the occasional union between a Kai soldier and a Beladine merchant's daughter, but the marriage of Kai royalty to either Gauri or Beladine royalty has never occurred until now. We are an odd couple. People will be curious."

Ildiko sighed inwardly. Another long evening of even longer stares and furious whispers from those attending the dinner. Their roles would be reversed, with many wondering how Ildiko could stomach the sight of her feral-looking spouse. She knew to expect it, but the knowing didn't make it any easier.

"Serovek is a curious sort then?"

Brishen led her to one of the comfortable couches set near the fireplace and sat down beside her. "Curious in that he believes knowledge is power. The more he knows the less likely he is to be unpleasantly surprised."

"A cautious man."

"An intelligent one."

Ildiko tilted her head to the side. "You like him."

Brishen nodded. "I do. He would make a valuable ally and a formidable enemy. Luckily for us both, we are amicable neighbors—for now."

They remained in the hall chatting of inconsequential things until Ildiko excused herself and rose. "I'm told two trade wagons have arrived from Haradis carrying food supplies. Your cook has stated one merchant's scales are suspiciously inaccurate. I'm off to resolve the problem."

Brishen abandoned his seat as well and escorted her to the doors. "And I'm riding with a guard to the southeast perimeters. For all that Serovek is friendly to me, others are not. There have been raids into the pasture lands. Horses and cattle stolen. It could just be thieves, but I have my doubts."

A frisson of worry tightened Ildiko's chest. She clasped Brishen's arm. "You'll be careful?" It was a silly thing to say. Brishen was an experienced soldier, as adept at fighting as any of the Kai under his command. She'd seen that for herself when he'd saved her from a Beladine raider. Still, she worried over him. He had become precious to her.

Brishen twined a lock of her hair around his claws, letting it slide over his knuckles. "You would come to my rescue if I needed it?"

She arched an eyebrow. "I'd be a terrible rescuer, but yes, I wouldn't hesitate to come to your aid."

"Don't sell yourself short, wife. I've seen you wield an axe."

Ildiko stepped closer and slid her arms over his broad shoulders in a loose embrace. His hair tickled her nose where she laid her head against his neck. "I'm serious, Brishen. Promise me you'll not get yourself killed or maimed out there."

His hands rested hot on her lower back, and he breathed gently against her before stepping away. He'd lost the smile, but there was a gentleness to his hard features. "I can't make that promise, Ildiko, but I can swear to do my best to come back with all arms and legs attached."

She frowned. "Your head too, if you please."

Brishen laughed then. "My head too."

"When will you return?"

"Just before midday if I leave now. Plenty of time to sleep before we must ready ourselves to attend Serovek's supper."

Ildiko couldn't care less about some Beladine noble's supper gathering. She just wanted to make sure she was awake when Brishen returned home.

They parted ways outside the great hall, she to the bailey and he to the barracks and stables. She ate lunch and dinner alone, seated on the balcony that led from her room and overlooked the wild orange grove that spread from the back of the estate's main house to the edge of a bramble field.

Brishen had given her a brief tour of the grove, or at least as much of a tour as the tangled undergrowth and a pair of slashing sickles allowed. The trees hung heavy with unpicked fruit and swarmed with wasps still flitting about in the encroaching twilight.

Her husband had graciously braved a branch spiny with thorns and picked an orange for her. It was juicy and sour enough to make the back of her jaw clench and her eyes squinch closed. She loved it.

Brishen had eyed her with a look of disgust. "Humans eat the most repulsive things."

Ildiko chose not to point out the many revolting aspects of baked scarpatine. Instead, she spat an orange seed in her hand and gave Brishen a sweet smile. "I'm guessing the Kai don't like oranges."

"No, not at all."

Ildiko had surveyed the wild grove with a measuring eye. "We like oranges, even the sour ones; and the flowers make a lovely perfume and water coveted by women. While not as valuable as your amaranthine, oranges are a currency crop for farmers. It might be worth putting the labor into this grove and selling the produce."

He'd shown interest in her idea but hadn't yet been convinced. Saggara's labor force was split between its military presence and the civilians who made the amaranthine. He didn't think he had enough population to spare for the grove, but he'd consider it.

Ildiko admired the orange trees, their dark silhouettes gilded in silver from the moon's light. Now and then a crow would shoot up from the canopy of leaves, circle the treetops only to disappear once more into the branches' hidden sanctuary. The shadow of an owl flew past on silent wings, its eyes as bright as Brishen's when he laughed at something she said.

This was the first time they'd been parted from each other for more than an hour or two that wasn't reserved for sleeping. She missed his presence—the smooth cadence of his voice, the graceful movement of his narrow hands with their lethal black claws, even the scent of his hair when he held her close, and she breathed him into her nostrils.

She'd sensed the anger simmering inside him from the moment he'd witness her kill the scarpatine until they'd reached Saggara. He'd said nothing to her about the incident other than to inquire about her well-being, but it wasn't a stretch to assume Secmis had something to do with the nasty insect hiding among Ildiko's bed sheets. Pride had made her offer up a half-hearted argument against leaving for Saggara right away, but she'd been more than happy to acquiesce to Brishen's insistence they leave that evening.

Saggara was an austere place compared to Haradis and lacked many of its creature comforts. It also lacked Secmis which, for Ildiko, made it a place far superior to the Kai royal palace. When Sinhue came to help her undress and get ready for bed, Ildiko waved her away and sent her to her own room. She was neither tired nor sleepy, but she did miss her husband. His chambers adjoined hers, and he'd told her more than once she was welcome to enter any time she wished. She did so now, pausing at the doorway to admire the space.

The furniture was plain but comfortable, the bed large with a thick mattress and piles of blankets and furs. As with his bedroom in the royal palace, this one had a hearth with a table and two chairs set before it. A half finished game of Butcher's Covenant lay on the table. Brishen was a far better strategist than Ildiko and had won every game so far except one. She suspected he'd let her win that one.

Ildiko returned to her room to strip out of her clothes and slip on her nightrail. From the chest at the foot of her bed, she retrieved one of the three precious books she'd brought with her from Pricid—a tome of psalms and poems. She'd read it so many times, she'd memorized most of them, but they were no less enjoyable with each reading. She'd read in her husband's bedroom until he came back from the border.

The linens on Brishen's bed were cool and crisp, the furs soft as she tucked herself in and piled the pillows behind her back so she could read. She left the doors leading to his balcony open. His bedroom faced east, and early morning sunlight spread across the plains until it spilled over the balcony and into the room.

Ildiko blew out the single candle by the bed and settled in to read by the light of the sun.

She was halfway through the book, her eyes heavy with sleep, when the bedroom door opened. Brishen stood at the threshold, dressed down to undertunic and trousers, his feet bare and his hair damp. He leaned against the door frame and crossed his arms. "Woman of day, you waited for me."

Ildiko closed her book and offered him a drowsy smile. Relief and happiness coursed through her. "Prince of night, you've come back to me—your head intact."

"I promised I'd try." Brishen strode across the room, motioning for her to stop when she made to swing out of bed. "Move over."

Surprised, she did as he said and made room for him on the side of the bed she'd previously occupied. He slid in next to her and covered them both with the blankets. Ildiko turned on her side and murmured her approval when he tucked her into his body and nuzzled his face against the slope where her shoulder met her neck. They'd slept like this during their travels to both Haradis and then Saggara, his lithe body both a comfort and a pleasure to lie against in slumber.

Ildiko was halfway to a dead sleep when Brishen's soft words in her ear brought her awake.

"Sleep here each day, Ildiko."

A sweet warmth suffused her. She entangled her legs with his and hugged his arm to her waist. "As you wish. Just don't steal the blankets."

CHAPTER SIXTEEN

High Salure nestled in a col cut between the steep sides of a pair of mountains. Endrisi oaks marched up the slopes, enrobing the sides in a dusky green cloak. These trees were different from the Solaris oaks that fronted Saggara. Shorter, with thick trunks and small leaves shaped like pendants, the Endrisi oaks grew low and wide instead of tall and were interspersed with more statuesque firs. The encroaching twilight cast their shadows long, and Brishen pointed out the shapes of red-shouldered hawks perched in their canopies to sleep while the silent owls took their place in the hunt.

A narrow path snaked up the windward slope with multiple switchbacks that made it easier for horses to navigate the slope's pitch. Trees lined the path on either side with an understory of thorny bramble thicker than a hair mat and guaranteed to rip anything bigger than a fox to shreds. A rider wanting to reach High Salure with his and horse's hides intact had to stay on the road—and the road was observed.

Twilight had given way to night by the time Brishen, Ildiko and their escort crossed a gentle stream and passed through a narrow wind gap to reach the fortress carved directly into the mountain. High Salure's battlements and graceful towers rose above them, dark silhouettes against the evening sky. Lanterns and torches blazed along the walls and lined the cobbled path that

145

led to the main gate. Brishen squinted against the light and announced himself and Ildiko to the guards at the gate.

Once inside, they crossed a pomerium to another high wall and heavily guarded gate. Brishen didn't have to announce himself a second time. The gates swung wide, and he guided his party into a courtyard edged by workshops, a stable, a smithy and a small temple.

Brishen relaxed in the saddle. So far, the Kai remained peaceable neighbors with the kingdom of Belawat. The raiders who attacked him and Ildiko on the trade road had worn the coat of arms of the Beladine royal house under their armor. Whatever hostility the Beladine king held for Brishen's marriage to a Gauri royal, that hostility had not yet made it to these borders or this Beladine lord. No one had yet demanded Brishen and his Kai guard disarm. It was a display of trust, and one Brishen reciprocated by bringing his wife to this dinner.

A steward greeted them at the great doors that opened to High Salure's interior. Brishen dismounted and helped Ildiko off her horse. He gave instructions to the soldiers who'd accompanied them on their journey, and they followed another livery servant to a stone building jutting from the inner wall and occupied by Beladine soldiers who watched their Kai guests with wary but curious gazes.

For all that High Salure was unmistakably a fort, much like Saggara, its interior was luxuriously appointed. The servant left Brishen and Ildiko in a receiving room fit for royalty. Heavy tapestries, free of moth holes and layers of dust, lined the walls, and numerous chairs and benches had been set around the chamber, inviting large numbers of guests to sit. Tiny ceramic pots rested on iron tripods. Stunted candles placed below them heated oils, perfuming the air with the scent of herbs that overrode the reek of tallow from the lit torches lining the wall.

Brishen glanced at Ildiko. "What do you think?"

She scraped her hood back, revealing the intricate braiding and beads Sinhue had woven into her hair. Her eyes moved back and forth as she surveyed their surroundings. "I suspect it's well defended and likely well stocked with provisions and a heavily guarded water source beyond the stream."

Startled, Brishen blinked and then laughed.

Ildiko gave him a look he could actually interpret now. He was growing used to his wife's face. "What's so funny?"

"You." He traced the embroidery on her cloak's edge with one claw. "You never fail to surprise me. I thought you'd remark on the architecture or the furnishings. Serovek is well-heeled, and it shows. Instead, you note the defenses and conjecture about High Salure's ability to withstand a siege. Plans of conquest, wife?"

She snorted delicately and raised her chin. "Hardly. I'm as much an admirer of a pretty garden, fancy windows, and a fine couch as the next woman, but there's also beauty in purpose. An enemy would lose many men trying to conquer this place."

Brishen couldn't dispute that observation. Saggara had its own strengths that High Salure lacked, and the reverse could be said of High Salure. They were equally matched in their abilities to launch attacks and defend against them. Such equality kept him and Serovek on friendly terms, and Brishen hoped it remained that way.

The doors separating the receiving room from the rest of the interior were thrown open, and a man dressed in brown leather and silks the color of fresh blood strode through them. Brishen caught Ildiko's soft gasp as Serovek, Lord Pangion of Belawat grasped Brishen's arm and yanked him into a brief, crushing embrace. Had Brishen been human instead of Kai, Serovek would have cracked a few of his ribs.

Serovek grinned, flashing the square human teeth that were often a source of amusement among the Kai of Saggara. Brishen had the instant realization that it was Serovek himself who had made him think of Ildiko's smile as equine. Lord Pangion was a big human—a little taller than Brishen—with massive shoulders and a slight bow to his legs that indicated he'd been tossed onto a horse's back at a young age and rarely left it since.

Brishen's greatest exposure to humans had been mostly isolated to Serovek and his cavalry, with its horse culture as strong as the Kai's. The humans even rolled their eyes in that bizarre way that horses did when frightened. They sometimes flashed their square teeth in laughter that reminded him of a whinny.

Serovek slammed a hand between Brishen's shoulder blades hard enough to make a weaker man stagger. "Brishen, welcome!"

Brishen bowed briefly. "Serovek. We appreciate the invitation." He glanced at his silent, wide-eyed wife. "My wife and *hercegesé*, Ildiko."

Serovek executed a courtly bow with flourish. "A pleasure, Your Highness." His gaze passed swiftly over Ildiko, and his voice softened and deepened even more. "Word reached us of your marriage. Your husband is a fortunate man. Welcome to High Salure."

Brishen felt his smile stiffen. He pressed his hand against Ildiko's back. He might not be able to discern the subtle emotions in a human's gaze, but he wasn't deaf. Blatant male interest saturated Serovek's voice.

Ildiko bowed. "Lord Pangion, Brishen has spoken most favorably about you. Thank you for inviting us to your lovely home."

Serovek motioned for them to accompany him through the doors and into a brightly lit hall crowded with humans and bisected by a long trestle table set for dinner. The other dinner guests were low-ranking noblemen and squires from the Beladine towns that received protection from High Salure. They gawked at both Brishen and Ildiko. As the only Kai in the crowd, Brishen had an idea of what Ildiko had dealt with at the palace and the circumstances she lived in at Saggara. His admiration for her unflappable aplomb grew. It wasn't an easy thing being an object of such focused curiosity, especially when that curiosity was mixed with distrust and revulsion.

Serovek made the necessary introductions, and soon Ildiko was whisked away to another part of the hall by a flock of wives and daughters eager to hear how the niece of the Gauri king ended up the wife of a Kai prince.

Brishen found himself alone with Serovek, the other men reluctant to interact with him beyond the initial introductions. They were of no concern to him beyond the possibility they might be future military targets.

Serovek lifted two goblets of wine from a tray presented by a servant and passed one to Brishen. "I won a sizeable wager thanks to you." They toasted each other in Common and drank.

Brishen peered into his cup. The wine was exceptional. "How so?"

He caught Serovek's smirk. "Bets were placed that a certain Kai prince would balk at the last minute and refuse to take a human woman to wife."

Bets were placed throughout the Kai kingdom on the same thing except it was whether or not the Gauri bride would balk. "The odds?"

"Sixty to one."

Brishen whistled. "Those are plump winnings."

Another servant passed with a tray. Serovek drained his cup and replaced it with another full one from the tray. His entire demeanor oozed satisfaction. "They are. I used the winnings to buy a young stallion from Nadiza's lightning herd as breeding stock."

Brishen made a note to himself that should another wedding between a Kai and a human take place any time soon, he wanted in on Serovek's betting pool. "You'll get fast ponies from that one."

"I'm counting on it." Serovek's expression turned grim. "Rumor has it you encountered trouble on your return to Haradis."

Unease rippled up Brishen's back. He trusted Serovek as much as he trusted any human, except for Ildiko. "Rumor is correct in this instance. You've those among your kinsmen who don't approve of the marriage and the alliance it forges, though I think the king of Belawat worries for nothing. We sell our amaranthine to any willing to pay. Gauri or Beladine, you are all simply humans to the Kai."

Serovek snorted. "I think we both know it has nothing to do with the dye. Your father's kingdom is the barrier between Belawat and Gaur. The Kai were neutral until this marriage."

Brishen snagged a second goblet of wine but this time only sipped at it. "Our deaths would be useless. The marriage is simply a gesture of good faith." He didn't say aloud what both he and Serovek knew—many a war had started over gestures of good faith.

He watched, intrigued, as his host suddenly pasted on a false smile and slid a brief glance at the clusters of other guests who watched them. "You and I are having an amusing conversation." Brishen took the hint and flashed an equally false smile of his own. "Any warning I might give you would be seen as treason, and I don't fancy having my head mounted on a gate spike outside the palace walls," Serovek said between his teeth. "But as one comrade to another, I would tell you to watch your back. Belawat disapproves of this alliance and will try again to make that disapproval known in the most obvious way it can."

Brishen's eyes narrowed. Kill the least important members first and move up the hierarchy until someone finally got the message. "It won't stop with me and Ildiko."

"No. Your deaths are simply the warning trumpet. The Beladine and the Gauri were equally matched in martial prowess until this latest trade alliance. The pendulum swung in Gaur's favor when Bast-Haradis agreed to more than just friendly trade."

Removed from court machinations and political negotiations by both distance and disinterest, Brishen hadn't thought much of their neighbor's sudden enthusiasm for offering access to their ports and moving Kai goods, especially the valuable amaranthine dye, on their ships without heavy tariffs and fees.

"The Gauri must have received information that Belawat was planning an offensive against them. My father would have considered the promise of assistance a fair trade for moving the dye without tariff. Both countries could fatten their coffers in no time. But to the Gauri, the military alliance is far more important than the trade one."

The false smile slowly slipped from Serovek's face. "Indeed. Djedor is known throughout the kingdoms as a stubborn, wily king. However, wipe out the heir and spares to this throne, and he'll break."

Brishen remained silent. What the human kingdoms believed was partially true. Djedor was a stubborn, wily bastard, and the continuation of his line meant everything to him. They, however, had not taken Secmis into account, and the Kai king's weaknesses didn't mirror those of his formidable queen.

"Why are you telling me this?" he asked Serovek. "You could kill me and Ildiko now and earn the gratitude of your king."

Serovek snorted. "King Rodan's gratitude doesn't manifest as coin, lands or favor. The most I'd get from it is a parade." Disdain curled his upper lip. "As if I crave such a thing—crowds throwing laurels at me and scaring my horses." The lip curl transformed to a sly smile. "You, on the other hand, make me rich with your dyes and your friendship. You're far more valuable to me as friend than foe."

Brishen laughed. The first time he'd met Serovek, he liked him. He was as odd as any other human in both appearance and expression, but he was a soldier with a mind for strategy and a penchant for honesty that was sometimes noble, sometimes opportunistic, sometimes both. It was these that Brishen related to and admired.

He clinked his cup against Serovek's. "To the value of profit and friendship." He drank the wine, the fear coating his tongue giving it a metallic taste. Brishen didn't fear for his safety. He could handle himself in a fight and would be difficult to kill, but he wasn't the only target. While Ildiko had the heart of a warrior, she was untrained, untried, and unprepared to fend off an attack from a determined assassin. He'd lay down his life for her, protect her with sword and axe, teeth and claws if necessary. Still, he was only mortal and there was a chink in even the best made armor.

Serovek pulled him from his grim musings with a tap on the shoulder. "We'll speak of more pleasing things." He turned his gaze to Ildiko nearby, laughing in the company of other human women. "Your wife is a stunning creature. How is it such a woman, with ties to the Gauri royal house, remain unmarried until now?"

Brishen shrugged, unsure if listening to his host wax enthusiastic about Ildiko's beauty was a pleasanter turn of the conversation. "She occupies the same role in the pecking order that I do. We are of no importance to the royal line, but we're useful in political maneuvering and kept in reserve for just the right moment." He had never resented the notion. In fact, his relative unimportance had offered him far more freedom than any given to his brother and bestowed on him an exceptional wife. Unfortunately, someone now considered him and Ildiko of great importance in the worst possible way.

His conversation with Serovek remained light-hearted until the dinner announcement. Serovek sat at the head of the table with Ildiko and Brishen on either side of him as guests of honor. Brishen split his attention between the mayor of one of the

Beladine towns who doggedly engaged him in conversation despite his obvious unease at being seated next to a Kai and Ildiko, whose laughter and animated responses to Serovek's bantering slowly soured the wine on his tongue.

She was comfortable here, in her element amongst humans like her. The differences between them never seemed so obvious as now, and they went far deeper than appearance. Brishen had told himself that as she grew used to him and his people, she'd adopt their ways, understand their culture and slowly become more Kai herself. Watching Ildiko interact now with the Beladine guests made him realize he'd fooled himself into thinking such a thing. She displayed a natural ease he never saw at Saggara though the relationship between her and his household was both peaceful and respectful.

Her ability to speedily adapt to new people and circumstances had lured him into a false sense of contentment. His own sense of isolation amongst Serovek's guests made him wonder if Ildiko was lonely.

It was close to dawn before the gathering broke up, and guests gathered their things in preparation to leave. Ildiko hid a yawn behind her hand as Brishen helped her with her cloak.

"Did you enjoy yourself?" he asked.

She rested her hand in the crook of his elbow and leaned her head on his arm. "Thoroughly," she said. "And your luck held. No potatoes at dinner."

He nuzzled the top of her head. "Proof that there are merciful gods. Or at least a merciful cook."

Serovek approached them after bidding farewell to another couple. "It's been a long time since I've visited Saggara. Has your wife had much time to put a woman's mark on it yet?"

Brishen recognized a hint when he heard one, and Serovek's was less than subtle. "A little. Let me return the favor and invite you to share a meal with us."

Serovek's reply came as no surprise. "I heartily accept. Name the day and time. I'll be there. I look forward to meeting your lieutenant again. A fascinating woman, that Anhuset."

By the time they'd descended the mountainside and tracked a path through the tall dropseed grass toward Saggara, it was early morning, and the sun cut a blinding swath of light across the plains. While the entire Kai troop retreated into the depths of their cloaks and hoods, Ildiko dropped her hood and turned her face to the sun. Eyes closed, she bathed in its rays with a smile.

Brishen watched her silently for a moment before speaking. "Do you miss human companionship, Ildiko?"

She opened one eye to stare at him. "Sometimes. Your people, however, have been very welcoming to me."

"Except for my mother."

"Your words, not mine," she said with a smile. "But it would be nice not to flounder so often or listen so closely to voices because I can't always read Kai expressions."

"It's been a trial for you." The words felt heavy on his tongue. He wanted her to deny them.

Ildiko shook her head. "No, simply a challenge. There's an easiness to being among familiar things and people. You don't have to try as hard."

Though he agreed with her about the difficulty in reading expressions—he dealt with the same when interacting with humans—he offered a counter argument. "We smile as you do. Frown as you do. Laugh and joke as you do."

This time she opened both eyes and sat straighter in the saddle. "True, but I think a lot of human expression comes from the eyes—how they move, blink, change color with emotion. We learn to read such signs from birth. It becomes second nature. I have a difficult time with the Kai because your eyes don't change. If they move, I can't tell. If they change color, I don't notice it. Do the Kai weep when they grieve?"

It was if she'd cracked the lock on a chest he'd been trying to pick for years. The eyes. The key to understanding humans was learning to read their dreadful eyes. The same could be said of the Kai.

"You have that mysterious smile again, husband." She arched an eyebrow.

"You've made me consider something I hadn't before. We have a lot to learn from each other, wife."

Ildiko stared at him for a moment before pulling her hood back over her head. "I'm eager to learn."

"So am I," he said.

By the time they made it through Saggara's inner gates, Ildiko was asleep in the saddle, kept upright purely by her body's instinctive memory of how to ride. Brishen carried her upstairs to her chambers and left her with an equally sleepy Sinhue to prepare for bed.

He didn't expect her to join him later, so she surprised him by appearing before him as he sat on the edge of his bed pondering the information Serovek had given him.

Dressed in one of her white nightrails, she nudged his knees apart until she stood between his legs. Her scent—cloves and the green of dropseed—seeped into his nostrils. Brishen tilted his head up. "I thought you'd be asleep in your bed."

Her hands were soft on his cheeks, fingertips stroking delicate lines and swirls across his cheekbones and temples. He closed his eyes as she threaded his hair through her fingers. "Am I no longer welcomed in your bed?"

Brishen sighed his pleasure as her hands tracked paths down his neck to his shoulders and began to knead. "Don't be foolish, wife."

"What troubles you, Brishen?" Ildiko's magical hands traveled into his scalp, massaging gently. Brishen moaned. "You've been acting strangely, ever since the dinner at High Salure. What did Lord Serovek tell you?"

It was hard to think while Ildiko caressed him into a stupor. Who knew that something so simple as a scalp massage would reduce him to a clod-pated idiot? He wrestled his thoughts together. At some point he'd have to tell her of Belawat's plans. While he disliked the idea of scaring her, ignorance had killed more than its fair share of people, and he wanted her aware of the danger.

Still, there was time enough to disturb her sleep tomorrow. For now, he'd offer something else—something that would disturb his sleep for many nights to come.

"Lord Pangion called you stunning."

For a moment the massaging stopped, only starting again when Brishen clasped her wrists and nudged her to continue. The feeble light cast by stray sunbeams that crept through the closed window shutters revealed the shadow of a blush on her cheeks. "Did he? That was very kind of him."

His homely wife—beautiful, yet not. Stunning to a man whose gaze had caressed her from head to toe and whose voice had proclaimed both approval and interest. "Or simply very truthful."

Ildiko laughed and tugged teasingly on a few strands of his hair. "Ah, my husband, what a silver tongue you have." Her fingers traced the curves of his ears, sending gooseflesh across his back and down his arms. His eyes closed as he sank into the sensation.

A question that lingered in the back of his mind since Serovek had first come through the doors to greet them rushed to the forefront. Brishen opened his eyes to meet Ildiko's smiling gaze. "And Serovek, Ildiko? Would human women think him handsome?"

Twin frown lines marred her brow before fading as she pondered his question. "Honestly? Extremely handsome." A seeping cold settled into Brishen's blood at her words. "That he's wealthy and intelligent as well doesn't hurt. That he's also unmarried puts a target on his back for every Beladine matchmaker in a nine-league radius." She gave Brishen a lighthearted grin. Such a human smile. So much like Serovek's. "Why do you ask?"

He couldn't answer her. The impetus for his question had been sparked by a jumble of emotions and thoughts. He needed time to sort them out, make sense of them to himself before he could make sense of them to her. The clearest emotions he had now were regret—regret that he'd returned the offer of dinner to the Beladine lord—and the unshakeable certainty he'd invited a wolf among them.

"Brishen?" Ildiko's smile had vanished. She worried her lower lip between her teeth. Brishen had the stray thought that if a Kai had done such a thing, they'd turn their mouth into a bloody mess.

He shrugged. "Just curious. I've had little interest in humans until now. With a human wife, it will do me good to learn more about them."

She started to answer him but was stopped by another yawn which she hid behind her hand. Brishen rose and folded back the bedcovers. "In with you," he said. "You're asleep on your feet, and my head aches from all the sunlight."

Ildiko scooted across the bed to the side she claimed. She was asleep the moment she snuggled into her pillows. Brishen used that boon to strip naked. Unsure of how she might react and not wishing to scare her back to her chamber, he always slept half clothed beside her. It was hot and uncomfortable but worth it to have her in his bed. This time he'd sleep as he usually did when he was alone.

He slipped under the covers and pulled her against him. Her braid slid across his arm, a colorful serpent. He captured it and wound its length around his forearm before letting it unwind and fall away to shelter behind Ildiko's slender back.

"I'm not human, wife," he whispered into the darkness.

Shock rounded his eyes at Ildiko's response, slurred with sleep and nearly incoherent. "But you're still mine, husband."

CHAPTER SEVENTEEN

If there was anything more odorous than an amaranthine dye house, Ildiko had yet to learn of it. She covered her nose with a handkerchief and followed the master dyer into the billowing clouds of choking steam that poured off the tops of open kettles suspended over fires. The smells of salt, soda ash, and shellfish combined to make her eyes water and her throat close.

Kai laborers worked in teams, taking turns at tending fires, dunking cloth in boiling vats of amaranthine, and setting the cloth to dry on wooden horses. The house's muddy floor looked like an emptied battlefield before all the blood washed away in a rainstorm. Puddles of water in shades from palest pink to deep ruby splashed across her boots as she trudged through the muck. She was far too busy trying to keep her balance to pay much attention to the stares her presence drew.

Anhuset muttered under her breath as she followed Ildiko. "It would have been easier to have someone deliver samples of the cloth to the fortress."

Ildiko chose not to answer her, preferring to keep her mouth closed and the odor of the dye off her palate as long as possible. It would indeed have been much easier to order samples brought to the fortress, but Ildiko wanted to see the dye houses and learn how the Kai made the valuable commodity that made the human kingdoms covet the vivid amaranthine.

She listened closely as the master dyer, a weathered Kai with hands permanently painted reddish-purple, described the process of extracting the dye from the freshwater bitter mollusk they fished from the nearby lake and dying the stacks of bleached linen, wool, and silk stored in another room. It was messy, smelly, sometimes dangerous work involving boiling the mollusks, racking the slime and impurities from the top, straining the dyes and boiling them again with salt and soda ash.

Fabric dyed in the jewel-toned magenta was stretched on the wooden horses in various states of drying. The master dyer had explained to her and Anhuset how the amaranthine didn't fade after years in sunlight as other dyes did, but instead, grew more vibrant over time with the saturation of light. Ildiko thought it ironic how a people who shunned the daylight were known for creating something that grew more beautiful with exposure to it.

Mollusk slime racked from the top of the boiling dye was pushed into a noxious pile near one of the middens. The congealing heap glistened in the moonlight, glowing green from the thousands of buzzing flies that swarmed its surface. The smell sent Ildiko's stomach into an endless tumble, and she turned away before she lost her breakfast.

Anhuset stood beside her, hand over her nose, a thunderhead of disapproval darkening her brow. "That bow-legged Beladine rooster isn't worth this."

Ildiko silently agreed, but she wasn't here solely to handpick a gift of hospitality for Serovek's visit. This was one of four principal dye houses in the Kai kingdom and under Brishen's guardianship. Ildiko felt it her duty as his wife to learn some small thing about the product that had secured an alliance between her people and his and this marriage between them.

She inhaled a grateful breath of clean air when the dye master led them outside and away from both middens and the pungent steam roiling out of the kettles. He pointed to another set of vats, these planted on the ground with no fires beneath them. Kai dyers used pulleys to raise and lower dripping cloth into more of the dye.

"This is the cold dye stage, Your Highness. The color has been racked and strained and left to sit in the sun for eleven days. We dye the silks in this amaranthine."

Ildiko drew closer to one of the vats and peered into a contained sea of magenta-colored liquid. The dye shimmered under the glow of hanging lanterns strung from poles driven into the ground. Her typical everyday garb reflected the colors she preferred – blacks and greens, dove grays, and the ambers and browns of autumn. She had never before favored reds or pinks, but staring at the lustrous amaranthine tempted her to consider a scarf in that color at a later date.

She leaned farther into the vat.

"Be careful you don't fall in, Your Highness."

The dyer's warning came too late. While Ildiko didn't pitch headlong into the vat, the necklace she wore slipped its clasped and fell into the color with a gentle plop. Its onyx cabochon and chain sank, leaving behind an expanding pattern of circular waves to mark where it fell.

"Oh no!" Ildiko didn't hesitate and plunged her arms all the way in into the vat until the dye lapped at her collarbones. Heedless of the dyer's and Anhuset's cries, she flailed in the dye, fingers clutching until she caught the tail end of the sinking chain on which the cabochon hung. She jerked it out of the vat, splashing dye across her neck and the underside of her jaw. The necklace hung from her dripping fingers, and she lifted it to show Anhuset. "Got it!" she crowed triumphantly.

The master dyer stared at her silently, features pinched. Anhuset also stared at her but with eyes narrowed and lips alternately twitching and compressing as she held back her laughter.

Ildiko glanced down at herself, soaked to the skin in dye. Her green tunic had turned a muddy brown, and where the color had washed bare skin, she was painted an interesting plum shade. She looked again to Anhuset whose sharp teeth flashed in a wide grin. The master dyer didn't share in her amusement. The pinched look had been replaced by a wide-eyed stare and a face gone pale as old ash. Even Ildiko couldn't mistake his dread.

She hastened to assure him. "No harm done, Master Soté. Nothing a good scrubbing with soap and hot water won't fix." Ildiko almost smiled but changed her mind at the last moment. She might not possess the fangs the Kai sported, but that didn't mean they found her smile any more reassuring than she found theirs.

Anhuset snorted. "Don't count on it, Highness. Remember what Soté said earlier, and you've seen the dyers here. The amaranthine holds fast. Cloth, skin, hair. You'll be an even more unusual color for several days."

Brishen had once said her skin reminded him of the bitter mollusk the Kai boiled to release the dye. Ildiko raised a bright pink arm, turning it one way and then the other. Her clothing was ruined, but at least now she could brag she had color to her skin.

She shrugged and tucked the broken necklace into her bodice. "Might I borrow a dry cloth, please?" she asked the dyer.

Master Soté leapt to do her bidding as if shot from a crossbow. In moments, she clutched two towels while Anhuset stood attendance, holding a spare set.

Her dip into the dye vat cut their tour short. Once dried, Ildiko apologized for the trouble and promised a fearful Master Soté that the *herceges* would not be angry and skin him for saddle leather just because his wife managed to tint herself pink in his dye house.

Soté was all that was polite and accommodating as he escorted her and Anhuset to where their mounts waited, but Ildiko had the distinct impression he couldn't get rid of them fast enough. She mounted her horse, ignoring the raised eyebrows and gawking stares of the rest of their escort.

Anhuset handed her cloak to her. "You're still damp, Highness. The cloak will keep you from getting cold." And keep her from distracting the Kai guardsmen who'd accompanied them from Saggara to the dye house and tried not to be too obvious in their gaping at her.

Ildiko sniffed and wrapped the cloak snugly around herself. She didn't regret her actions. They had been instinctive and careless, true, but the necklace was precious—a last gift from her mother before she died. Ildiko would have dived headfirst into a vat of boiling horse piss to retrieve it. Still, she didn't relish the idea of her neck and arms being stained the color of young plum for a fortnight.

They travelled the main road to the manor, the young Solaris oaks silent sentinels to their passing. The trees gave way to a series of earthenworks and masonry walls that formed Saggara's outer redoubt. Behind the barriers perched one of two stables that housed the many horses kept at Saggara and a set of barracks that provided hearth and roof for those soldiers who'd chosen not to live on the lakeshore.

Cheers, whistles, and catcalls sounded nearby. Ildiko had heard them before when she'd ventured out onto one of the balconies to admire the landscape or the pattern of stars that wheeled above her. She glanced at Anhuset. "What is that?"

Anhuset called out a command, and their party turned as one toward the sounds. She pointed to a low earthen wall on which several Kai either stood or sat and watched something beyond Ildiko's line of sight.

They followed the curve of the wall and paused at a wide entrance that opened onto a makeshift training arena. Archers' targets shared space alongside one wall with straw men in various states of dismemberment. Weapons of every type, from wood to steel, occupied another space. There were other contraptions as well, items that looked like they were used for training from horseback, but in the dim torchlight flickering across the arena, Ildiko could only guess at their purpose.

The cheers and shouts that drew her here were for the combatants in the middle of the arena. Nine pairs of Kai faced off against each other, each man or woman intent on grappling their opponent into submission. The men were dressed down to simple linen cloths that girded the loins and were knotted at the waist. The women wore similar clothing except for the addition of a sleeveless gambeson cut to above the navel. Quilted and layered, it protected the breasts like a padded breastplate.

Sinuous and muscular, the battling Kai reminded her of cats. The light from the torches cast the combatants in high relief. Their skin glistened with sweat as they crashed together, bent, twisted, and threw each other to the ground in multiple attempts to win the match.

Anhuset tapped Ildiko on the shoulder and pointed to one of the battling pair. "There is Brishen, Your Highness. He fights Nefiritsen. A difficult opponent to wrestle."

Ildiko guided her horse to a better spot so she could see. Brishen and Nefiritsen were locked in a knot of arms and legs, muscles straining as they each tried to bring their opponent to the ground.

Not cats, she thought. Eels, very much alive and aggressive. They wound around each other, wavy and serpentine as if their bones had softened and stretched until they could bend and twist in a combat so supple it seemed more dance than fight and looked utterly inhuman.

Like the other Kai in the arena, Brishen wore only the linen loincloth. He'd scraped his hair back and tied it at the nape. The style highlighted the sloped almond shape of his eyes and the high curve of his cheekbones. He was shiny with sweat and streaked with dirt. A handsome man still, despite the grime.

The thought brought Ildiko up short. This wasn't the first time she'd noted her husband's appearance in such a way. She'd done so before three evenings past, and then she'd called him beautiful.

They had shared a bed, though they had done nothing more than sleep. Ildiko had quickly grown used to Brishen's presence beside her, the heat of his body beneath the covers. He was a peaceful sleeper—no thrashing or sighs, no snoring. She sometimes wondered if he or any of the Kai dreamed as humans did.

After their return from High Salure and Serovek's dinner, she'd fallen asleep as soon as Brishen ordered her under the covers. Unlike every evening prior, she'd awakened before him and discovered a man sublime in slumber.

He stretched recumbent on one side, facing her, one arm tucked against his chest, the other extended toward her. A few locks of black hair partially obscured his features, but Ildiko could still see the sharp line of his jaw and equally sharp bridge of his nose. For a man who smiled and laughed so easily, his mouth had a distinct downturn, a gift of heritage from the cold-blooded mother he so despised.

His deep-set eyes were closed, the thick lashes fluttering with the occasional twitch of his eyelids. A faint frown marred the stillness of his face for a moment, lowering the slant of his eyebrows. It faded as quickly as it appeared, and he sighed softly in his sleep. Ildiko reached out to smooth his brow. She pulled back, unwilling to disturb him and end her chance to openly admire him.

He had rolled in the covers at some point. They bunched at his waist and twisted around one leg, leaving the other exposed to the cool night air that drafted in thin streams into the room through the window shutters' narrow slats.

Ildiko blinked, and a surge of heat climbed from her belly to her chest, making the breath catch in her throat.

He was naked under the sheets. She'd seen him bare-chested before, but he usually came to bed partially dressed in loose breeches of parchment-thin linen. That long leg, bared to the evening air from ankle to flank revealed he'd chosen to forego such modesty.

The Kai were a tall, graceful people, their willowy physiques deceptive. It was known among the human nations that the Kai were immensely strong, with bones like iron and just as heavy. The Beladine lord Serovek was a big man, powerfully built and looked like he could carry a draft horse on his shoulders. Brishen, by contrast, had seemed almost delicate, yet Ildiko suspected his weight equaled, if not surpassed Serovek's, as did his strength.

Resting beside her, he seemed to Ildiko a living statue, carved from dark granite into a form of supple elegance and power. He was beautiful, and the tremor change in her perception of him robbed her lungs of air.

He opened both eyes suddenly, making her jump. Two shimmering gold coins stared at her unblinking. "Good evening, wife," he said in a voice raspy with the remnants of sleep. A closed-lip smile curved his mouth upward and deepened the tiny lines that fanned from the corners of his eyes. "You're staring. Do I have a fly on my nose?"

Fighting down a blush at being caught gawking at her own husband, Ildiko lightly tapped the tip of his nose with one finger. "I was trying to find a way to kill it without punching you in the face. Lucky for you, it flew away."

He clasped her wrist and brought her palm to his mouth for a kiss. Generous with his affections, he'd done this many times before, but this time was different. This time the brush of his lips across the sensitive center of her palm sent hot shivers down her arms and back. Ildiko freed her hand from his grasp and sat up to fluff the pillows behind her. She avoided his gaze and smoothed the covers over her lap. "I'm sorry to have woken you."

She caught the faint narrowing of his gaze from the corner of her eye. She was acting oddly, and he knew it.

He started to sit up and recline beside her but paused. A gravid silence hovered between them before Brishen cursed softly in bast-Kai. He yanked the covers over both legs and sat up. His fingers on her chin were light as he turned her head to face him.

The firelight yellow of his eyes had paled, and the smile that greeted her when he awoke was gone. "Forgive me, Ildiko. It was too hot yesterday for bedclothes, and I usually sleep unclad. I meant to be up and dressed before you." He dropped his hand and motioned for her to turn away. "This will only take me a moment."

He tried to rise, halting when Ildiko grabbed his arm. She'd heard it in his voice, threads of disappointment, embarrassment. He thought her disgusted by the sight of him naked beside her and barely covered by the bed covers. The opposite couldn't be more true.

That persistent blush did a slow crawl up her neck. This time Ildiko ignored it. "Don't be foolish, Brishen. I should be the one embarrassed. You caught me eyeing you like prized horseflesh." She chuckled as his eyes rounded. "Don't look so shocked. I may be human, but I'm not blind. I've come to appreciate Kai beauty." She raised her chin. "And I refuse to apologize for indulging in admiration of my own husband."

Brishen's wide grin matched her own, even if his teeth far outmatched hers in intimidation. He tucked his pillows behind his back and recaptured her hand. Ildiko didn't pull away this time.

"And here I thought I'd married a shy, blushing maiden," he teased.

Ildiko sniffed and tugged aside the collar of her night rail to reveal her neck, now feverish to the touch and no doubt bright red. "You're partially right. I'm blushing right now." She released the collar and gave him an arch stare. "I am not, however, a maiden."

To a Gauri nobleman intent on siring heirs of his blood, confirmation of a new bride's innocence was paramount. Ildiko's cousins had been guarded like prisoners by an army of governesses and bodyguards as if their maidenheads were made of precious stones instead of flesh. Any man deemed unworthy as suitor material by the royal family risked life and limb by so much as casting an admiring glance toward one of the prisoners.

Ildiko's own virtue was far less prized and as such, her aunt didn't act quite the zealot toward protecting it. Brishen had never inquired, and she hoped it was from lack of interest more than an assumption that she was yet uninitiated into the physical intimacies between men and women.

Brishen wiggled his eyebrows at her and crossed his arms. "Ah, a tale of your past. You keep your secrets close, wife. Tell me this one. What lovers taught you the pleasures of the flesh?"

She squeezed his fingers, relieved that her admission incited only curiosity. Maybe the Kai didn't place the same value on such a silly notion as the Gauri did.

"Lover," she said. "Just one and I didn't find it all that pleasurable." Brishen lost his slight smile but remained silent. Ildiko shrugged. "It was nice but certainly not worth drinking lorus flower tea beforehand." She shuddered at that memory.

"Did he force you?" Brishen asked the question in a voice gone guttural. Tiny white sparks flashed in his eyes.

Ildiko patted his arm and eased her hand out of his before he forgot he could crush her fingers with one squeeze. "Of course not. He was a pleasant lad, the youngest of a minor nobleman's eight sons. Neither one of us knew what we were doing really. It was messy and awkward and not worth bothering with after the third time."

Brishen's mouth contorted into strange shapes as he struggled to hold back his laughter. "Why didn't you try someone else? An experienced lover would have taught you much. It's called 'pleasures of the flesh' for a reason, Ildiko, and goes far beyond clumsy fumblings under the covers."

She waved a nonchalant hand. "It still wouldn't have been worth it in my opinion. Lorus flower tea prevents a man's seed from catching in the womb, but it tastes so foul even the memory of it makes my stomach turn. Surely, there is nothing so pleasurable to make it worth drinking that swill."

Her comment made Brishen laugh outright, his fangs gleaming white in the room's twilight. He reached for her braid and wrapped it loosely around his forearm. "Ah, my Ildiko, what a practical soul you have."

"I consider it an attribute, not a fault. More people could use a dose of practicality now and then."

He tugged on her braid. "I don't disparage you. I find such a trait one of your charms."

The color of his eyes had deepened once more to the lamplight gold he'd shown her when he first woke. While Ildiko couldn't track the movement of his eyes except for the slight jerk at the edges of his eye sockets, she had the sense his gaze touched long on her hair, her shoulders and neck, her bare arms.

The fine tingle dancing along her skin transformed to a sizzle. Ildiko inhaled sharply as Brishen leaned close to nuzzle the sensitive spot at her temple with his nose. His breath tickled her ear. "One of many," he whispered, and his words were a caress along her back.

Brishen's lips fluttered along the edge of her ear to her earlobe. Caught between the sensual beguilement of his light touch and the unconquerable fear that he might inadvertently snap off her earlobe with his teeth, Ildiko sat frozen, her breath riding through her mouth and nose in jagged exhalations.

As if he sensed her wariness more than her desire, he pulled away slowly, shoulders rigid, face wiped clean of expression. He uncoiled her braid from his arm and smoothed it over her shoulder, his movements controlled and careful. He drew away from her in both body and spirit.

Ildiko clutched his arm, unwilling to have him leave her side. "I enjoy your touch, Brishen."

The stiffness eased from his shoulders. He gave her a wry look and pressed his palm to the pale expanse of skin just below her collarbones. His hand rose and fell in quick time to her breathing. "I believe you, but this tells me you fear it as well."

She winced. "Your teeth are so...sharp."

"They are, but I'm not careless, wife. And if, for some unfathomable reason, I accidently bite you, you're welcome to bite me back."

His attempt at humor worked, and Ildiko chuckled. "Brishen—" She offered him a toothy grin. "These wouldn't do much damage."

He traced the line of her collarbones with the rough pads of his fingers, their dark claws a whisper of movement across her flesh. "You have obviously never been badly bitten by a horse."

Strange as the analogy was, she had no argument to rebut it. Instead she contented herself with lifting strands of his hair from his shoulder and letting it slide between her fingers. Brishen's eyes drifted shut at the caress, and he shifted position so that he laid crossways on the bed, his head in her lap, his back to her.

If they both didn't have a hundred tasks to complete once they rose, she'd be content to stroke his silky hair for hours. A lock of hair snagged in her loose grip. "Sorry," she said. "You've a few tangles back here."

"You can brush it for me when we get up."

Very clever, she thought. "I'll brush your hair if you tell me about your first lover. Hopefully, the encounter was more memorable than mine."

She felt the tensing of his cheek on her leg when he smiled. He stayed quiet, and she pulled on one of his tangles. "I told you a past tale, Brishen. Your turn."

"Wouldn't you rather hear about how my nurse caught me practicing how to write my name by pissing on my bedroom walls?"

Ildiko rolled her eyes. "No, I wouldn't. You just told me too much already."

Silent laughter shimmied down her leg. Brishen turned onto his other side to face her. His head pressed into her belly, warm and heavy. He took her hand and placed it back on his head. She took the hint and resumed carding his hair.

"My first lover was thirteen years older than me and the most famous courtesan in all of Bast-Haradis. My father felt if anyone was to teach his sons the skills of the bedchamber, it should be someone well known for them." Ildiko halted, and Brishen tapped the back of her hand to continue. "You asked," he said.

Ildiko wasn't shocked by his revelation and in many ways understood Djedor's logic. She twirled strands of Brishen's hair around her finger, let it unspool and twirled it again. "I should have hired myself a courtesan," she mused. Men, as well as women, sold their favors in Pricid's flesh markets. Though how she might have sneaked one into the palace was another subject altogether.

Brishen startled beneath her hand, and he sat up clumsily, half swaddled as he was in blankets and sheets. He gaped at Ildiko. "You are an odd creature," he finally said.

She wished for a lit candle so she might better see him in the slowly darkening room. "You'll adjust," she said in her sweetest voice and promptly swatted him with a stray pillow.

He toppled to the side only to spring up, a matching pillow in his hands. "That is a declaration of war, Ildiko."

"Of course it is." She took another swing at him with her pillow only to be interrupted by a pounding at the door.

Instead of his servant's voice as she expected, Brishen's steward called from the other side. "Your Highness, the constable from Halmatus township has arrived and seeks an audience."

Brishen's shoulders drooped, and he dropped his pillow with a sigh. "I've not wasted my hours here with you, wife, but I've matters to attend to, and no one waits at the leisure of a lowly prince who isn't the heir apparent."

Ildiko shared his disappointment. She had a task list longer than her arm to take care of herself, but it didn't lessen her regret at having to end these moments with Brishen. She knee-walked across the bed to him and slid her arms around his neck. "I owe you a hair-brushing," she said.

He enclosed her in a loose embrace. "You do. I'll collect later. Count on it." He kissed her forehead and lowered his arms. "Off with you. With any luck, we can share lunch."

She left him for her room, giving him a last glance and nod as he watched her leave from his spot in the middle of the rumpled bed. Her ear still tingled where he'd kissed her, and her back felt feverish at the memory of his touch.

Anhuset's quick tap on her shoulder brought Ildiko back to the present and the reality of horses, torchlight and Kai fighters trying to kill each other on a dusty training field.

"Highness, do you want someone to summon him?" Anhuset nodded at Brishen still locked in martial embrace with his opponent.

Ildiko flinched, barely able to watch. Someone was going to end up with a broken neck or broken something before this was done. "No," she said. "Let's leave. I don't want to distract him, and I'll see him soon enough at the house." She turned her horse amidst the soldiers who accompanied them to the dye house. They followed her but stopped when she held up a hand. "Stay if you wish. We're within the redoubt. I don't need an escort."

She nudged her mount into a trot, Anhuset riding beside her. They weren't far from the iron gates that opened to a manicured loggia and more orderly landscape. A flash of motion teased the corner of her eye. Ildiko turned in time to see Anhuset draw her sword, utter a swear word and resheathe the weapon.

Brishen loped toward them, long legs flexing as he cut across their path. Ildiko had barely slowed her horse when he caught up, grasped her saddle pommel and landed behind her in a smooth, running mount.

"That is the worst display of showing off I've ever seen," Anhuset said in forbidding tones.

"Of course it is." Brishen wrapped an arm around Ildiko's waist and pressed himself against her back. "I'm trying to impress my wife."

"I'm very impressed." Ildiko flashed him a smile over her shoulder.

Brishen's hands wandered over the folds of her cloak. "Why are you damp? And you smell like salt. Did you fall into a dye vat?"

"Dived in is more like it," Anhuset volunteered in cheery tones.

Ildiko narrowed her eyes. "You can leave now, sha-Anhuset. I'm sure Brishen can get me safely to the front door in the next fifteen steps by himself."

Anhuset's unrepentant cackle echoed in the night air as she saluted and wheeled her horse back toward the outer redoubt.

Ildiko guided her horse to a waiting groom. Brishen dismounted first, and Ildiko waved away his offer to help her down. She was perfectly capable of climbing off her own horse.

Hoping to delay her confession and avoid showing off her new skin color to Brishen, she asked him about his wrestling bout. "Did you win?"

"No. Nefiritsen is my best wrestler. He remains unbeaten in all matches so far. If any of us must face an enemy in unarmed combat, we want him beside us."

They entered the castle, passed through the great hall and climbed one of the two stairwells that flanked either side of the high-ceilinged chamber. Candlelight lit their way down the corridor. Ildiko didn't stumble around in the dark as often these days, but she was glad for the candles and their anemic luminescence.

She stopped in front of her door, turned to face Brishen, and adopted what she hoped was a nonchalant expression, especially when he was standing before her half naked. She tried not to let her avid gaze linger on him too long. "You'll want a bath I'm sure. I'll meet you later for a meal or some wine?"

Brishen placed a hand over hers on the door latch. "You'll not get rid of me that quickly, wife. My cousin said you dove into a dye vat. I'll be on my way once you satisfy my curiosity."

Resolved to the inevitable, she motioned him inside. Sinhue was elsewhere, probably getting an earful from another servant or soldier about how Brishen's homely wife tried to make herself more pleasing to the eye by dying herself pink. If horses traveled as fast as gossip, they'd blow their riders clear off their backs.

Brishen laughed only a little when Ildiko removed her cloak, shrugged off her ruined tunic and revealed her arms, neck and shift dappled in varying shades of the summer rose.

"I look ridiculous," she huffed.

"You look pink," he replied. He circled her slowly. "And you chose to bathe in amaranthine why?"

Ildiko told him the story of her necklace. "I didn't want to lose it. I know someone could have fished it out of the vat for me, but I panicked." She lifted the necklace from where it nestled under her bodice laces and handed it to Brishen. "I think it's worth very little in coin but is precious to me. The clasp broke as I leaned over to get a closer look at the cold dye."

Brishen raised the chain for a better look. "It's a good piece. Remember the constable from Halmatus?" Ildiko nodded. "A jeweler resides there. He can repair the clasp or fashion a new chain for your necklace."

Ildiko eyed the necklace longingly. Her hand itched to snatch it out of Brishen's grasp, but she squelched the urge. He deserved her trust, even with those things precious and irreplaceable to her. She clasped her hands behind her back. "Would it take long to fix the clasp?"

He must have heard something in her voice, something hesitant and fearful. "Not long. I can deliver it myself if you like."

Ildiko clapped her hands. "Oh yes, please, would you?" Mortification rushed in hard on the heels of euphoria. "I'm sorry, Brishen," she said. "You're not a messenger boy. Someone else can go."

Brishen offered the necklace to her, his head cocked in a way that Ildiko was fast recognizing as a sign of his amusement. "You misunderstand me, Ildiko. I'm not going alone. You'll go with me. I've no eye for the delicacies of a woman's trinkets. You can deal with the jeweler. I'll just be there to keep you company and cross the man's palm with the coin he demands for his work."

She scooped the necklace out of his palm and held it close. "That is a wonderful idea. I know you're worried about the dangers of Beladine raiders, but I'd love to visit more of the towns and villages under Saggara's protection."

He'd been reluctant to let her venture to Lakeside, convinced only by Anhuset's promise to bring a small army as escort and the fact the town was within walking distance of the estate and redoubt.

Brishen lifted her hand, turning it one way and then the other. "At least it wasn't nettle dye," he said and kissed her knuckles before leaving her for a much-needed bath.

He was right. Nettle dye was green. There were worse colors to sport than pink.

They met again for their supper in the great hall and afterwards in his chamber for another game of Butcher's Covenant in which Brishen out-maneuvered her and slaughtered every man on her side of the board without losing more than three on his side.

"You're getting better," he said as she lay the intricately carved pieces into a silk lined boxed and closed the lid.

Ildiko snorted. "That's a lie and you know it. Just when I think I've outsmarted you, you kill off one of my men."

Brishen poured them both a goblet of wine from a nearby pitcher. "You've outsmarted me on several occasions in the game. Your weakness is you over-think your strategy and question yourself until you react instead of plan." He handed her one of the goblets along with a comb. "You are, however, far better with a comb than you are with Butcher's Covenant."

Ildiko took the comb. "That doesn't comfort me. One is an exercise in strategy, the other carding wool."

He dropped down onto his haunches in front of her chair and tilted his head back to gaze at her. "I am no sheep."

She gathered his hair into a waterfall that spilled down his back and set to combing out the dark strands. "Trust me, Brishen, no one with eyes will ever mistake you, or any Kai for that matter, for sheep. More like wolves."

Brishen sat passive before her, his wide shoulders slumped, his breathing slow as Ildiko glided the comb through his hair in long strokes.

"Tell me a tale," she said.

It was their bargain. She groomed his hair, and he told her stories of his childhood in Haradis. Some were funny, others grim, though he told them in a matter-of-fact voice as if it was quite commonplace for mothers to lash their children with a horsewhip because they had a slight lisp and couldn't quite master one of the simple spells all Kai children learned.

Ildiko guessed Brishen had been rambunctious, resourceful and clever. And he'd been born with a compassion and nobility of character neither of his parents possessed.

"What would you like to hear?" he asked.

She thought about it for a moment. Her request was more for an answer to a question than a story of the past. "Why are you nothing like the man who sired you and the woman who bore you?"

It was as if she touched him with a hot brand. Brishen jerked forward, back stiff as a spear haft. He gained his feet in one fluid motion and turned to Ildiko with his hand outstretched. "Come with me," he said.

She stared at him, then took his hand without question. He led her through the manor, down to the first floor and out a door that led from a buttery to the bristling thicket of brambles and wild oranges that hemmed in one side of the estate.

A pale moon hung thin in the sky and did nothing to illuminate the earth below it. Ildiko stumbled along behind Brishen, blind as a mole in daylight. Her husband moved surefooted in the suffocating darkness, guiding Ildiko toward a destination she assumed would answer a question she was starting to regret asking.

They stopped before a patch of wall that surrounded part of the manor's loggia. Brishen uttered a word in a language Ildiko was certain couldn't have been bast-Kai. A shadow, paler than its siblings, parted from the stone, exposing a set of three indentions cut shallow in one of the masonry blocks.

Brishen placed the three fingers of his right hand into the depressions and whispered another arcane word. Ildiko gasped as the block softened until it melted into the stones on either side of it, leaving an opening black and deep.

She almost batted his arm away when he reached inside the hollow. For all she knew, something with teeth longer and sharper than a Kai's lurked in that space. Brishen didn't hesitate and pulled out a small urn. He faced Ildiko, gently cradling the urn.

"What is it?" she asked.

"The answer to your question."

He lifted the lid. For a moment nothing happened, then suddenly a feeble light no bigger than a dandelion puff and just as delicate floated upward until it hovered above its housing.

The glow of Brishen's eyes provided the only illumination between them, but it was enough to gild the tiny light as it flickered and bobbed between them. "My sister," he said softly. "Or her memory at least."

Ildiko gasped softly. His sister. He'd never spoken of another sibling, only the indifferent brother she met briefly in Haradis. Brishen's revelation begged more questions, the first being why would his sibling's mortem light be here at Saggara, hidden away by spellwork, instead of at Emlek where the Kai held the memories of their dead?

"She was never formally named, but I call her Anaknet. I'd seen eleven seasons when she was born." The tiny mortem light floated toward him and balanced on the back of his hand. "She was born with a club foot, an imperfect child and unacceptable to Secmis. I thought her pretty."

A sinking dread grew in Ildiko's chest. He would tell her something terrible, something to bind her insides into knots . She was tempted to cover her ears, tell him to stop and apologize to him for asking her silly questions, but she stood silent before him and waited for this childhood tale to unfold.

"Secmis murdered her four days after her birth. She broke her neck. I saw her do it."

"My gods," Ildiko breathed, horrified at Secmis's monstrous cruelty and the knowledge that Brishen, a young boy, had witnessed it.

Brishen continued, his voice flat and distant. "Secmis is a mage-leech. She gains power and long life from forbidden spellwork and the consumption of souls and memories. She was old when my father was a child, though now she goes by a different name and claims lineage from another clan." Anaknet's mortem light danced over his palm.

"I took Anaknet's light and released her soul before my mother could steal both. Anhuset and my old nurse Peret helped me with the lamentation and got me through the memory sickness. Peret kept the light for me tucked away in the hollow of a birch tree in her sister's garden. When I was given Saggara, I brought Anaknet here."

He coaxed the mortem light back into the urn, closed the lid and returned the vessel to its hiding place. Different spells reformed the masonry block until it hardened, leaving only an expanse of blank wall.

Brishen faced Ildiko fully, and even through a vision compromised by darkness and tears, she still saw the sparks of red that danced in his eyes. "I hate my mother, Ildiko," he said in that same flat voice. "Down to the marrow of my bones. One day I will kill her. She knows this." He looked at the place where the urn rested. "Anaknet is why I am who I am, wife. Because I refuse to become like the monstrosities who bore us."

Ildiko sniffled and scraped her sleeve across her cheeks in the futile effort to staunch the flow of tears. She reached out to Brishen, carefully, as if he were an injured animal caught in a trap. He accepted her touch, and soon she was wrapped in his embrace.

"I'm sorry," she sobbed into his shoulder. "So very sorry." She stroked his hair, holding him for what seemed like hours, listening to the rapid hammer of his heartbeat and the shallow breaths that sometimes verged on sorrowful moans. The Kai didn't weep, but they mourned just as deeply as humans.

When he finally stepped away from her, his eyes had lost their red sparks and Ildiko's had dried of their tears. She grasped one of his hands in both of hers. "I swear I will take this knowledge to my deathbed, Brishen."

One corner of his mouth turned up, and he meshed his fingers with hers. "I know. It's why I told you."

They walked back to the manor in silence just as a thin line of crimson spread across the far horizon to announce the dawn. Sinhue greeted Ildiko at her door. "Your Highness, are you unwell?" She ushered her charge inside and made her sit on the bed while she poured water into a cup and handed it to her. "This might help. Do you need a cloth for your eyes? They're swollen and red."

Ildiko sought and found the a partial lie to tell. "I was crying." She hiccupped a giggle at Sinhue's bewildered look. "Humans weep when they're sad. I was missing my family. I'm fine now, though I'll take that cloth."

By the time she'd bathed her hot face and changed into her nightrail, the sun had risen enough to turn the plains into a golden sea. Ildiko slipped quietly into Brishen's room and found him, still dressed, standing in a clot of shadows near the open window. He stared eastward, into the blinding dawn and didn't turn as she padded closer to him.

"Stop, Ildiko."

Startled by the abrupt command, she halted. "Brishen?"

A faint sigh, and his voice gentled. "It will be best if you sleep in your bed alone today."

An icy rush of hurt punched her in the gut. She staggered inwardly for a moment, then righted herself. This had nothing to do with her. His recounting of his sister's death had left her emotionally wrung out. She suspected that for him it had torn open old wounds that had scabbed but never healed. He wanted to tend them in isolation.

Solitude, however, wasn't always the best comfort. She eased another step forward. "Are you sure you wish to be alone in your grief?"

His dry chuckle held no humor. "If it were just grief, no. I'd want you here." He still refused to face her. "I'm not only grieving, Ildiko. I'm bitter; I'm angry and I'm lusting." His voice deepened on the last part of his declaration and sent Ildiko's heartbeat into a gallop. "Those emotions together offer nothing but misery and violence for both human and Kai. It's dangerous for you to be in here with me. Go to your room. I'll talk with you tomorrow."

She fled, carrying with her his words before she shut and bolted the door between them.

"Thank you, sweet Ildiko."

CHAPTER EIGHTEEN

There were times when the day lasted forever and night never came. For Brishen, this was one of those times. He stared unblinking at the bolted door between his and Ildiko's chambers until his eyes burned. He'd caught it—the brief flinch of hurt tightening the skin around her eyes before it disappeared, and her pale features eased into an expression of concern.

Brishen thanked the gods he and Ildiko had begun this marriage with such unadorned honesty between them. She'd taken his warning at face value and done exactly as he hoped by fleeing and bolting her door. No cajoling or long explanations for why he wasn't fit—or even safe—company at the moment. She might not be able to discern emotion in his eyes, but she knew him well enough now to know his words weren't empty ones.

Even through the thick walls and closed door, he heard her soft voice and Sinhue's as they both prepared to sleep. The words were indecipherable, but he found their cadence soothing. They soon faded, leaving only a heavy quiet that leached from the walls to join the shadows that fled from the encroaching sunbeams and pooled at his feet.

Twenty-two years had passed since he witnessed his mother murder his sister, and the memory remained as clear as if it happened the previous night. Secmis's hands cupping Anaknet's head, fingers like spider legs that curved around the tiny skull until her claw tips touched. The baby's fists curled in innocent sleep. Partially concealed behind the nursery door and made mute with horror, Brishen watched as the queen gently held Anaknet's head for a moment and gave one quick twist.

He shook his head to clear it of the memory. He could block out the image but not the grotesque sound—a soft snick, barely more than a whisper that over time gained the volume of a thunderclap in his dreams and recollections.

Brishen never imagined he'd tell another person about Anaknet. Only two other people knew what he'd seen and done those many years ago. One died a decade earlier of old age; the other would cut out her own tongue before she surrendered her knowledge. Both had been pivotal in helping him abscond with Anaknet's mortem light and release her fragile soul before Secmis claimed it, and he remained forever grateful to them. His old nursemaid and his cousin were braver than any ten Kai warriors combined. Had Secmis discovered their roles in his plan...he shuddered at the thought.

Now Ildiko knew as well. Brishen turned away from the door separating him from his wife. She was like a skein of raw silk, strong as steel with a luster woven into her blood and bones. She held him in her arms as he keened an old grief. Like all Kai, he didn't shed tears. Ildiko; however, had shed them for him, and he'd caught the taste of salt and sorrow on his lips when she brushed her mouth across his in a gesture of comfort.

The need to embrace her, clasp her hard to every part of his body had almost overwhelmed him then. She was solace enrobed in smooth flesh and scented hair. He had kept his hands light on her back, knowing that to hold her the way he wanted, he might injure her in his enthusiasm. Her very human body was far weaker than her character.

Such knowledge hadn't stopped the lust rising inside him. Warped by anger and simmering hatred for the queen, that lust poisoned the growing desire he had for his wife, turning it into an ugly thing.

When Ildiko appeared in his chamber, dressed in her nightrail and prepared to sleep with him as she did each day, he'd almost lunged at her, blinded by the desperation to sink into her, body and soul. Every part of him ached with the need. Brishen pummeled the temptation into submission, chilled to the core by images of a woman bloodied and broken by a man possessed.

He meant every bit of his thanks when she fled his chamber and bolted her door. Solitude did nothing to cool his rage or his desire. He paced. He drank wine. He called down every curse he knew on the queen and finally, he grabbed his cloak and quit the chamber where he was certain he could smell Ildiko's flowery scent on his sheets.

Saggara was quiet. Most of its inhabitants slept except for a few hooded guards who saluted Brishen as he strode through the corridors and into the brutal morning daylight. The short walk to the redoubt and its deserted arena did little to soothe his restlessness. He stripped down to his breeches and eagerly took up one of the practice swords set in racks that lined the arena walls.

Swords were not his preferred weapons, and straw men made laughable opponents, but he hacked away at them in a sun-blinded frenzy until straw hazed the air, and body parts lay strewn across the dirt floor. Muscles quivering with fatigue, Brishen glanced up briefly, startled to see the sun had climbed almost directly overhead. He'd been training in full battle mode for two hours, and the sweat streamed off his arms and legs in rivulets. His lungs burned and his body ached, but his head was clear. Mock combat had done its job. The rage had subsided. The lust was still there but mellowed into a desire that bubbled in his belly. He still wanted Ildiko—fiercely, but to savor instead of conquer.

"You'll be blind for good if you don't cover up, cousin."

Brishen turned and squinted at Anhuset. She stood to one side, his discarded cloak draped over her arm. She unlaced the hood from the cloak and tossed it to him. "I'm amazed you can still see at all."

He caught the hood but held off from pulling it over his head until he could rinse off the grime and bits of straw coating his skin. The cold water shock from the nearby well banished any exhaustion. Water from his dripping hair and breeches puddled at his feet. While the hood offered relief from the punishing light, it weighed hot and stifling on his head and shoulders.

"You look like a half-drowned magefinder," Anhuset said.

He scowled at her. "Be glad I didn't shake the water off, or you'd be as drenched as me." He used his cloak to wipe down his arms. "What are you doing here?"

She shrugged. "You know I've never been a good sleeper. I thought I might come to the arena and train for a little while. Imagine my surprise at finding you here." Her eyes narrowed to glowing slits within the shadows of her hood. "Where's the *hercegesé*?"

Brishen gazed at his cousin. Anhuset. Sharp, intuitive, she knew him better and longer than anyone. Something about his

demeanor alarmed her. "Asleep in her bed, unlike either of us."
He withstood her silent scrutiny. She'd have her say, and his best
course of action was to wait until she did.

"Unless your sword arm needs improving, there are better
ways to spend a sleepless day. I know a dozen women who'd be
happy to cool the fire for you."

He'd briefly entertained the thought. Ildiko had once hinted
she didn't mind if he took a mistress, yet he wondered if that still
held true. Three days earlier they had lain together in his bed. He
hadn't imagined the delicate shiver that raced down her body as he
nuzzled her temple, and that shiver had not been fear.

"I wouldn't survive the affections of a dozen Kai women,
cousin. Besides, only one can cool the fire."

Anhuset's lips twitched. "And that one isn't Kai. What has
Ildiko become to you?"

"The fire." He nodded once to her and started to leave the
arena.

She called to him. "Don't you want to spar with me?"

Brishen shook his head and kept walking. "No. I miss my
wife."

"Are you sure you're not trying to avoid me beating you into
one big bruise?"

He waved away her taunt. "That too." If he didn't dawdle,
he'd have a few hours to bring Ildiko back to his bed where she
belonged and sleep the last daylight hours away with her by his
side.

Anhuset wasn't finished with him yet. "Your Highness, when
Lord Pangion arrives at Saggara this evening do you wish for us to
escort him from the main road or from the gates of the redoubt?"

He halted, cursing under his breath. Serovek. The dinner. He'd forgotten. He pinched the bridge of his nose between thumb and forefinger. The headache he suffered from the sun just grew worse. Brishen was tempted to tell Anhuset to kindly escort their guest back home the moment he arrived. Such an action though guaranteed a neighbor no longer amiable or forthcoming with information.

"Meet him and his party at the main road." He was glad for the hood which hid his smirk. "Anhuset, you'll attend the dinner and the dancing afterwards." The low snarl that met his command widened his smirk to a grin. Brishen walked away, listening closely for the tell-tale snick of a sword unsheathed or the breath of air cleaved by a flying dagger.

He returned to the manor unscathed and found its occupants still deep in slumber. His personal servant slept in a modest chamber nearby. Brishen let him sleep, unwilling to rouse the man in the middle of the day just to bring him water for a bath. A face cloth and the water in his wash basin and pitcher would have to do. The sodden breeches were discarded and tossed in a heap in one corner. He scrubbed away the dirt the well water dousing missed, donned a pair of the linen breeches he was truly starting to despise and made his way to the door between his chamber and Ildiko's.

Sleeping naked next to her that one time had been a mistake. Ildiko had caught him off guard by waking up before him. Luckily, neither of them were prone to cuddle in their sleep, or she would have discovered very quickly that his deep affection for her was changing into something far beyond the platonic. Trapped under the covers until she left to change in her room, Brishen had collapsed on the bed with a frustrated groan once he was alone and vowed they'd sleep separately after that. His vow lasted less than a day. He wanted her beside him.

Were he his father, Brishen could turn the door thin as parchment and walk through it to retrieve his wife. Were he his grandfather, he could pass through the solid wood, as ethereal as any wraith, but the magic was fading in the Kai with every generation born. Brishen conserved the magic he possessed and limited the use of his power to a few chanted words that slid the bolt free on the other side.

He eased around the door and discovered a bleary-eyed Sinhue rising from her bed in the shallow alcove in one corner of the room. He held a finger to his lips for silence. She nodded and lay down, her back to him.

Ildiko sprawled in the middle of her bed. Asleep on her stomach with half her face buried in the pillows, she presented him with a profile that shone as pale as the sheets in the darkness. He once called her a hag of a woman. Leached of color except for the bitter mollusk pink that surged under her skin in uneven patches when she was angry or embarrassed, he'd found her both ugly and peculiar to behold. Had it only been a few months earlier that he bore such thoughts of her?

Looking at her now, Brishen wondered how he could have thought her unsightly. Her eyes still brought him up short on occasion, especially when she teased him by crossing them toward her nose, but he'd ceased comparing them to parasites. They were just eyes, different from his and fascinating in their own way with their colorful irises and black pupils that shrank or expanded depending on the light or her emotions.

Her eyes were hidden from him now, behind closed lids edged in bronze lashes. Serovek had called her beautiful, and Brishen hadn't missed the long stares cast upon her by the Gauri noblemen who attended her wedding. He tried to see her as a Gauri man might but failed in the endeavor. A sudden realization made him smile a little.

One of his wife's greatest strengths, and a thing he most admired about her, was her ability to adapt to a situation and still remain steadfast in her own sense of worth and place. Brishen no longer viewed her with the eyes of a Kai and couldn't view her with the eyes of a human male, but that held no consequence now. He saw her as she'd always seen herself—as simply Ildiko. For her, it was enough; for him, a gift beyond price.

He reached down to thread her loose hair through his fingers. She murmured in her sleep and rolled onto her back, exposing delicate collarbones and the outline of her breasts beneath her nightrail. She lay before him, a study in shade and shadow-play.

She didn't startle when he slid his arms beneath her and scooped her up from the bed. Her eyes opened slowly, and she nestled against his chest. "Is it evening already, Brishen?"

Brishen kissed the top of her head as he padded from her chamber to his and kicked the door closed behind him. "No. Still midday. Unlike you, I no longer sleep well without you next to me."

Ildiko patted his chest with one hand. "Your fault. You told me to go."

He tightened his embrace. "I did and was right to do so." He climbed into his bed still holding her. The sheets were cool on his legs, Ildiko hot on his torso.

Her hand wandered along his shoulder and up his neck until she cupped his jaw. Her dark pupils nearly swallowed the blue in her eyes. "Secmis is a vile and evil woman, Brishen."

He turned his face into her palm and planted a kiss in its curvature. "Don't bother with lavish compliments, wife," he said. "You'll never endear my loathsome mother to me."

Ildiko shook with sleepy laughter. Her amusement faded, and in the room's tenebrous shade her eyes glistened with sympathy and something else that ignited the desire simmering restlessly in Brishen's veins. "My noble prince," she said. "You are..." She frowned, searching for the words.

"A dead eel?" His hands tracked their own paths over her body, learning each curve beneath the thin nightrail.

"No," she said. "More like a raven. Dark and elegant."

"A clever scavenger."

Ildiko gave him a mock scowl. "A beautiful bird." She thumped him on the arm. "Stop fishing for compliments, you vain creature."

Brishen rolled, taking Ildiko with him until she lay fully under him. Her thighs opened, and he sank against her. They both gasped and stilled, all traces of humor gone. If she had no awareness of his body's reaction to her before this—and Ildiko, by her own admission, was neither that innocent nor that foolish—she couldn't mistake it now.

Forearms braced on either side of her head, he kept most of his weight off her, careful not to crush her into the bed. Ildiko's eyes were wide, her breathing thin and quick, an accompaniment to his own labored breaths.

He played with the curling strands of her hair that caught on his fingers like spiderweb. "I am no poet possessing honeyed words," he said. "But you have always known me to be forthright with you." Gods, his muscles shook as if from cold in his effort to stay still and not thrust hard against her. "I want you, Ildiko. Want to sink so deep into you that neither of us will know where one ends and the other begins." Only the darker blue rim of her irises still shone around her pupils. His voice had gone guttural, and he worked to soften it. "I've never forced a woman, Kai or human, and I never will. If you refuse me, this will stop, with no ill will between us."

Please, he prayed—and he didn't know if he prayed to Kai gods or to the statue-still woman pressed against him—*don't refuse me.*

Ildiko's black-eyed stare sharpened, and she peered into his gaze as if searching for something. Whatever she found transformed her expression. Her lids lowered, sinking to half-mast. Her breathing deepened, and her lips parted, revealing the edges of her upper front teeth. Hardly daring to hope and half dizzy with want, Brishen watched, fascinated, as the tip of her tongue darted out to swipe across her lower lip.

The silence yawned between them as she continued to stare at him. "What is it, Ildiko?" he asked. "What do you see?"

His question acted as a catalyst, breaking a spell that held him beguiled and her enthralled. She opened beneath him; not just her body. All of her. He sensed it in every part of him.

She twined her arms around his neck and tilted her head until her lips brushed the corner of his mouth. "My beautiful husband." she said. "I see radiance."

He groaned low in his throat as her mouth captured his. Ildiko buried her hands in his hair, pressing him closer to slide her tongue across the sensitive skin under his top lip and then his lower one. Brishen returned the caress, plying playful swipes at the edges of her lips and along the corners until she rocked in his arms, hips bumping against his in clumsy rhythm while he learned her taste and she learned his.

Ildiko didn't kiss as a Kai woman did. Her kisses were forceful—a sucking, nipping dance along his lips with her tongue seeking entrance past the barrier of his teeth clamped tight against intrusion. It was as if she'd forgotten the sharpness of his fangs or simply no longer cared.

Brishen pulled away despite Ildiko's protesting gasps. He pressed a finger to her lips, the tip of one black claw barely brushing the end of her nose. The air felt thin in his lungs. "I've seen humans kiss. You mate with your mouths." Just the words sent a spear of heat straight to his groin. He was so hard, he ached. "I can't do that, sweet wife. I'll slice you bloody."

Oh did he regret such an obstacle. For once, and probably the only time in his life, he wished for more human attributes. Horse teeth didn't seem so bad or so ridiculous at the moment. He'd take Ildiko's mouth the way he would take her body—deep and slow with hours spent dedicated on nothing more than savoring the taste and feel of her.

Undaunted by his warning, she tugged him back to her. "Maybe you can't," she said. "But I'm not limited by a mouthful of sword blades." Her pupils glittered in the shadow he cast across her face and body. "Part your lips." Spellbound, he did as she ordered. Ildiko rested her mouth lightly on his. Her lips tickled his when she spoke. "Slide your tongue out—just a little."

She'd be the death of him before they ever consummated this marriage. Brishen's body screamed to be done with it and slide inside her. His mind begged patience, delighted by this journey she took him on as the day waxed bright beyond the closed shutters.

Ildiko's lips closed around the tip of Brishen's tongue and sucked. He jerked in her arms, shivering at the new and pleasurable touch. Her tongue brushed his, a seductive caress that coaxed him to offer her more. He did and was rewarded by a longer suckling. Brishen moaned into her mouth, giving her more until his tongue twined with hers in the mating dance he'd so envied and coveted earlier.

She echoed his moan. Her arms, linked loosely behind his neck, fell away so that her hands could busy themselves with stroking him from shoulder to waist, pushing him to rise up so they could travel the hard planes of his abdomen.

Her fingers traced the ridges of his ribs, wandering higher and closer until her thumbs glided across his nipples. Brishen ended their kiss with a one-word prayer, back arching like a drawn bow as a lightning bolt of sensation shot across his chest to encircle his back and rake down his spine.

Ildiko's calves crossed over the back of his thighs and locked him in place. One hand splayed across his back, pressing him down so that she bore more of his weight. Her lips followed where her hands had played, teasing a trail from the hollow of his throat to the line of one collarbone and down the planes of his chest.

Brishen's claws gouged furrows into the pillows on either side of her head as she alternated between worrying his nipple with her tongue and blowing gently across the sensitive tip. His hips ignored the dictates of his mind to stay still. He thrust against her, enamored with the sleek feel of her thighs cradling him and the hot wetness that dampened both her nightrail and his linen breeches. Human women were obviously much like Kai women in that regard. Ildiko wanted him as much as he wanted her, and somewhere in his fogged brain, Brishen recognized that it was she who savored him at the moment and not the other way around as he originally planned.

He pulled himself out of reach, ignored her protests and captured her wrists in one hand. Her odd eyes were glassy, the blue of her irises completely surrendered to her pupils. A darker flush painted her pale skin. Brishen caught sight of the ragged amaranthine stain on the underside of her jaw from her earlier foray to the dye house. He bent and traced its outline, first with the tip of his nose and then his lips. Ildiko moaned softly in his ear.

Her eyebrows rose when he scooted them both down toward the foot of the bed and stretched her arms above her head, her wrists still manacled in his light grip. "You'll be my undoing before I can take another breath, and I want this day to last far beyond a breath," he said.

She frowned and wiggled teasingly beneath him. "But I've only had a taste."

"That's more than I've had," he countered. "Have you enjoyed me so far?" He preened at her enthusiastic nod. "Then be fair, wife, and let me enjoy you."

Ildiko unfurled along his length, a silk ribbon tipped from a spool to ripple and stroke him from chest to knees. "Oh, well then," she breathed. "I don't wish to be unjust."

She stopped him before he could return the touches that so inflamed him. Her hand stroked his hair. "Close your eyes," she said.

Brishen frowned. If Ildiko worried he'd find her the hag he first met in Pricid's royal gardens, she had nothing to fear. His vision of her was irrevocably changed. "Why?" he asked, wary of her reasons.

"Because I'd have you see me with your touch." Her mouth curved into a smile. "It's how I see you in this blind darkness, Brishen, and it is a wondrous thing."

He'd been the recipient of heady praise from mistresses as in lust with his title as they were with his body. No such honeyed words ever came close to these and their power over him.

She kept her arms above her head, even after he released her wrists. Brishen closed his eyes and let his other senses overtake his willing blindness. He took his time, exploring every hollow, swell and nook of Ildiko's neck and shoulders. She smelled of flowers and the scented oils imported by the caravan peoples who traded such indulgences for spells and charms from Kai shaman. She tasted...human.

He could think of no comparison. Soft skin with a hint of spice and a sweetness he'd tasted nowhere else in either food or on the supple, muscular limbs of the Kai women he'd bedded before his marriage. Her differences intrigued him, seduced him.

He didn't remember removing her nightrail or his breeches, but they somehow ended up in a discarded heap on the floor by the side of the bed. Free of any barrier between them, Brishen indulged himself by easing more of his weight onto her.

"Ooh," Ildiko said on a sigh, her heavy-lidded eyes almost closed. "You feel good." She drew swirls on his back. "We should have done this much sooner."

Brishen's chortle vibrated between them. His forthright wife. "I couldn't agree more," he whispered in her ear.

He set her to squirming in his arms, her soft moans a sensual cadence in his ear, while he kissed and licked a path from her shoulders to her belly, stopping for long moments to repay her torture of him by flicking his tongue back and forth across the tips of her breasts. That she didn't pull away from fear of his teeth spoke of her faith in him and the sure knowledge he would never hurt her.

A subtle quiver of tension passed through her body under his hands as he kissed a path downward toward the juncture of her thighs. Brishen opened his eyes. His heightened senses warned him that delicate vibration had been one of unease instead of eagerness.

Ildiko gazed at him steadily, her features somber. She lowered her arms to card her fingers through his hair. She didn't try and wiggle out of his reach. This wasn't a matter of trust so much as experience, or its lack. Brishen knew that while his wife wasn't completely ignorant of bed play, her introduction to its many intimacies by her previous lover had been limited. Her statement that three romps in the bedroom or the hayloft had not made the effort of a fourth worth the trouble revealed a great deal.

He'd have to tamp down on his eagerness to explore every part of her in a single day. The knowledge that he had a lifetime to draw out the anticipation of familiarizing himself with his wife's lovely body evaporated any of his initial disappointment.

Brishen bent and traced the circumference of her navel before kissing a return path up her belly, to the valley between her breasts and finally to her chin. Ildiko gave him an abashed look. "I haven't tried that yet," she said.

He framed her face in his hands. "So I gathered." He smoothed away the lines between her eyebrows with his lips. It's not a failing, Ildiko."

"I know, but—" She broke off to return the kiss he pressed to her mouth.

"Consider it your gift to me," he said, noting her confusion. "I have the opportunity to be your teacher and show you the pleasure of that particular act, one of the finest between a man and a woman."

She relaxed under him once more. Her knees clamped against his sides. He exhaled a surprised grunt that changed to a groan when her hips lifted to rub against the erection that was robbing the blood from every other part of his body. Her hands glided down his back to cup his buttocks and keep him in place.

Her heavy-lidded expression returned, one Brishen quickly recognized as her passion for him and one he found more seductive by the moment. "What will I teach you?" she asked, hips thrusting, pressing, tempting him toward madness.

"Patience," he said in guttural tones that made a mockery of the word. His arm slid under her buttocks, lifted until her hips tilted toward him. "Endurance." His limbs shook with the strain of holding back. Ildiko's hands moved to his arms, clutched his biceps. The mollusk-pink of her skin deepened, blending with the amaranthine stain. His cock nudged the entrance to her body, slick and hot. "Ecstasy," he whispered and slid deep.

They gasped in unison, and Ildiko arched in his embrace, her short nails digging into his arms. Drowning in the pleasure of being inside his wife, feeling slippery muscles gripping him, drawing him ever deeper, Brishen fought to breathe, to pause. Patience. Endurance. And oh gods, the ecstasy.

He settled them both and waited, even as the waiting killed him. "Ildiko?"

Ildiko gave him a quick smile. Her hands abandoned his arms for his lower back. She kissed him, tongue flicking over his lower lip. Brishen pulsed inside her, and her smile widened. "I'm fine, my lovely prince," she said and kissed him a second time. "Don't stop." Her clasp on his back tightened, and a soft moan threaded her voice. "It feels too good to stop."

Grateful and relieved, Brishen needed no further reassurance. She was fire in his arms, hot and sweet. Her moans and softly worded encouragements, the feel of her surrounding him as he thrust inside her—slow and deep, shallow and fast—destroyed any lingering coherent thought he possessed.

Every near withdrawal had her clawing at his back; every hard pump of his hips made her croon her pleasure in his ear. Brishen angled his hips, a minute change in his position. Ildiko's eyes grew wide, and she emitted a strangled sound.

Brishen froze, horrified. He'd hurt her. He stared down at her, eyes equally as wide. "What's wrong?"

She held his hips prisoner when he made to pull out of her. "No!" Her legs flexed on him. "Do it again."

204 | GRACE DRAVEN

"Do what?" He gawked at her, bewildered. She didn't act as if he hurt her.

"That thing with your hips," she said and wriggled hers to coax him into action.

He tried to recall exactly what he did. The angle, a mere shift in his body that forced his pelvis down onto hers and stroked a different spot with each thrust. Brishen repeated the motion, and Ildiko did her best to climb up his body.

His jaw dropped. "That?"

She nodded frantically, her thighs clamping so tightly against his torso, his muscles protested. "Again," she commanded him between pants. "Do it again."

"Yes, Your Highness," he teased, exultant that he could make his wife burn the way she made him burn.

Whispered affections, drugging kisses and the steady rock of hips: Brishen balanced on the edge of release, struggling to read Ildiko's ever-changing expressions as she met his thrusts and moaned her pleasures.

She suddenly stiffed, her arms tensing as her fingernails carved tiny crescent moons into his skin. Her moans flattened to harsh gasps, and her eyes closed. "Brishen. Brishen." She chanted his name, and whether it was a desperate prayer or affectionate curse, it didn't matter to him. Ildiko came apart in his arms, her body flushed and hot, and arched until he thought he'd hear her spine crack.

The sleek muscles gripping his cock tightened and pulsed with her release. Brishen buried his face in her neck and surrendered his control. His groans chorused with her gasps as he came hard inside her.

His climax rolled through him, leaving him both blissful and utterly stripped of vigor. His heart pounded in his chest, and he sucked in sweet gulps of air like a man saved from a drowning. Were Ildiko a Kai woman, he'd collapse on her, letting her take his full weight. He braced on his elbows instead and raised his head to regard his silent wife.

The flush to her skin had receded a little, though her chest rose and fell in shallow pants. She regarded him with an expression in her eyes even he could read: stunned amazement. She opened her mouth, closed it and opened it again only to say nothing.

Brishen brushed the tip of his nose across hers. "Breathe, Ildiko," he said between his own short gasps. "Just breathe."

She exhaled a strand of his hair away from her face. Her smile held the smug satisfaction of a cat that had caught a particularly juicy mouse. "That was neither awkward nor messy."

His eyebrows climbed, and he tucked his hips even closer to hers to stay inside her. "Oh, it will get messy, wife, the moment we move."

One small heel roamed up his calf to his knee. She traced his cheekbones with her fingertips. "I don't mind," she said softly.

"Nor do I." He kissed her, and she kissed him back, her mouth working its magic so that his blood heated once more, and his cock hardened inside her.

He took her a second time as the sun marched west and then a third when they were both drowsy and exhausted from their lovemaking and lack of sleep. The third time was a slow melding of bodies and low sighs. When it was over, Brishen rolled to his back with Ildiko draped over him. She was asleep before he could cover them haphazardly with the bed linens.

He followed her into sleep only to be awakened what seemed like moments later by a brisk knock at his door. Those moments must have been more like hours. The candle he kept lit for Ildiko had melted into a pool of wax, the flame extinguished. Full darkness enveloped the room, and the air had grown colder. Ildiko was nowhere in sight, and he frowned.

The knock came again. Brishen rubbed at his scratchy eyes and sat up. "What?" he barked at his annoying visitor.

"Your Highness, you're past the gloaming. You can't sleep anymore." Anhuset's admonishment was muffled by the door's thick wood.

Brishen scowled and swung out of bed to pad naked across the room. He slid the bolt aside and yanked the door open to the sight of his cousin's smirk and his personal servant's flinch. "What are you doing here?" he snapped.

Her gaze made a slow journey from the top of his head to his feet. "Cousin or not, you're a fine figure of a man." Her smirk deepened at his impatient growl. "Etep here fetched me. He said you didn't respond to his calls or knocks. He thought you might be ill." She looked past him to the bed and its rumpled sheets. "Obviously he worried for nothing. You've only been conquered."

Brishen bared his teeth at her. "Don't you have something to do other than vex me?"

She shrugged, unconcerned by his forbidding mood. "Not nearly as much as you do and more time to do it. The Beladine lord is due to arrive. The manor is in an uproar preparing for his visit."

He groaned and raked his hands through his hair. "Poor timing," he muttered to himself. He pointed a finger at Anhuset. "I'm not looking for your agreement." She and Etep followed him into the chamber when he trekked back to the bed and pulled on the thin trousers he'd discarded earlier. Ildiko's nightrail was gone, vanished like its owner. "Where is Ildiko?"

"Unlike you, your *hercegesé* is awake, dressed, and elbow-deep in supervising the preparations for your guests. And here I thought humans weaker than the Kai." She flashed him a fanged grin, her eyes sparking bright with amusement.

Brishen growled. His cousin reveled in her chance to flense him with her mockery and draw a little blood—revenge for him ordering her to attend tonight's dinner and the dancing that followed. He allowed her the indulgence, too tired and sated to do more than shoo her off with a flick of his hand and a sour "Go away before I have you flogged." Her laughter drifted to him, even after she and Etep left his room, closing the door behind them.

He wasn't alone long. Etep reappeared, leading a parade of servants carrying buckets of water to fill the bathing tub in the corner. One built the fire in the hearth. The servant bowed to his master. "A cold water bath tonight, *Herceges*. We don't have time to heat that much water."

Brishen shrugged. He lost count of the number of dousings he'd had in the icy waters of a lake or mountain stream. He'd save the hot water bath for a more leisurely time when he didn't have to rush and Ildiko could share with him. The images of such a scenario banished the sleepy fog shrouding his mind. He stripped and hopped into the tub, allowing himself one hard shiver before submerging in the cold water to scrub himself clean.

In less than an hour he was dried, dressed and headed to the great hall. His chest swelled with pride at the sight. His servants had outdone themselves and brought Saggara's great hall back to the days when it was the summer palace of a Kai king. More torches were lit for the benefit of their human guests and the trestle tables draped in embroidered cloths dyed in jeweled shades of cerulean and crimson, nettle-green and aubergine, and the coveted amaranthine that was the greatest source of his people's wealth. The tables were set with the costly ceramics carried over the mountains via caravan and goblets made of silver mined out of the Serpent's Teeth hills far to the south.

Not a speck of dust dared to collect in the corners, and the tapestries hanging on the walls had been taken down, beaten clean and rehung to tell their stories of an ancient past—Kai battles won and magic unleashed.

The scents drifting from the kitchens made Brishen's empty stomach rumble and his mouth water. He had no idea what the cooks would serve. Though she was human in a Kai household, its maintenance and organization was Ildiko's domain. He knew his place in the order of things, and in this, his only requirement were to stay out of the way, praise her efforts and show up on time to eat the food she ordered prepared. He only prayed she didn't order potatoes.

His steward approached him. Mesumenes was Saggara's steward long before Djedor gave it to Brishen. He knew it better than anyone—every stone, every corner, every roof tile. Loyal to the estate more than to any of its owners, he had patiently mentored Brishen into becoming a capable overlord and did the same for Ildiko when she arrived as its new mistress. He bowed. "Does this meet with your approval, Your Highness?"

Brishen nodded and clapped Mesumenes on the back. "Very much so. You and the servants have outdone yourselves."

"The *hercegesé's* hand is in this as well. She knew what would please and impress humans."

Brishen complimented Mesumenes a second time and continued his tour of the manor. There were many, many benefits to having a human wife, or at least his human wife. He would thank her for her insight when he saw her. If he managed not to lift her skirts while he did so, it would be a testament to his control. His need for her ran like molten streams just under his skin. His cold bath had dampened his ardor only so long. He missed her and wanted her in his bed once more—preferably now.

It wasn't to be, and he distracted himself by inspecting the bailey and training yard and ignoring Anhuset's snide comments when he came across her saddling her horse in preparation to ride out and meet the Beladine party at the entrance to the estate road.

She wore ceremonial military leathers and beneath those a pearl colored tunic over teal trousers spun of silk. Brishen wondered how many times she cursed him while dressed in the formal clothing reserved for court and which she hated.

He twisted the knife. "You look beautiful."

Her lips thinned and her eyes narrowed. Brishen kept his gaze on her dagger which she toyed with at her waist. "I don't understand why I have to attend this thing. It's a dinner with a Beladine warlord. More court maneuverings and double talk with sly innuendo and hidden meaning. Ask me to meet him in battle, and I will happily comply. This though...I hate this."

Brishen sympathized with his cousin's sentiment. He wasn't fond of such gatherings either, but they weren't at court. And while Serovek's loyalty lay with a kingdom displeased with the Kai at the moment, he had always been a friend to Brishen. Until they met on a battlefield—and he prayed that would never come to pass—they would invite each other to dinner, socialize and trade valuable information no spy could ever retrieve from bribed sources.

"This isn't court," he said. "And you need to be there because you are my second and an important member of my household. Your presence is expected." He didn't mention that Serovek had asked after her when they traveled to High Salure to dine with him. Sha-Anuset was his trusted lieutenant and a woman of exceptional martial skill and leadership abilities. Had she been human, Brishen had no doubt Serovek would have attempted to lure her away to act as one of his commanders.

"I refuse to dance," she proclaimed in a final show of rebellion and swung into the saddle.

Brishen shrugged. "That is your choice." His lips twitched. "The last time I recall being forced to dance with you, you crushed every one of my toes. We'll consider it a favor if you just watch this time."

She glared at him and nudged her horse into a brisk trot toward the barracks where the rest of the escort awaited her.

Brishen returned to the house and made his way to Ildiko's room. He could hear the gentle peaks and troughs of female conversation through the door. His knock was met with silence before a set of footsteps approached and the door swung open. Sinhue bowed and motioned him inside.

Ildiko sat on a stool before a looking glass. Dressed as a Kai noblewoman, she wore the split skirt-tunic and trousers in the dark colors she typically preferred—this time a combination of brown dark as tea steeped long in a pot and lustrous amber that shimmered in the candlelight.

She met his gaze in the mirror's reflection. Her face was paler than usual, marred by lavender shadows under her eyes and the amaranthine splash edging her jaw. Her fiery hair was partially up, bound into braids woven with tiny pearls. She was stunning, and Brishen's breeches grew uncomfortably tight the longer he stared at her.

"I think we still have a little time, yes?" She indicated the servant with a tilt of her head. "Sinhue is almost finished with my hair."

Sinhue offered another bow to Brishen before skirting around him to return to her mistress. Her nimble fingers worked magic with a comb, and in no time Ildiko's hair was coiffed, beaded and pinned. The servant left them alone then, a knowing look on her face as she eased out of the room, leaving the door open.

Ildiko rose from the stool to face Brishen and spread her arms. "What do you think? Presentable for our guests?"

Brishen narrowed the distance between them until they were toe to toe. He leaned down and placed a soft kiss on the tip of her earlobe. Even though he didn't touch her beyond that small caress, he felt her shiver. "Beautiful, though even more so without clothes." They smiled at each other. "Regrets?" he asked.

She shook her head. "Only that I fell asleep."

He nuzzled the soft hairs at her temple. "Who cares about the guests. Come to my bed. Now."

He knew she'd say no. It was a foregone conclusion, and the worst thing she could do was say no. But if she said yes...

She turned her head toward him until her cheek pressed against his. "You'll ruin my hair," she teased.

"And you're ruining my peace," he countered. He laid his hand on her slender waist. "What say you?"

"Later," she replied. "We're the hosts, Brishen. We can't be late."

He sighed, stepped away from temptation, and offered his arm. "Let's get this over with then." He escorted her into the hall and toward one of the staircases that led to the great hall.

Ildiko squeezed his arm. "I don't miss the Haradis court, but I do miss your court garb. You will be the handsomest man in the room."

Brishen gave her a small smile. "You mean the handsomest Kai." She had earlier complimented Serovek's looks when asked. In her eyes, he would be the finer looking of them.

Her mouth turned down a little. "No," she said. "The handsomest man."

"Lord Pangion will be there."

Ildiko shrugged. "So? My opinion remains unchanged."

He halted abruptly and hauled Ildiko into his arms. She gasped, then sighed when he kissed her. Her arms slid over his shoulders to play with the long braid of hair he'd queued at his neck.

Brishen forgot about time, about guests, about dinner, about the world around him. He cursed his inability to kiss her the way she kissed him—that soft mating of tongues and lips so sensual and alluring, she made his head swim.

He groaned when the warning peal of the gate bell rang throughout the estate, signaling the arrival of visitors. Ildiko's blue eyes had darkened once more, and her lips were red. Her arms slid off his shoulders, and she put some much needed distance between them. "We'll never make it to the hall if we keep doing this."

"I don't view that as a problem," he groused.

"I don't either, but others will." She tugged on his arm. "Come, Your Highness. We need to make our grand entrance."

Brishen schooled his features into a polite mask, placed his wife's hand over his and escorted her toward the hall. A long, long night awaited him.

CHAPTER NINETEEN

Standing this close to him, Ildiko was struck by Serovek's impressive size. He was a big man—a little taller than Brishen—with massive shoulders and long, muscular legs. He looked as if he could crush anvils with his bare hands. She wondered if his gregarious personality contributed even more to the sense of physical power he exuded.

He'd come to Saggara with a small entourage of Beladine soldiers. Their sparse numbers signaled a gesture of peace and trust in Brishen that this dinner would be as safe and friendly as the one the Kai attended at High Salure.

The Beladine guests mingled with Kai officers and councilmen of the Kai villages and townships under Saggara's protection. Ildiko admired the ease in which the two groups socialized, so different from her wedding where Gauri and Kai almost drew swords on each other. Such actions seemed counterintuitive to the realities at hand: The Kai were allied with the Gauri through trade while hostilities with the Beladine brewed hotter every day. Serovek and those under his command were unique in the political fray. Ildiko wondered how long his friendship with Brishen would last after a declaration of war or accusation of treason. She hoped neither came to pass.

"You are a fine hostess, Your Highness, and your cooks in danger of abduction to High Salure." Serovek inclined his head to where servants cleared the remains of the earlier dinner from the tables. In one corner, a quintet of Kai musicians strummed instruments, the haunting melodies accompanying the din of several conversations. "I especially enjoyed the scarpatine pie."

Ildiko shuddered. Her hope to never again see or eat the Kai's most beloved and revolting delicacy had been in vain. When Brishen informed her that the dish was one of Serovek's favorites, she resigned herself to another culinary battle with her food and put the scarpatine on the menu. She ordered roasted potatoes as well, much to the head cook's disgust.

When servants brought out the food and set it on the table, Brishen leaned close and whispered in her ear. "Revenge, wife?"

"Hardly," she replied, keeping a wary eye on the pie closest to her. The golden top crust, with its sprinkle of sparkling salt, pitched in a lazy undulation. "But I'm starving, and I have no intention of filling up on that abomination."

Their guest of honor didn't share their dislike of either food. As deft as any Kai, Serovek made short work of the scarpatine and its whipping tail, cleaved open the shell with his knife and took a generous bite of the steaming gray meat.

Ildiko's stomach heaved. She forgot her nausea when Serovek complimented her. "An excellent choice to pair the scarpatine with the potato, Your Highness. They are better together than apart."

Beside her, Brishen choked into his goblet. He wiped his mouth with his sanap. "What a waste of good scarpatine," he muttered under his breath.

What a waste of a nice potato, she thought. However, the more she thought on Serovek's remark, the more her amusement grew.

"And what has you smiling so brightly?" Brishen stared at her, his lambent eyes glowing nearly white in the hall's torchlight.

She glanced at Serovek, happily cleaning his plate and shooting the occasional glance at Anhuset nearby. Brishen's cousin refused to meet his gaze, but Ildiko had caught the woman watching the Beladine lord more than a few times during dinner.

"That's us, you know," she said.

"What is us?"

"The scarpatine and the potato. Better together than alone. At least I think so."

One of Brishen's eyebrows slid upward. "I thought we were hag and dead eel. I think I like those comparisons more." He shoved his barely-touched potato to the edge of his plate with his knife tip, upper lip curled in revulsion to reveal a gleaming white fang.

Ildiko laughed and stabbed a piece of the potato off his plate. She popped it into her mouth and chewed with gusto, eager to blunt the taste of scarpatine still lingering on her tongue.

The crowd broke into groups after dinner, and Ildiko soon found herself in conversation with Serovek and on the opposite side of the hall from Brishen.

The lines at the corners of the lord's eyes fanned and deepened. "Will you favor me with a dance, Your Highness? The Kai think humans are clumsy creatures. Shall we prove them wrong?"

Ildiko glanced at Brishen who stood conversing with a mayor of one of the nearby Kai villages. He didn't look directly at her, but she sensed the weight of his gaze. Gauri society dictated that a woman either ask her father or her husband permission to dance with another man. Kai society did not. To the Kai, it was perfectly acceptable for Ildiko to take up Serovek's invitation without Brishen's approval. Still, she hesitated.

Serovek's chuckle returned her attention to him. He nodded toward Brishen. "Were we both Kai, I don't think he'd care. If I were Kai, he wouldn't care. But we're both human, and that presents something very different. I desire a dance with you, but I'd also like to leave Saggara alive."

Ildiko clinked her goblet against his in silent agreement. She had no idea how one might read the more subtle hints of jealousy in a Kai, but there was a certain rigidity in Brishen's stance that reminded her of an owl watching prey from the branches of a tree. "As I'm still learning Kai protocol, I think I'll ask my husband what the proper response is to such an invitation."

His grin transformed Serovek's already handsome face into an even more striking visage. Ildiko tried not to gape. "I await your answer, madam."

Ildiko left him to seek out Brishen. He was no longer where she first saw him, and she kept to the outer perimeters of the room, searching for broad shoulders garbed in indigo silk and a long, black braid. She jumped when his voice suddenly sounded behind her.

"I'm told Serovek is known as the Stallion in the Beladine court." A muscled arm slid around Ildiko's waist, and she leaned back against Brishen's chest. He rubbed his nose along the curve of her ear. "He's an exceptional horseman, but I doubt the title was bestowed on him because of his skills in the saddle."

His cheek was cool and smooth pressed to hers. "I suspect, my husband, that is exactly why he was given the title."

His low laughter rumbled in her ear. A clawed hand outlined the curve of her waist before settling at her hip. "You stalk this hall with purpose, Ildiko. What do you seek?"

"Serovek has requested a dance with me. I know the Kai don't follow the Gauri customs, but he thought it best I ask you first."

She felt it then, a stiffening in his body as he pressed against her. It faded as soon as it appeared, but Brishen's voice had lost its sensual warmth and turned clipped.

"He has a finely honed sense of survival. It makes him a good warrior. Do you wish to dance with him?"

Ildiko turned in his embrace so she could face him. She stroked his arm and gazed into his eyes. "I wish to dance with you, but I think it only hospitable as one of his hosts if I dance one dance with him." She winked. "Or you could dance with him."

Brishen snorted, and his features softened. "There is hospitable, and then there's ridiculous." He brushed his mouth across her forehead. "You don't need my leave to dance with another, wife. But I reserve the right to steal you away at any time."

Beladine and Kai guests paired off as the musicians segued into the beginnings of a more high-spirited tune. Ildiko wove through the crowd and found Serovek where she left him. He watched her approach with a slight smile.

"Will I live another day?" he asked.

She handed him her goblet so he could set it on the table behind him. "That depends. If you trample my feet, *I'll* kill you." Her grin matched his laughter. "You'll forgive me, of course, if I trample yours. I'm not familiar with Kai dances. Until recently, I didn't even know they danced."

Serovek grasped her offered hand and led her toward the center of the hall. "They are exceptional dancers. Think about it. Strong, fast, and nimble, they are made for it. And you may recognize many of their tunes. The Gauri and the Beladine have taken a few as theirs over the centuries."

They waited amidst a throng of other couples who had paused after the first tune ended and before the next one began. Ildiko glimpsed Brishen across the hall, watching them. When the second tune started, she clapped her hands. "You're right! I know this song."

Serovek lifted her hand, bowed and swept her into a loose embrace. "Your Highness, it is my honor."

They fell into familiar steps. Serovek had spoken true when he said the Gauri—and the Beladine as well—had borrowed a few things from the Kai. She had learned to dance to this particular song when she was very young. It was a popular dance at the Gauri court and one of her favorites.

Serovek's familiarity with the dance was obvious. He guided her smoothly through the steps, graceful as any Kai, especially for a man of his stature. Her feet were in no danger of being crushed; her partner was an adept dancer. It would have been perfect if she danced with Brishen instead of Serovek.

The dance soon came to an end, and Serovek surrendered her to a Kai officer who bowed low and requested a dance. It was followed by another with a Kai town councilman and one after that with one of Serovek's Beladine soldiers.

She was flushed, winded and thirstier than a willow tree by a dry lake bed when Brishen sought her out, carrying a much welcomed goblet of wine. Ildiko took it with heartfelt thanks and drained it in two swallows.

Brishen blinked and offered his wine. "Would you like mine?"

Ildiko shook her head. "No. You've rescued me. I thought my tongue would stick to the roof of my mouth if I didn't stop dancing soon and find something to drink." She handed her empty goblet to a passing servant.

"Are you enjoying yourself?" He downed his drink and sent the cup off with Ildiko's.

"I am." Ildiko reached out to play with one of the lacings on his tunic. "Though I'd have much more fun if you paused a moment from all your political machinations and plans to dance with me. Just one dance, husband. It isn't much to ask." She winked at him. He had promised to claim her from any of her dance partners but so far had refrained, choosing instead to circulate through the hall, talking with both Beladine and Kai guests, including Serovek when that lord wasn't dancing himself.

Brishen grasped her hand and brought it to his mouth for a soft kiss. The caress sent tingles from the tips of her fingers to her toes and set a hot pool of desire swirling inside her. She hadn't chosen this husband of hers, nor had he chosen her, but fate or kind gods had brought them together, made them friends and then lovers. While her Gauri peers might shudder at the idea of a Kai mate and give thanks they weren't her, Ildiko considered herself the most fortunate of women.

Her expression must have revealed something of her thoughts. Brishen tilted his head, a puzzled furrow appearing between his eyebrows. "What is it?"

"I want to dance with you now," she said in a low voice only he could hear. "But I want to make to love to you more." Her cheeks burned hot at her own blunt declaration and the reaction it caused.

Brishen's back snapped straight, and his eyes paled. Her fingers went briefly numb at the sudden grip he closed on her hand. His lips flattened against his teeth; nostrils flared, and the skin drew tight across his cheekbones. He said nothing, but Ildiko suddenly found herself jogging to keep up as he pulled her across the hall toward the stairwell leading to Saggara's private wing.

"Brishen, wait." she whispered, caught between panic and laughter. The weight of several curious gazes rested on her shoulders, no doubt wondering why the *Herceges* of Saggara suddenly decided to whisk his wife out of the hall.

She stumbled into him when he halted abruptly and turned. He caught her in his arms and helped her regain her balance. His eyes still glowed white-hot, and his breathing paced shallow from his nostrils. His voice, by contrast, was cool and uninflected. "Are you trying to kill me, Ildiko?"

Were they not standing in the middle of the hall with a crowd of people watching, she'd twine her arms around his neck and kiss him senseless. Brishen's parted lips revealed the tips of his fangs. Carefully senseless, she corrected.

She settled for squeezing his hand and offering an apologetic smile. "Killing you is the farthest thing from my mind, and were we alone, I'd race you to the stairs." His claws were dark against her knuckles, lethal as spear points knapped from obsidian. "But we aren't alone, and we are the hosts. We're obligated to stay."

Torchlight caught his eyes in a different pattern as his gaze flickered from her face to the crowd behind her and back again. "And who will stop us if we leave?"

No one would. In Haradis, Brishen was the unessential spare prince. At Saggara, he was king and subject to no one. Still, Ildiko didn't relish the gossip such an act would incite. She traced the line of his knuckles with her free hand.

"I don't regret my words, only their timing," she said. "Dawn isn't far off. Dance with me until then, and you can bid your guests good riddance."

His lids closed for a moment, black lashes thick against his cheeks. When he opened them again, his eyes were once more their lamplight yellow. "As you wish, but it will be another day of no sleep, wife," he warned in a voice no longer cool but sensual. He kissed her hand for a second time, leaving a damp line as his tongue stroked across her fingers.

Ildiko gasped, her knees going weak at the caress. She exhaled a shuddering breath. "I'll hold you to that promise, husband."

He claimed her for the rest of the night, either dancing with her or keeping her by his side when others drew him away to discuss the various issues of the townships and villages under Saggara's guardianship.

Night gave way to day, and the wine flowed fast and generous. Servants escorted some of the more inebriated guests to spare rooms prepared in a ground floor wing near the kitchens. Brishen offered Serovek one of the chambers on the second floor, along the same hallways as his and Ildiko's chambers.

Serovek refused and slapped Brishen on the back. His dark eyes were glassy with drink, but he remained steady on his feet, and Ildiko suspected anyone foolish enough to think him vulnerable to attack would find themselves suffering or dead for making such a mistake.

"A generous offer, my friend, but I'm for home." He smiled, and Ildiko was once again struck by the beauty of his features. "And unlike you Kai, I enjoy the feel of the sun on my face when I ride." He gestured toward Anhuset who stood among her compatriots, tugging ceaselessly at her finery and scowling. "I will, however, accept an escort to your gate."

The Kai might not be able to read human expression any better than Ildiko could read theirs, but Serovek's interest in Anhuset was plain to her. He caught her knowing look and winked in return. Brishen stiffened beside her.

Thanks for Saggara's hospitality, wishes for a safe journey and promises of mutual aid if needed were exchanged before Serovek and his party left, escorted by a sour-faced Anhuset sporting a telltale dusting of color on her high cheekbones.

They watched him leave. Brishen slowly pivoted to survey his nearly empty hall. The sun-flare returned to his eyes when he settled his stare on Ildiko. Her breath caught in her throat. "And now I can say good riddance."

This time it was she who yanked him to the stairs and raced down the corridor. His door banged open against the wall and just as quickly slammed back on its frame. Brishen slid the bolt home and turned in time for Ildiko to shove him against its expanse.

She was desperate to touch him, feel the solid strength of muscle beneath her hands, the smooth expanse of gray skin. The fire that had smoldered inside her since his aborted attempt to seduce her before they went downstairs to greet their guests flared to an inferno. She caught his braid in one hand and used it to pull his head down to her. The gleam of fangs didn't deter her from kissing him—hard. He groaned and offered his tongue. She took him deep, tasting sweet wine and the honey harvested from the wild hives built in the bramble-strangled orange grove.

Brishen hoisted her in his arms, hands cupping her buttocks. His breath sounded harsh in her ear as she nibbled his neck and caught his earlobe in between her teeth. Another groan was her reward. "So eager, wife?" he said between pants.

"How can you tell?" she whispered to the sweet space behind his ear. She rocked against him, seeking the erection that proclaimed his desire for her was as great as hers for him. His fingers flexed, claws piercing layers of cloth. Ildiko gasped from the pleasure-pain.

He froze. "Forgive..."

"Nothing to forgive." She tore at the lacings on his tunic, loosening some and knotting the others. Her mewl of frustration drew a chuckle from him.

"This is when claws come in handy, wife."

He made short work of the tunic, splitting it down the center with one swipe of his hand to reveal a sculpted chest that made Ildiko breathe an admiring "oooh." He didn't stop there, and soon their finery hung off them in sliced ribbons.

Brishen's chest was hot against her breasts, the room's air chilly on her back. He'd rucked up her long tunic to her waist and shoved her silk trousers below her hips. His own clothing was equally twisted and shoved aside.

Ildiko arched her back and gasped Brishen's name when he thrust inside her. Every muscle clenched, eliciting a low growl from him as he clutched her hips, braced himself against the door, and set a hard pace.

"My gods, Ildiko," he managed to gasp out between thrusts. "You're a hearth fire. Were you like this downstairs?"

She wondered vaguely how he could possibly remain coherent. She was reduced to mewls and moans. "Yes," she said. "Needed you. Need you now."

She punctuated her demand by scoring the corded tendons of his neck with her teeth. Brishen's knees buckled, and he nearly dropped her. Had he done the same to her, he would have laid open her jugular. Her teeth, though, were no danger to him. She wasn't Kai and heartily glad of it.

He employed the trick he discovered when they first lay together, angling his pelvis so that every thrust rubbed in just the right way. She climaxed in his arms, uncaring that her guttural cries likely carried down the corridors and all the way out to the redoubt's defenses. A few more deep thrusts and Brishen joined her, his own moans low, almost bestial.

They sagged against the door, Ildiko boneless in Brishen's grasp. He rested his forehead on her shoulder, breath hot as it gusted across her breasts. He finally straightened and staggered to the bed, careful not to trip or lose his hold on her.

Their clothes landed in a heap on the floor, and it was only moments before she welcomed him once more into the sanctuary of her body as well as her heart. Afterwards, they lay together, pressed skin to skin from shoulder to ankle.

Brishen picked a broken strand of beads out of her hair and tossed them to the floor. "Your hair—"

"Is a mess," she finished for him.

"A spectacular mess," he said. "Your maid has her work cut out for her later."

Ildiko took no offense. If being loved like this by her husband meant a ruined coif, well, there were some things worth sacrificing. She pulled the edge of one of the sheets toward her and paused at the sight of the jagged rents. She frowned. "You have to stop destroying the bed linens."

He shrugged, blithely unremorseful. "Only when you stop destroying me."

They exchanged slow kisses while sunlight seeped through the partially open shutters and bathed their bed. Brishen started to untangle himself from Ildiko to rise and close the shutters.

She stopped him with a hand on his hip. "Wait. I'd like to see you in the sunlight." He'd had the advantage of twilight's gloom and the full dark of night to see her—naked, vulnerable, undeniably human. It was only fair that she see him. Naked, never vulnerable, undeniably Kai.

Brishen paused to stare at her for a moment before relaxing into the mattress and rolling on his back. He covered his eyes with his forearm. "As you wish, wife."

Ildiko peeled the sheets away from where they gathered at his shins. He was completely bare to her, painted in daytime's golden light.

Beautifully made, lithe and powerful, he reminded her a little of a cat—all sleek muscle beneath skin gray and smooth as the dolphins that rode the bow wave of the Gauri merchant ships sailing into harbor.

"I am no friend to the sun, Ildiko." His voice was tense, his body as well as he stretched out on the bed.

"That's unfortunate," she said softly. "It's certainly a friend to you." She traced a line of muscle from his knee to his inner thigh and felt him shiver under her palm. Sunlight filled the room. Ildiko took mercy on him, leaving the bed long enough to close the shutters and pitch the chamber into its usual candlelit-shadows.

Brishen enfolded her in his arms as soon as she returned and rolled her beneath him. Even with most of his weight on his elbows, he pressed her into the mattress, heavy on her. "And what do you think of your dead eel in the daylight?"

Ildiko brushed a feathery strand of his hair away from his eyes. "He pleases me greatly. The handsomest of eels." His high cheekbones angled sharply under her palms. "So says this hag."

"Who is most beautiful in the darkness." Brishen kissed her then, lingering on her mouth for several moments before bestowing more of the fluttering caresses along the edge of her hairline and over the bridge of her nose. He murmured something else against her cheek.

Caught up in the languorous sensations, Ildiko almost missed what he said. She blinked. "Pardon?"

Brishen tucked his head down to nuzzle her cleavage before answering. "If you're up to it, we will journey from here to Halmatus township tonight. Remember the jeweler I told you about?" She nodded. "He will repair your necklace, and you can see more of my lands than just Saggara and the lake. Some of Serovek's as well. High Salure is the fortress, but his territory runs a fair length alongside mine."

Excitement took hold. She'd been at Saggara for months now, consumed with her duties as its new mistress and the all the adjustments living in a Kai household entailed. The short visit to the dye houses on the lake shore had only whetted her curiosity regarding the Kai kingdom and its people. She was eager to learn more. "Is it far?"

"Two hours by horseback through hilly terrain."

Not far at all. She almost said yes but hesitated, remembering all that Brishen had told her of his conversation with Serovek when they returned from High Salure. "Is it safe?"

His brow stitched into a frown. "You have my shield and protection, Ildiko."

She smoothed away the lines marring his skin with her thumb. "I'm not just thinking of me."

He turned his face into her hand and kissed her palm. "I know. You've witnessed the Kai in battle. We're formidable enough, and we protect ourselves and our own."

That was an understatement. Hard, heavy bones, fangs, claws, and a superior agility, the Kai were uniquely suited for battle.

"You don't have to go if that is your wish," he continued at her prolonged silence.

She started. "No! I want to go." Ildiko had left all that was familiar to her to accompany a stranger who wasn't even human into an alien kingdom where she became the outsider, the stranger. She had learned, thrived and found both love and friendship. No filthy pack of lawless mercenaries would make her a prisoner in her new home.

Brishen glided a hand down her arm before trekking a path over her collarbones and down to cup a breast. His hips rocked gently on hers, and she spread her thighs so he settled more firmly into the cradle of her body. "It will still be a long journey with the return trip. You should sleep."

Ildiko looped her arms around his neck and caressed the rope of hair hanging down his back. She gave Brishen a mock scowl. "I'll sleep when I'm dead. Now kiss me. We're wasting good daylight."

Their laughter soon changed to sighs and whispered encouragements spoken against skin sheened in perspiration. Ildiko embraced her lover, her husband, her best friend and counted herself a most blessed wife.

CHAPTER TWENTY

Brishen hoped he might one day take Ildiko somewhere without a quarter of his regiment accompanying them. Caution, however, dictated that they have an escort. The attack made on their company on the great trade road as they traveled from Pricid to Haradis combined with Serovek's earlier warnings meant he and Ildiko went nowhere alone outside Saggara. He had reduced their escort to twenty of his more experienced fighters. Unlike the journey to High Salure, they traveled at night. An unfriendly time for any group of raiders who might think of attacking. While they'd come near Beladine borders, those lands belonged to Serovek whose troops vigilantly patrolled and protected them. An unfriendly place for any who wanted to cause trouble.

Brishen glanced at his wife as she rode beside him. She held a confident seat in the saddle, even with the challenge of navigating the hilly paths that led to Halmatus township in the dark. She wore her heavier cloak for the cold nights, but her head was bare. The red hair, which he at first thought garish but now beautiful, shimmered multiple shades of gray under the moonlight. She'd kept her hood down at his insistence.

"You don't need this," he told her earlier as they readied to mount and ride out of Saggara. He pushed back the hood, exposing her braided hair and pale features. He'd spent the last hour before sundown studying her face as she slept next to him. Had he truly ever thought her ugly?

Ildiko tucked a few strands of hair that had come loose from her braid behind her ears. "There will be a lot of stares and talk." Brishen took her hand to lightly trace the lines of her palm with one nail. "Let them talk; let them stare. It matters not. Besides, you are the *hercegesé*, wife of Saggara's *herceges*. You hide from no one."

They crossed a bridge spanning a narrow ravine. Far below, a lazy river wound like a black ribbon to disappear around a bend of sheer rockface. A waterfall's dull roar sounded nearby, background resonance to the creak of wood under horse hooves as their party rode single file over the bridge.

They arrived in Halmatus shortly before midnight. Built in a sheltered dale, the town glimmered like a nest of fireflies under a tree canopy. Pleased to discover that he'd inadvertently chosen the weekly market night to visit the town, Brishen escorted Ildiko through the narrow streets lined with temporary stalls filled with various wares and food offered by Kai farmers and merchants.

Their presence drew a curious crowd, and the stares and talk Ildiko predicted rested heavy on his shoulders and thick in his ears. Ildiko paid no attention, and instead engaged the various vendors in nearly flawless bast-Kai.

Only once did she hint of her awareness of the town's singular focus on her. She stepped away from the protection of Brishen's silhouette so that she was in full view of the crowd. Her closed-lip smile gave away her intent.

"Ildiko," Brishen warned and blocked the crowd's view just as her eyes slid toward each other and met on either side of her nose.

They slid back in place just as quickly, making Brishen twitch and the Kai soldiers closest to them exclaim under their breaths. Ildiko sighed. "You've ruined a perfectly good opportunity to provide gossip for years to come."

"And saved a few people from being trampled by those trying to get away from you." He nudged her toward the next stall. "Try not to start a panic, wife."

The low sound of her laughter teased his ears and recalled a moment hours earlier when she'd laughed the same way while torturing him with soft kisses planted down the center of his back. His nostrils flared, and he shoved the memory away before his breeches grew uncomfortable and he began searching for a secluded spot where he might swive his wife. Her sorcery shredded his ability to think sensibly.

They found the jeweler's shop at the end of one of the lanes. Unlike his fellow townsmen, the merchant never revealed shock or surprise at Ildiko's appearance. He inspected the necklace and broken clasp she presented to him and promised the repair was simple enough. A price and delivery date was agreed upon. A shrewd business man, he offered to show her more of his work. Brishen fled outside to wait by the door.

When Ildiko emerged from the shop, he tucked her hand into the crook of his arm. "Am I a pauper now?"

She gave him an arch look. "I doubt it. I bought one thing."

He surveyed her person, noting neither bauble on her neck nor package in her hand. "What is it?"

Ildiko lifted her chin. "You'll see it when they deliver it with my necklace."

Word of the *herceges's* visit traveled fast through Halmatus, and the town's mayor was quick to issue an invitation to dine. Anhuset abandoned Brishen and Ildiko to their fate with a salute and a grin. "You'll find the rest of us at the Crooked Shank tavern where the ale is thick and the company better."

Her words proved prophetic. The food at the mayor's home was fair; the company tiresome and ridiculous. Brishen liked the man well enough. The mayor's wife was another matter. Despite Ildiko's best efforts to put her at ease, the woman couldn't stop staring round-eyed at her. Too busy gawking to mind what she was doing, she nearly poured wine into Ildiko's lap twice.

Brishen breathed a sigh of relief when it was over and they made their escape. Ildiko looked no worse the wear for their trouble. "They didn't serve scarpatine," she said. "I consider it a successful meal."

"Do you want to visit the tavern? I think Anhuset is right about the food and company."

Ildiko shook her head. "No. I'll cause too much of a stir. Let our escort enjoy themselves. You can give me a tour of the town, and I'll have you to myself for once."

He happily acquiesced to her wishes. Halmatus was small, surrounded by thick woodland. At its outskirts, Brishen paused and took advantage of the brief privacy afforded them. He tilted Ildiko's face up to his with a gentle thumb under her chin. Her skin glowed lustrous as a pearl in the moonlight.

"Kiss me," he commanded softly. "I've craved the touch of your mouth ever since we left Saggara."

It didn't matter to him if all of Halmatus heard his satisfied groans as she made love to him with her lips and the fine caress of her hands. They couldn't quit this place or get home soon enough to satisfy him. His human wife had become a fire in his blood and spirit, as hot and bright as her red hair.

"We leave them alone for what? Two hours? And now we're chasing after them like nannies after toddlers." Anhuset's waspish tones carried over the whispering lullaby of trees rustling in the breeze.

Ildiko's mouth drifted over his in a fading kiss. "I think we're in trouble," she murmured.

"Fan out and find them," Anhuset ordered. "Knock on every door if you have to."

Brishen growled, annoyed and yet pleased by his cousin's vigilance. He set Ildiko from him and took her hand. "Come. We'll need to reveal ourselves before she puts the entire town in an uproar."

Anhuset's scowl forewarned Brishen he was in for a tongue-lashing. He halted whatever admonishment hovered on her lips. "Thought is often wiser than speech, sha-Anhuset," he said in his coldest, loftiest tones. "Lest we forget who rules here and who does not."

Her lips thinned to a tight line, but she bowed, along with the rest of their escort. "Are you ready to depart, *Herceges*?" she asked in an equally frigid voice. He nodded, and she sent the soldiers off to gather the horses and meet in the town square.

When it was just he, Ildiko and Anhuset, his cousin rounded on him. "Are you trying to worry me into an early death?" she snapped.

"Stop henpecking me," he snapped back. "I have a wife for that, and even she doesn't do it."

Muffled laughter sounded next to him. Ildiko stared at them both with watery eyes and a hand clapped over her mouth. She lowered her hand and compressed her lips in an obvious effort to contain her mirth. "Sorry," she managed to gasp out between giggles.

Anhuset didn't share in her amusement. Her expression darkened before she bowed a second time. "I will see you both in the town square."

Brishen remained unsure if that was a promise or a threat.

"You can trust us to be there, Anhuset," Ildiko called to her.

"We'll see," the other woman said shortly. She strode away, back stiff with outrage.

"She loves you, you know." Ildiko glanced at Brishen. "She would do anything you asked of her."

Brishen nodded. Ildiko told him nothing he didn't already know. "We're bound to each other by blood and secrets. She's the child of my father's sister and the only true sibling I've ever had." He met Ildiko's gentle gaze and sighed. "She's also older than me with an unfortunate tendency to either mother me or order me about if I allow it."

The mayor, his goggle-eyed wife and a bevy of councilmen were in the square to see them off. Brishen and Ildiko bid polite goodbyes and promised another visit soon. The moon had begun her journey toward the horizon by the time they rode the paths that led them back to Saggara.

The ravine and its bridge came into view. Their party had started out from Halmatus in high spirits with much small talk and joking exchanged. The atmosphere slowly changed, their group growing quieter, tenser. The trickle of unease that made the spot between Brishen's shoulder blades tingle became an icy stream that froze the length of his spine. He edged his horse closer to Ildiko. Anhuset did the same on Ildiko's other side.

Brishen caught his cousin's eye and spoke softly, using a pidgin Kai spoken by the lakeside dyers and understood by very few who weren't Kai. "Do you feel that?" Anhuset nodded. "We're being watched."

They all felt it, a distinct scrutiny edged with malice. All around him, hands eased toward sword pommels and shifted shields into protective position. The horses picked up on their riders' unease, snorting and prancing their agitation as they rode toward the bridge.

Ildiko's eyes flicked first to Anhuset, then to Brishen. "What's wrong?" she asked softly.

Brishen signaled behind her, and two of his men closed the space behind her horse, creating a shield wall of man, metal and steed. It was likely too late to disguise her now. She stood out among them like a beacon, but better late than not at all.

"Ildiko," he said in his most casual tone. "Raise your hood as if you're just keeping the wind off your hair and do exactly as I tell you when I tell you."

What little color flowed under her pale skin, leached away to a pallor grayed by fear. She did as he instructed, making a show of fussing with her braids before pulling the hood up until her features were hidden.

Brishen loosened the leather guard covering the blade of the hand axe he wore at his hip. The air around them hung thick with tension—an unnatural silence broken only by the steady clop of horse hooves.

A battle cry shattered the stillness, followed by a bright flash of light. Brishen bellowed a curse at the sudden light blindness and turned his face into his hood. His mount slammed into Ildiko's mare.

"Down, Ildiko!" he bellowed at her, shoving her face toward the mare's withers, just as a thin ripple of cold air shot a breath away from his face. A thunk sounded, followed by a heavy groan and the creak of a saddle.

They were easy targets for arrows while mounted, and Ildiko cried out when Brishen dragged her off the saddle with him to hit the ground amidst the chaos of soldiers struggling to control panicked horses. They were partially shielded by equine bodies from the pulsing flare of light that left him and his fellow Kai virtually sightless.

Anhuset barreled into him, sword drawn. Her lips were drawn back from her fangs in a grimace. "Beladine!" she shouted just as a volley of arrows rained over them from the trees. "The fletching is Beladine."

A chorus of howls rang from the shadows. Brishen clutched Ildiko to him, crouched low among the milling horses. Magefinders. The scum had brought mage hounds.

He pried Ildiko off of him and thrust her toward Anhuset. "Take her and get across the bridge. Now!" The arrow volleys were simply the first phase. If he didn't get her out of here now, she'd die.

Ildiko clutched at him, her strange eyes huge and dark with terror. "No, Brishen!"

Anhuset didn't hesitate. She wrapped her arm around Ildiko and slung her over her shoulder. Her own expression was as fearful as Ildiko's and full of rage. "Stay alive," she ordered before sprinting away with a struggling Ildiko.

Brishen caught Anhuset's horse, looped the reins over the saddle horn and slapped the animal on the flank. It shot out of the mayhem towards its mistress. Riderless and seemingly out of control, it darted toward Anhuset unscathed by arrow fire. His cousin altered her path to run parallel, and he lost sight of her for just a moment. Silver hair and muted red mingled in the shadows as Anhuset leapt atop her mount's back, dropped Ildiko before her into the saddle and kicked the horse into a dead run.

They were past the first hurdle, but the bridge ran long and arrows flew fast. More cries echoed from the forest, this time led by the trumpet of a horn. Brishen drew hard on the sleeping magic bequeathed to him by his sire and all those who came before him. It rolled through him, pooling into his hands. Somewhere a battle mage lurked among the trees, casting light spells to render the Kai blind.

He uttered an ancient word, one spoken by Kai sorcerers who built its spell from the power of shadow and Kai reverence for all things born of the night. A blast of darkness shot from Brishen's fingers and snuffed out the light flares. Cries of dismay and surprise mingled with shouts of triumph.

Brishen forced down the wave of weakness that threatened to buckle his knees. He could finally see well enough to fight. He shouted to his men. "To the trees! Kill their mage! Kill their dogs!"

A Beladine attacker burst out of the underbrush toward him, swinging a short-handled scythe. Trained for war as all his kin were, Brishen met the attack with knife and axe. The two men slammed into each other, Brishen's heavier weight forcing his opponent backwards. Brishen slashed his throat and was sprinting through the trees before the spray of blood even touched him.

All around him Kai battled Beladine in bloody skirmishes. He cleaved the skull of an archer and hobbled a swordsman before decapitating him with one swing of the axe. He leapt over the head as it rolled under his feet.

Battle rage coursed through his veins in a hot river, even as he methodically cut a bloody swath through the ranks of enemies swarming out of the forest's understory and dropping from the trees.

Someone shouted, and their message sent Brishen's heart jumping to his throat. "The Gauri bitch! She's crossing the bridge!"

Brishen tore through the forest, bolting out of the tree line in time to see an archer take aim at the fleeing horse and its two riders as they raced toward the other side of the ravine. Every sound around him faded to silence, every movement narrowed to the archer's flexing shoulder as he drew the bowstring.

The prince of Saggara didn't pray to gods but to the bloodied axe he held. "Be true," he whispered and flung the weapon as hard he could.

The archer slammed forward—the axe blade buried between his shoulders—and teetered on the ravine's edge before pitching into the abyss.

Brishen sprinted for the bridge just as a dozen Beladine riders galloped onto its span. Oh gods, no! He was fast, but he'd never catch them. He could outrun a human but not a horse.

"Commander, what do you need?" Two of his Kai, splattered in blood, raced to his side. A pack of Beladine attackers pursued them.

"Hold them off as long as you can," he ordered. The magic would get him killed, but he had no choice. If he didn't use it, Anhuset's pursuers would catch her. She'd kill half before they took her down, but she'd still die and so would Ildiko.

He set his hands on the bridge's first plank. More words of power, these a sizzling wash of pain that threatened to peel his skin back from his bones. He waited precious seconds until Anhuset's horse touched the ground on the other side of the ravine. He closed his eyes, dizzy from relief and the blazing agony that poured down his arms. He unleashed the last part of the spell.

A rolling tide of flame roared across the bridge, consuming it with a ravenous hunger and engulfing screaming horses and their horrified riders.

Brishen staggered to his feet only to be thrown sideways. He and his attacker wrestled across the ground. Weakened and slowed by the ravages of spellwork, Brishen struggled to free himself from the grip of a Beladine sell-sword twice his size. The man slammed Brishen's hand against a protruding rock. His fingers went numb, and he lost the grip on his knife. His enemy snarled in triumph.

Brishen snarled back before lunging up to sink his fangs into the man's neck. A gurgling scream set his ear to ringing, and the sour tastes of unwashed human sweat and blood filled his mouth. He jerked his head, tore out flesh with his teeth and half drowned as gouts of hot gore splashed his face and neck.

He spat out the hunk of meat and shoved the dead mercenary off him. Half blinded once more, this time by blood instead of light, he stood. The Kai who'd come to help him fought hard but were overwhelmed by sheer numbers. Brishen took up his opponent's sword and ran toward them, no longer fleet and sure-footed. A menacing growl was his only warning before a whirlwind of dusty brown fur shot toward him.

He spun at the last moment, sword blade slicing upward. A canine yelp told him he'd hit his target just as a dead magefinder landed nearby in the dirt.

The same voice that alerted others of Ildiko's and Anhuset's escape shouted again. Enraged. Desperate.

"Bring him down! Bring that Kai bastard down!"

He heard the warning hisses of air, but his body refused to obey his mind's screaming commands to get out of the way. The first arrow took him in the right shoulder, the second in the upper left thigh, the third in the right. Brishen crashed to his knees. His vision blurred, and he swayed under the sudden heavy weight of a net. It tangled around his limbs, a living thing as sinuous and gripping as the tentacled sea creatures he'd heard of in stories.

The side of a club was the last thing he saw before the inside of his skull exploded in a shower of hot agony. Darkness followed, and in this blackness he could not see.

CHAPTER TWENTY-ONE

The trees did their best to claw Ildiko and Anhuset from the saddle, their outstretched limbs whipping and scratching as Anhuset's gelding galloped hard into the dark forest. Ildiko, wedged between Anhuset and the saddle pommel stared blindly into the blackness, its edges feathered away by a distant glow that teased the corner of her eye.

Brishen.

Her last glimpse of him had been a wavering view of his back as he plunged into the chaos of horses, blind Kai and a hail of arrows. She'd struggled in Anhuset's hold to break free, to run back to her husband, to do something other than flee. The Kai woman's unyielding grip proved unbreakable. Ildiko had been a breath away from vomiting after the violent pitching she suffered while thrown across her captor's shoulder. Her vision spun when she was upended and slung into the saddle of the still galloping horse.

A metallic glimmer caught her eye—moonlight on steel. Anhuset thrust the handle of a dagger into her hand.

"Take this," she ordered in a grim voice that warned against argument. "Stab anything that moves."

Ildiko barely had her fingers around the handle when a rippling shadow shot out of the dark from her left side and rushed the horse. Their attacker emitted a screeching cry, one echoed by

Ildiko. Grasping hands tore at her skirts and leg while the horse neighed and danced sideways.

She did exactly as Anhuset instructed, plunging the dagger toward the figure hanging off the saddle. An agonized scream, the give of flesh as the dagger sank deep and the warm wash of blood coating her hand were her rewards.

Their attacker fell away only to be replaced by another and another who swarmed out of the underbrush like insects from a disturbed mound. Anhuset's mount joined in the fight, kicking and rearing. One attacker slammed into a nearby tree and curled into the fetal position, clutching his belly.

Anhuset shoved the reins into Ildiko's hands. "Guide the horse!"

Ildiko grabbed the reins, lost the dagger and kicked the gelding hard in the sides. He leapt into a gallop, dragging someone beside him. Behind Ildiko, Anhuset twisted one way and then the other, her arms stretched out on either side, swords in hand as she swung at their attackers. She slammed hard into Ildiko's back twice with a grunt but held her seat to slash their way free.

They plunged through the wood, Ildiko as blind as a Kai at noon and praying she hadn't turned them around and ridden straight for the ravine and a fast descent to their death. Escaping the last raider, they rounded a copse of trees and raced into a clearing.

Wide open and ablaze in moonlight, the clearing left them more exposed. Ildiko turned the gelding back toward the tree line. They couldn't go back the way they came, but if they hugged the border that traveled an eastern path, the low-hanging branches of some of the trees would shield them. She had, at least, led them away from the ravine instead of toward it.

Her companion was ominously silent behind her. Ildiko glanced over her shoulder. "Anhuset?"

The other woman answered with a slow exhalation and promptly slid out of the saddle, taking a startled Ildiko with her. They both hit the ground, Ildiko's fall partially cushioned by Anhuset's arm. The horse tossed his head and pranced to the side before trotting a small distance away, reins dragging behind him.

Ildiko stumbled to her feet and gasped.

Anhuset lay on her side, facing Ildiko. An arrow shaft protruded from her left shoulder, another just above her left hip. She inhaled and exhaled slow breaths, and her gold-coin eyes were dull.

Ildiko crouched before her, bloodied hands drifting over, but not touching the places where the arrows had embedded themselves in armor and flesh. "Anhuset! Why didn't you say something?"

The woman tried to shrug but only managed a twitch of one shoulder. "Because there was nothing to say. I think the arrows are dipped in marseret sap." Her voice was as dull as her eyes, the words oozing off a thickened tongue.

Ildiko closed her eyes. If the arrowheads were dipped in marseret as Anhuset predicted, she'd be numb from her shoulders to her feet in moments, unable to move. Even if she weren't dead weight from the poison, she was far too heavy for Ildiko to lift and hoist onto the horse. They were doomed, stranded here while whatever surviving raiders lurked in the woods caught up to them.

A gust of hot air, thick with the green scent of grass, flooded her neck and the side of her face. She opened her eyes to find Anhuset's horse had ambled back to them, one liquid-dark eye trained on her as if to ask how long they planned to sit there. Ildiko might have laughed if she didn't so badly want to scream.

Anhuset's head lolled. "I can't feel my arms or legs."

A dog's triumphant howl followed her declaration and sent Ildiko's heart drumming in her chest. "Oh gods, more magefinders."

"Run." Anhuset's eyes gave a slow owl's blink. "They're scenting me, not you. Take the horse. Run," she repeated.

Ildiko sprang to her feet. "I'm not leaving you here." The glimmer of moonlit steel caught her eye, and she found the two sabers Anhuset had wielded against their attackers during the wild ride through the woods. They lay in the grass, one behind Anhuset, the other near her outstretched fingers. Blood, made black in silver light, streaked the blades.

Ildiko retrieved the one closest to her, surprised by its overall lightness in her hand and the weighted tilt toward the tip of the blade.

"Stupid human woman." Anhuset's words slurred together. "You'll die if you stay."

"Silence." Ildiko scowled but kept her eyes trained on the stretch of tree line from where the canine sounds originated. "Obviously the sap doesn't work on your disrespectful tongue."

Stupid or not, she had no intention of abandoning a helpless Anhuset on the cold ground to be torn apart by a pack of magefinders. The sword no longer felt light in her grasp, and she gripped it with both hands.

Her stomach plummeted to her feet when the first magefinder shot out of the tree line, a fur-clad lightning bolt built of long legs, glistening fangs, and eyes as yellow and fierce as any Kai's, but far more bestial. It was followed by another and then a third, and they loped across the clearing, their bays muted to snarls as they closed the distance between them and Ildiko.

"Bend your knees and swing as hard as you can." Anhuset's voice sounded far away in Ildiko's ears, but she did as the other bid and braced herself. Her lungs felt starved for air though she breathed harder than an exhausted horse. Rivulets of sweat streamed down her sides under her clothes and made her gore-sticky hands slippery on the sword grip. She forced herself not to flinch and close her eyes when the first dog leapt at her.

She screamed and swung just as a blurred dark line flew past her vision, followed by a meaty thunk. The dog's legs snapped together in midstride before it hit the ground and skidded to a stop, an arrow sunk deep in its neck. Another whine of air teased her ear before the second dog met a similar fate.

Ildiko pivoted in time to see a horse and armored rider gallop past her to take down the third hound with a sword.

"Highness, are you all right?"

Still clutching the sword, Ildiko turned toward the familiar voice. "Serovek?"

He strode toward her, lightly armored and carrying a bow. He'd been the one to kill two of the dogs, his soldier the third. His gaze assessed her for injuries, and he gave an approving nod at the sight of her clutching one of Anhuset's swords.

A half dozen more mounted Beladine warriors emerged from the trees across the clearing, one leading a riderless horse.

Anhuset's own mount whickered a greeting as they surrounded Ildiko and the fallen Kai woman.

Ildiko held onto the sword and refused to budge from Anhuset's side. The part of her brain that still functioned on reason assured her that if Serovek had ordered this attack, it wouldn't have failed. Still, her muscles quivered and her heart thundered as the Beladine lord drew closer.

He knelt before Anhuset who watched him with narrowed eyes gone from glowing gold to muddy yellow. He glanced at Ildiko. "We tried to reach you at the bridge. Too late. We killed the two handlers following the dogs, but expect more dogs, more raiders. You've crossed into my territory. They'll think themselves safe here. More fool them." He motioned to one of his men who dismounted and handed him an axe similar in size to the one she'd seen Brishen carry.

"What are you doing?" she asked.

He removed the blade guard. "We'll travel easier if I can cut down the arrow shafts sticking out of her ladyship here."

Poisoned and immobilized, Anhuset still managed enough movement to curl her fingers and take a weak swipe at Serovek. One claw caught a fold in his breeches near the knee and neatly split it open. "Don't touch me, Beladine pig," she mumbled.

Serovek sighed, and quicker than Ildiko could blink, snapped his knuckles against Anhuset's chin. Her head jerked before her eyes closed, and she went completely limp.

Ildiko gasped. "She'll kill you for that when she wakes up."

Serovek winked and took a flat rock one of his soldiers handed to him, along with a folded blanket. "No she won't. I'll tell her you did it."

He braced the blanket, with the stone on top, against her back. The arrow in her shoulder was lodged between two of the armor plates sewn to the gambeson. Ildiko flinched when Serovek brought the ax down on the shaft, shortening it to the length of a small spoon handle. Quick, efficient, and steady, he did the same with the arrow at her hip. The unconscious Anhuset jerked but didn't waken.

Serovek stroked her silver hair with a big hand. "Easy, my beauty. I'm done." He looked to Ildiko. "Can you control her mount?"

"Yes." The shock of facing certain, brutal death only to be rescued by the sudden appearance of Serovek and his men, left her lightheaded and unable to utter more than monosyllabic responses.

If the Beladine lord noticed, he didn't remark on it. "Good. Anhuset will ride with me." He scooped the Kai woman into his arms, his features darkening as he slowly lifted her. He staggered and exhaled a harsh breath. "Damn Kai," he said in a strained voice. "Heavier than a sack of wet bricks."

His reaction to lifting Anhuset confirmed what Ildiko had guessed. There was no possible way she could have moved her wounded companion or gotten her back on her horse.

Serovek made his way to the one horse with no rider. Bigger than the others, it snorted in protest and laid back its ears as its master mounted with his burden. Their party gathered supplies. One of the Beladine soldiers retrieved Anhuset's second sword where it lay in the grass and gently pried the other from Ildiko's stiff fingers. "Do you need help onto the gelding, Your Highness?"

She shook her head. She wasn't much good with blades, but she could at least swing into a saddle by herself.

Serovek eyed her as she rode up next to him. "Whose blood stains your hands? It isn't Anhuset's, and I see no wound on you."

"We were attacked in the woods. I stabbed one of them when he tried to pull me off the horse."

A flicker of amusement softened Serovek's somber face. "Soft Gauri noblewomen with hidden savagery." He kneed his horse forward. "I should visit Pricid one day."

Free from the forest's labyrinthine darkness, Ildiko had regained her sense of direction and a choking panic that blackened the edges of her vision. They were riding away from Saggara and help!

She trotted next up to Serovek and wheeled Anhuset's horse in front of his mount's to block their path. Serovek's horse snorted when his rider hauled back on the reins to keep from plowing into the other horse.

She ignored Serovek's scowl. "We have to go back to the bridge. Now. Help Brishen and the others! We can't just leave them there."

Serovek's expression softened. "That battle is long over by now, Highness. You need to trust me that what I'm doing will help Brishen." He pointed to an unseen path somewhere within the trees. "There's a hidden sanctuary not far from here, an old temple bound by magic to confuse the dogs. We'll stay there for now. I sent messengers to Saggara. If my guess is right, we'll have my men and more of the Kai here by morning." He gently adjusted the unconscious Anhuset in his arms. "Did you see what happened to the *herceges*?"

It was impossible to speak around the knot of tears lodged in her throat. Ildiko swallowed several times before answering. "No. He was in the thick of the fighting when I last saw him, and that was only a glimpse." For all she knew, the Kai would arrive, with one bearing the news that he or she carried Brishen's mortem light within them. The grim thought made it hard to breathe.

"Don't lose heart, Ildiko." Serovek abandoned his formality in an effort to comfort her. "They won't kill him. Not yet at least." His words did nothing to lessen her fear for Brishen.

The ruins Serovek led them to butted up against a gentle slope surrounded by trees. Ildiko had no sorcery of her own, but even she sensed the presence of power here. The Beladine mounts balked at moving closer. Accustomed to the thrum and whisper of magic that every Kai possessed, no matter how weak, Anhuset's gelding picked his way among the stones, unconcerned. The other horses soon followed.

Serovek motioned to the other riders, complicated hand signals that mystified Ildiko but that his soldiers understood. Three dismounted and melted into the shadows that ringed the temple's perimeter. The remaining three gathered up the horses and led them deeper into the ruin's sanctuary to shelter behind the ridges of broken half walls and copses of pillars. In the far distance a familiar howl rode the moonlight. Ildiko shuddered. Not again.

She followed Serovek who carried his unconscious burden through the low doorway of a tiny chapel within the temple ruin. The blackness inside hung thick enough to pour from a bottle, and the skitter and squeak of disturbed rats played on her ears. She leapt aside at the suspicious slither of something gliding along the floor near her foot.

"No light yet, Ildiko." Serovek's deep voice was more vibration than sound. "We wait."

They stood in the suffocating silence, listening as the rustle of leaves stirred up by running feet crackled nearby. Long sniffs and quiet growls joined them.

Ildiko clenched her teeth together and tried not to breathe. Her heartbeat drummed so loud in her head, she was certain their pursuers could hear her.

"Anything?" a voice called out in the Common tongue.

Another answered. "Fresh tracks, but it's a big party and the hooves are shod with shoes of Beladine making, not Kai."

"Patrol then. We're within Beladine territory, but it's High Salure. That bastard Pangion would as soon hang us with our own innards as wink at us. His troops won't be too friendly if they come across us. Let's go."

"Don't you want to search the temple?"

Ildiko felt Serovek tense even more beside her, and his soft breaths stopped altogether.

"Why bother? Look at the magefinders. They're just whining and sniffing about. Probably smelling badger or deer scat. The girl is riding with a Kai. If they were here, we'd know it by now. We'll keep going. I'm not too keen to cross a patrol anyway."

"I'm not keen on crossing that Kai. You saw what she did in the clearing. Took down all three hounds."

"Just means you need to be on your guard. Let's go."

The minutes of silence stretched into an eternity of stillness until a night bird's call sounded outside.

"They're gone." Serovek spoke in conversational volume. Shuffling noises accompanied his statement. "Outside, Highness, where we can see our hands in front of our faces."

The moonlight seemed like the noonday sun after her time in the chapel's sepulchral darkness. Ildiko blinked and caught sight of Serovek as he crouched to settle Anhuset gently on the ground. The Kai woman lay ominously still, but her chest rose and fell in easy rhythm, and Ildiko exhaled a relieved sigh.

Serovek rose. "Stay with her," he said. "I need to get supplies from my horse." He paused to give instructions to the two soldiers who stood guard nearby before disappearing into the foliage surrounding the temple grounds.

When he returned, he carried a small satchel, a blanket and a bottle. He dropped down next to Ildiko who was stroking Anhuset's hair from her face. He fished inside the satchel and retrieved an oddly shaped utensil. Diamond-shaped with a shallow lip folded inward on all sides, it vaguely resembled a spoon, though Ildiko couldn't figure out how such a design might adequately hold porridge and would never contain broth.

"What is that?" she asked.

Serovek took the knife belted at his side and cut away the laces on Anhuset's hauberk. "An arrow spoon. If our luck holds, I won't have to use it." He didn't expound further and split the stitching around the armored scales that were sewn to the gambeson and surrounded the shortened arrow shaft sticking out of Anhuset's shoulder.

He cut through the quilted gambeson next and the clothing underneath. He set the knife aside. "I'm going to lift her up. I need you to peel away the hauberk and clothes. Quick but gentle. Can you do it?"

She nodded, and the two set to work. Anhuset rested still in Serovek's embrace while Ildiko eased the hauberk, gambeson and shirt off her shoulders and away from the arrow shaft. Serovek laid the Kai woman onto her right side and bent for a closer look at the shoulder wound. "I think it's a bodkin tip. I won't know until I cut into her." Ildiko blanched, and Serovek's responding smile lacked all humor. "It's a mercy she's suffering through marseret poisoning. I'll have to work fast before it wears off."

He cut away Anhuset's trousers while Ildiko removed her boots. Naked in the cold air, her gray skin riddled with goose flesh, she shivered lightly. Ildiko covered her legs with the blanket for warmth and added her own cloak for protection.

Serovek pulled a small candle from his satchel and coaxed a flame from the wick using flint, steel and charcloth. He passed the candle to Ildiko. "I'm no Kai to be cutting into wounds in the dark, so hold that steady and don't let the flame die."

He doused the blade with the contents from the bottle he'd brought back with him. Smoke rose in tendrils from the blade. He glanced at Ildiko whose eyes had rounded at the sight. "Peleta's Tears. Good for drinking and keeps wounds from festering."

"You drink that?" She'd heard of Peleta's Tears. Named after the goddess of dragons, it laid low any who dared to taste its brew. Surely something that made metal smoke wasn't safe to imbibe.

"Sometimes. When I want to forget." Serovek positioned himself so that Anhuset lay recumbent between his knees, her chest pressed against one of his thighs while he braced her back with the other. He trickled more of the drink onto the wound.

Ildiko flinched, right along with the unconscious Anhuset. While the drink might smoke metal, it didn't burn the skin.

Serovek's legs flexed against his patient as he made incisions with the knife and widened the wound. Ildiko poured Peleta's Tears over his bloodied fingers as he felt for the arrowhead. Anhuset didn't move, but a small moan escaped her lips. Serovek's shoulders sagged in obvious relief. "Bodkin," he said. "Not broadhead. Bad enough but easier to remove."

Blood ran in thin rills down Anhuset's back, staining Serovek's breeches as he worked. The arrow shaft detached from the tip but not before he managed to extract the bodkin from the wound.

Ildiko gave up her overskirt to use as bandages. Serovek packed the wound with moss he pulled from his satchel and bound it with strips cut from the skirt. They repeated the process on Anhuset's hip. By the time they were done, her clawed fingers had begun to flex and relax against her palm, and dawn gilded the edges of the eastern facing trees with pink light.

"Will she be all right?" Ildiko tucked the blanket and cloak more closely around Anhuset. The shivering had stopped, but her breathing had turned more erratic.

Serovek stood and wiped away the perspiration on his brow with his forearm. "I think so. Kai are hard to kill."

"Have you killed them?"

His mouth quirked. "A few. We have our raiders; they have theirs. Your husband and I deal with both because they cross into each of our territories. It's just a matter of who gets to them first." He took a seat next to Ildiko, grabbed the bottle of Peleta's tears and tipped it to his lips. The first swallow made him gasp and shake like a wet dog but didn't stop him from taking a second swallow. He offered the bottle to Ildiko who shook her head, preferring not to torture her already queasy stomach even more. Serovek passed her a flask of water instead so she could rinse the blood from her hands.

"Why didn't the dogs sniff us out?" she asked.

Serovek placed the bottle of spirits between them and draped his arms over his knees. His gaze drifted to Anhuset's face and stayed. "They did, but their task was to hunt Kai, not humans. The sorcery lingering here confused them and made Anhuset hard to detect."

"Didn't their handlers know that such a thing might happen?"

He shrugged. "Only if they were familiar with this land or a Kai. This temple sits inside my borders, but it's Kai-built and once Kai-worshipped. Brishen told me about it a couple of years ago while we shared a bottle of Tears between us and commiserated on the vagaries of volatile mistresses." He winked at Ildiko.

Ildiko tried to smile at the idea of the two men crying on each other's shoulder over women, but her lips refused to obey. She couldn't get the image out of her mind of Brishen's set features when he thrust her at Anhuset and shouted for them to ride for the bridge. She'd seen death in that glowing gaze—his death.

She blinked to fight back the tears that suddenly blurred her vision. "How did you find me and Anhuset?"

Serovek tipped the bottle again before answering. "A rumor about the ambush reached High Salure. By the time I dispatched a rider to Saggara to warn the *herceges*, you were already at Halmatus township. We set out to meet you but were too late."

It did no good to dwell on what-ifs, but Ildiko couldn't help but think how their fate might have differed if they had waited one more day before leaving Saggara. "I wonder if this is the same pack that attacked us on the trade road after Brishen and I were married."

"Probably not. That attempt failed. Whoever is moving the pieces on this board doesn't want to fail twice. They've supplied this party with mage hounds to anyone or anything with magery, like the Kai. An expensive weapon and far outside the means of even the most successful raiders. I suspect half this group isn't even Beladine, so they're bringing in sell-swords with no allegiance except to the sacks of coins paid to them."

Ildiko recalled the brief exchange between Brishen and Anhuset when the night's darkness had exploded into blinding flashes of light. "They have a battle mage with them as well."

Serovek scowled. "That will be a problem when we retrieve your husband."

When they retrieved him, not if. His matter of fact reply gave her hope despite its dire prediction regarding the mage. "Do you really think Brishen's still alive?" She held on to hope that he was. Her husband was a formidable fighter, but who knew how many raiders they faced or the sorcery used against him and the other Kai by the mage.

Serovek held up one of the two arrowheads he'd extracted from Anhuset. Coated in dried blood, its dagger-like point bounced a stray beam of anemic sunlight off its tip. "These are marseret-tipped bodkins. If they wanted to kill Brishen—and you—right away, they would have used broadheads. The bodkins pierce armor and bring down horses, but a man shot with one can survive longer than if he were shot with a broadhead. Had it been the second, Anhuset would have bled out before she even fell from her horse."

He tossed the arrowhead aside. "I have no doubt that Brishen is alive and a prisoner. Your escape put a knot in their plans. They were in a better position to force either the Kai or the Gauri to renegotiate or break their alliance in order to save you. They only have one of you now, but that's enough to begin negotiations for his life with the Kai royal house of Khaskhem."

Ildiko almost burst into tears at that. Her hand trembled as she reached for Serovek's bottle of Peleta's Tears. The drink set fire to her tongue and throat and sent the tears pouring down her cheeks. Serovek snatched the bottle out of her hand and hid it behind his back.

She wiped her streaming eyes and gave a bitter laugh. "Then he's dead already. Neither of us is of any real worth to our families. The Kai throne is secured by Brishen's older brother and more sons than you can count on one hand. Brishen is a spare without value. Secmis will turn her back on him, and her husband will follow her lead."

Serovek looked beyond her into the ever-brightening tree line. "I've never met her and hope not to, but rumors abound. It's hard to believe that the Shadow Queen of Haradis birthed such a man as Brishen Khaskhem."

"It's hard to believe anything with a soul came out of that womb." In that moment Ildiko hated Secmis more than any person she'd ever known.

"Whoever in Belawat is paying these sell-swords doesn't know there's no love lost between them. So we have time. Not much.

A few days only but enough to find their hiding place and rescue your husband."

Ildiko twisted her tunic in her hands. "What can I do? Surely, there's something I can do." She hated the helplessness, the lack of martial skills. Common sense dictated that no one could have foreseen such circumstances for her, but the knowledge offered little comfort.

Serovek gained his feet and helped her rise as well. "There is, but I want Anhuset's opinion first. The effects of the marseret should fade, and she'll awaken soon."

"What about her wounds?"

He had kind eyes. A soft brown the color of roasted chestnut with flecks of gold radiating from the edges of the pupils, they shimmered with a steady humor. He was a good man, a brave one, and his attraction to Anhuset was palpable. "You should know by now the toughness of a Kai. Those wounds won't slow her down anymore than flea bites would." He patted Ildiko on the arm. "I'll bring you extra blankets. You can rest beside her."

"I can't sleep." There was no possible way she could sleep, not with Brishen out there somewhere, a hostage of Beladine mercenaries.

"Try," Serovek said. "I need you alert and sharp later."

She did as he requested and rolled into the blankets he gave her. She was asleep as soon as her eyes closed. It seemed like only a handful of moments before the sound of voices arguing in bast-Kai awakened her. Ildiko rubbed her scratchy eyes and squinted at the couple glaring at each other not far from where she lay alone. Anhuset, wrapped in a blanket tied at her good shoulder, was awake and arguing fiercely with Serovek.

"It's a sound idea," he said and crossed his arms.

Anhuset mimicked his actions, her features drawn into a scowl. "Until someone skewers her or puts a bolt in her."

"I saw her handle your horse. She's an adept rider. She can do this. If you want this to work, she needs to do this."

"Brishen sacrificed himself to save her. We risk making that sacrifice for naught."

Serovek blew out a frustrated breath. "Stop being so eager to kill him off. He isn't dead!" His body tensed as a furious Anhuset rounded on him, fangs bared.

Ildiko threw off her blankets and leapt to her feet. "Please," she said. The two forgot their fight and turned to her. "I'll do whatever you ask of me. Anything. I'm sorry I'm not a warrior. I wish I were."

Serovek gazed at her with an implacable expression. "We don't need another warrior, Highness. We need bait."

*****

The sun had burned away the last of the lingering morning fog. Ildiko reclined against one of the temple walls and tried not to gnaw her fingernails down to the quick with worry. Instead, she worked to repair the laces on Anhuset's gambeson and watched as the Kai woman paced back and forth with a hitched gait, her lips drawn back against her teeth as she glared at Serovek.

"This is taking too long," she snapped.

Seated cross-legged near Ildiko, he didn't bother to look up from his task of sharpening a knife on the whetting stone he held.

"It's taking as long as it needs to," he said calmly. "You might as well sit down before you wear a path in the stones."

No sooner had he finished the sentence than Anhuset went still, listening. "Horses," she said after a moment.

The scrape of blade on stone halted as Serovek joined her. "But no dogs," he said. A bird's whistle carried through the trees, and Serovek answered back with a similar whistle. He stood and sheathed the knife at his waist. "We've company, and it's friendly."

The temple ruin was soon filled with both Beladine and hooded Kai warriors and their horses. They split into two groups, the Kai to gather around Anhuset and Ildiko, the Beladine around Serovek. One of the Beladine bowed before Serovek.

"We think we know where the raiders are hiding. A honeycomb of caves no more than a league north of here."

Serovek's lip curled, contempt souring his words. "They're moving farther into my territory, thinking it safe."

One of the Kai addressed both Anhuset and Ildiko. "We recovered our dead on the other side of the ravine. Two fallen. The raiders fought only long to capture the *herceges* and flee."

Ildiko's shoulders sagged. She glanced at Serovek. "You were right."

He nodded. "Right now he's more valuable alive than dead. Now we just need to discover how many we'll face when we rescue him."

The soldier who gave the raiders whereabouts spoke up again. "We've captured one of them." He gestured with a nod over his shoulder when Serovek's eyebrows rose. "We broke up a raid on a lower holt just within our borders. They massacred the family steading there and stole the sheep and grain. We killed all but one and hanged them from the trees as a warning."

Ildiko closed her eyes. So much killing and over two people who were never supposed to matter.

The crowd parted as a Kai shoved a human to his knees before Serovek. An impromptu circle formed, caging in their captive. Filthy, lice-infested and splattered with blood, the man glared at Serovek before spying Ildiko who recoiled from his lascivious, black-tooth leer.

One of the Beladine grabbed his arm and shoved the dirty sleeve past his elbow, revealing a patterned marking tattooed in blue and green ink on his arm. "Clansman out of the Serpent's Teeth," the soldier said.

Serovek crouched before his prisoner. His voice was mild, almost friendly. All the hairs on Ildiko's nape rose in warning. "You've traveled a long way to butcher farmers for their grain and a few sheep. How many of you are hiding in the caves?"

The man's eyes slid away. "I don't know about any caves. We was just stealing because we was hungry."

"So the four of you made off with an entire herd of sheep and a full wagon of grain? You have big stomachs."

"Why do you care?" The raider thrust his shoulders back and his chin forward. His bloodshot eyes glittered. "They's just farmers."

Serovek's mild tone didn't change. "Because they were farmers under my protection, and now they're dead. I'll ask again. How many of you rats are hiding in those caves?"

The man clamped his lips together and refused to say anything more. He fell back on his haunches with a gasp when Anhuset lunged at him, claws curled.

"He'll talk for me," she snarled in bast-Kai.

Serovek checked her advance with one arm. "Patience," he said in the same tongue. "Here, I am the law, and he's broken it by murdering and stealing within my territory."

He turned to the captured raider and switched back to Common tongue. "You're far from home, and I know there are no Kai from where you hail, so let me enlighten you." The circle of Kai and Beladine tightened around them. Ildiko was unable to dredge up a drop of sympathy for the suddenly pale prisoner. Serovek cold smile would have frozen a candle flame. "A long time ago the Kai hunted humans for food. If you refuse to talk, I'm going to feed you to them. From what I know, they aren't concerned whether or not their meal is alive or dead when they start eating."

Were Ildiko not used to the toothy Kai after months of living amongst them, she would have fled in terror at the sight of so many fanged grins that flashed at the raider after Serovek's threat.

The man whimpered and promptly lost control of his bladder. The pungent odor of urine saturated the air. Words tumbled out of his mouth, so fast and stuttering that Serovek had to make him repeat himself several times over. By the time the interrogation ended, they all knew the number of enemies hiding in the caves, how many magefinders remained and which cave held Brishen.

Serovek stood and motioned with one hand. The raider was jerked to his feet. Ildiko gasped as the Beladine lord moved with breathtaking speed. A flash of hands, the brittle snap of bone and the dead raider dropped in a heap to the floor. In the time it took for Ildiko to inhale a breath, Serovek had broken the man's neck with one swift, practiced motion. She swayed and clutched Anhuset's arm, overtaken by dizziness and a distinct buzzing in her ears.

The Kai woman pressed a supporting hand to her back and leaned to whisper in her ear. "Strength, *Hercegesé*. Brishen needs you."

The words worked a magic no sorcerer could mimic. The dizziness evaporated, and Ildiko's back stiffened. She refused to look at the still body crumpled at Serovek's feet, but she no longer wanted to faint.

The charming, jocular man she'd first met at High Salure and danced with at Saggara was gone. The ruthless Beladine marcher lord stood in his place, judge and executioner of any who committed crimes within his borders. He nudged the dead man with his foot. "Take him back to the holt and hang him in the trees with the others. If they haven't soiled their clothes too badly, strip them. We need their garb."

Ildiko trusted whatever plan he had in mind, but the thought of wearing a dead man's clothes made her skin crawl. "What will we do now?"

The wolfish smile he gave her made her glad they were on the same side of this particular conflict. "Play raider," he said. "And you don't even need to ride a horse."

*****

"Are the knots too tight?" Anhuset tugged on the strips of cloth that bound Ildiko's hands together.

Ildiko shook her head. "No. I can twist out of them quickly if necessary."

They stood within the concealment of heavy underbrush and the overcast shadow of rocky outcropping. Within the shelter of the forest, Kai and Beladine waited together as Ildiko prepared to act as the bait Serovek needed.

Her clothes were ripped and filthy, her hair a wild mat of tangles, her face smudged with dirt and streaks of dried blood. Anhuset strengthened the look by shredding random spots of Ildiko's tunic. "I still don't think this is the best idea."

Ildiko shrugged. "I think Lord Pangion is right. If we want to be sure of entering the right cave, I'm the best thing to draw them out."

"Brishen will never forgive me if you die during my watch." Anhuset tied one of her daggers to the sash encircling Ildiko's waist.

The Kai woman's skin was clammy under Ildiko's fingertips, hints of fever in the darkened flush on her cheekbones. "I think he would forgive you anything, sha-Anhuset," she said softly. "Besides, I have no intention of dying today."

The other woman stared at her in silence for several moments. "I once thought you weak. I was wrong." She finished strapping the dagger in place. "Are you afraid?"

Ildiko nodded. "Terrified."

"Good. You'll stay alert that way."

Serovek joined them, accompanied by one of his men dressed in the clothes of one of the dead mercenaries. "Ready?"

Ildiko exhaled a shaky breath. "As much as I can be."

Their plan was simple. They'd ascertain the captive raider hadn't lied about his information by luring some of his compatriots out of the caves. Serovek's man, acting as one of them, would lead her before them in full view, the captive Gauri woman they so eagerly sought. That was all they needed from her. Every Beladine soldier would pair up with a Kai—one to fight in the light, one in the dark, neither helpless as long as the other covered their backs. They'd rush the caves, fight their way in and back out again, hopefully with a living Brishen in tow.

Twilight engulfed the sky by the time a stumbling, weeping Ildiko followed her false captor as he jerked her by a lead rope across the clearing toward the caves. Her stomach did somersaults under her ribs, and she peered through the screen of her ragged hair at the cave openings that seemed to watch them from eyeless sockets.

She stubbed her toe against a jut of rocks hidden within ankle-high wisps of yellow grass and fell to her knees. The soldier leading her slackened the line. "Highness?" he whispered.

"Pull the rope," she whispered back. "Call me names." If they heard his earlier question, the masquerade was finished.

The soldier yanked hard on the rope, dragging her across the ground. She yelped as gravel abraded the exposed skin of her side and the rope welted her wrists. "Get up, bitch," he snapped at her. "I don't have all night."

She stumbled to her feet, weaving drunkenly at the end of her tether. A flutter of movement caught her eye. Two figures emerged from one of the smaller cave openings, cautious in their approach, until her "captor" waved and raised the rope. "I caught her," he called out in a triumphant voice. Exultant whoops answered, and the two figures became a pair of bedraggled raiders who raced toward him.

Their celebration was short-lived. The ambush they'd earlier set upon the Kai was turned on them. Beladine and Kai warriors swarmed from the forest and rushed the cave opening. Ildiko caught only glimpses of Serovek and Anhuset as they plunged into the cave's darkness before a Kai warrior lifted her off her feet and fled with her into the forest.

This time she didn't struggle as she had with Anhuset. She waited, free of her bonds, amidst a circle of tense, heavily armed guards and watched the cave with eyes that watered because she was too afraid to blink.

Light flashes illuminated the darkness in brief bursts. The ring of metal on metal mingled with shouts and cries of pain. Her heart paused in its thunderous beating when the noise died, and all she heard were the soft hoots of howls and the rustle of rodents hiding in the leaves.

It was full dark, and the moon planished the landscape in silver armor. Ildiko laced her fingers together and prayed to gods she hoped would be merciful this night. Her prayer was answered when Serovek's and Anhuset's warriors spilled out of the cave. She cried out, feet flying across the brittle grass toward the war party.

Anhuset emerged from their midst to catch Ildiko about the waist and spin her around. "We have him, *Hercegesé*," she said in a tight voice.

Ildiko gripped the other woman's arms. "Where is he?"

"Ildiko, he's been tortured."

Her knees gave, and she sagged in Anhuset's arms. Shock quickly gave way to rage. "I want to see him. Now," she said.

Anhuset nodded and guided her through the flow of soldiers until they reached a small knot gathered near the cave entrance. Serovek stood when he caught sight of her. He blocked her path and her view.

"Do you have a strong stomach?" he asked. He looked even more severe than when he'd snapped the raider's neck. Blood dripped off the sword he held, and his dark eyes glittered hard as diamonds in the moonlight.

"Get out of my way, Lord Pangion," she snapped. He stepped aside, and she brushed past him to fall to her knees beside the prone figure in the grass.

Brishen lay before her, quiet and still. At least she thought it was him. A scream swelled in her chest, roiled into her throat, and seeped through her clenched teeth, an inhuman cry of anguish.

Anhuset hadn't lied, but she hadn't expounded either. Brishen's face, elegant, regal, and sublime by Kai standards, was swollen beyond recognition, mottled with bruises and cuts and washed in blood. It streaked his cheeks in cracked black ribbons that ran from his hairline to his chin. His mouth had been split multiple times, and the high bridge of his nose was crooked and swelled to twice its width. His right eye had swollen shut, and where his left eye should have been; only a sunken eyelid over an empty socket remained.

She clapped a hand over her mouth but refused to close her eyes. Bruises covered every part of his body she could see, and her gaze froze on his hands. They hadn't stopped with his eye. Ildiko traced a delicate line over the back of his left hand. The lethal claws that could split a man from gullet to navel yet tease her skin with the lightest touch, were ripped out, leaving behind only bloody, mangled nail beds. His right hand matched his left.

Ildiko stroked the air just above his head with a trembling hand, afraid to touch him, afraid his beaten, brutalized body would disintegrate before her eyes. She didn't know what she wanted to do more—scream her anguish or shriek her rage. "My poor love," she whispered. "Why?"

Serovek spoke behind her. "We think the leader got away. We slaughtered all but a half dozen who say they can tell us who hired them in exchange for mercy. What do you wish to do, Highness?"

Ildiko stared at Brishen, at the shallow rise and fall of his chest as he breathed gurgling breaths. He stank of blood and agony. The wind lifted a strand of his hair, and she caught it between two fingers. It stuck to her skin, matted with gore. She didn't care who hired animals to unleash their savagery.

"Kill them," she said in a flat voice. "Kill them all."

*****

When they returned to Saggara, she sequestered herself in Brishen's chamber and didn't leave for four days. She bathed there, ate there, and dressed there. Except for brief dozing spells, she didn't sleep there.

The small troop of healers who tended her husband came and went, each time assuring her that time, rest, and regular doses of marseret tisane would see him through his ordeal. Ildiko found it ironic that the poison sap used to bring Anhuset low served a more merciful purpose in staving off Brishen's pain.

He slept peacefully, his bandaged hands resting across his stomach. More bandages covered the arrow wounds in his shoulder and legs. Ildiko sat for hours in a chair next to the bed, content to watch him. The swelling had slowly receded, and the blood and dirt were gone. His right eyelid twitched as he slept. The left she couldn't see. White cloth swathed that side of his face, hiding the deep cut that ran from below his lower lashes to the top curve of his cheekbone, testament to the brutality used when his captors cut out his eye.

Delirium didn't plague him, and he drank the tisanes the healers coaxed on him without waking. Ildiko read to him sometimes and ventured a song or two before her voice warbled too much to continue. Anhuset often visited, updating him on the fortress's daily activities as if he sat before her, awake and demanding a status.

She didn't stay long. Ildiko always knew when Anhuset was about to bolt from the chamber. Her hands flexed on her sword pommel as if she wanted nothing more than to kill Brishen's torturers a second time. Ildiko knew exactly how she felt.

"You'll send for me as soon as he wakes?" The same question each time before Anhuset escaped.

"Of course," Ildiko promised each time she asked.

No longer afraid to touch him, she caressed the unbandaged side of Brishen's face. Ildiko had once admired him, naked and glorious on his bed within a corona of golden sunlight, and thought him invulnerable. How terribly wrong she had been.

"This should never have happened, Brishen." The inevitable, annoying tears threatened, and she blinked hard to force them back. "We were unimportant, you and I. We weren't supposed to mean anything to anyone."

A slow, deep sigh escaped his lips, and his right eyelid opened, revealing a glowing, lamplight gaze. Brishen's voice was hoarse from disuse but still clear. "Woman of day," he said slowly. "You mean everything to me."

No amount of blinking this time held back Ildiko's tears. They streamed down her cheeks to drip off her chin and onto Brishen's shoulder. "Prince of night," she said in a watery voice that echoed another moment when she'd greeted him with the same words. "You've come back to me."

CHAPTER TWENTY-TWO

B rishen was a man who chose to see the good that came of any situation. He had yet to find it with the loss of his eye, but he had discovered it with the loss of his claws. While his recollection of his torture remained murky, his fingers still throbbed sometimes, as if the memory of a terrible pain had imbedded itself in his flesh. The nailbeds had healed over the months, the claws slowly growing across the exposed skin. They were still short—well below the quick—but lengthening and hardening every day. He'd have a full set of scythes on both hands within a year.

For now though, he took advantage of his disadvantage by drawing invisible murals across his wife's naked back and buttocks with his sensitive fingertips.

She lay on her stomach in his bed—their bed now—her head resting on her folded arms, her face partially shielded from his gaze by locks of red hair. He lay recumbent beside her, sketching looping designs along the graceful indention of her spine, down to the pair of dimples that decorated her lower back. Her skin pebbled under his touch, and a patch of muscle contracted involuntarily as his fingers glided over her body.

It was a sensual pleasure to touch her this way, a fine thing that sprang unexpectedly from brutality. She was in no danger of being scratched or lacerated, and Brishen had discovered that

273

fingers with short nails could do things that ones with claws could not. Things that made Ildiko writhe in his arms and leave claw marks of her own on his shoulders. If he didn't depend on the martial edge his claws gave him, Brishen would keep his short for that reason alone.

Ildiko pushed her hair away to look at him.

"What?" he asked. He'd stopped searching for revulsion in her gaze weeks ago. There was none to be found. Except for the sympathetic kisses she placed on his eyebrow and the flattened lid over his empty eye socket, she remained untroubled by his mutilated visage.

She watched him now with an expression softened by post-coital languor. "I think I fell in love with you during our wedding."

Her statement sent a rush of euphoria through Brishen that left him lightheaded. His hand flattened on her back before sliding up between her shoulder blades to bury itself in her hair. Her every action, every laugh, every caress spoke of her great affection for him, but this was the first time she said she loved him. An upbringing in the Kai court had taught him to control his emotions. A good thing too or he would snatch his wife into a hard embrace and accidently break every bone in her body.

He settled for hooking an arm under her side and dragging her closer to him. "It took you that long?" he teased. "You are difficult to win. I tried very hard during our first meeting in the gardens."

Ildiko sputtered. Her leg slid between his knees, riding higher to rest against his thigh. "Calling me a hag is not the best courtship gesture."

"As I recall, you threatened to bash my skull in because of my appearance. And that was when I was magnificent to behold." He wiggled his eyebrows at her.

His smile faded when she didn't return it. She traced the bony ridge of his cheekbone, fissured by scars inflicted by a knife. "They took your eye, Brishen," she said. "Not your character. You're still magnificent."

His control only went so far. Brishen groaned and rolled to his back, taking Ildiko with him. It was a long hour later before he peeled himself out of his wife's embrace and kicked the blankets away from them both.

Ildiko grabbed for the closest sheet. "What are you doing?" Her skin glowed, washed a shade of pink similar to the bitter mollusk. Brishen curled his clawless hands into fists to keep from caressing her and losing yet another hour.

He sat up and swung his legs to the floor. "My mother will be here soon."

Ildiko flopped back onto her pillow with a groan. "Don't remind me. I've already warned Sinhue to check the bedding and clothes chests in both rooms once she's gone."

He hadn't been any more thrilled than Ildiko when a messenger from Haradis had arrived a week earlier to warn them of Secmis's visit. "At least she is only here for two nights."

"Those will be the longest two nights of our lives."

He couldn't agree more.

They helped each other dress in the quiet of the chamber. The halls below them were a hornet's nest of frantic activity in preparation for the queen's visit. Brishen had wanted to tell his servants to leave Saggara and visit family, friends, anyone for a few days. Secmis could fend for herself. Ildiko had met that suggestion with an expression of nostril-flaring indignation.

"I will not be known as a rude, unwelcoming hostess," she said in a voice that Anhuset told him later sounded exactly like when she ordered his captors' executions.

Brishen had hidden his smile and backed quickly away from the idea.

He paused in lacing his tunic when Ildiko handed him the eye patch he wore outside their bedroom. "I thought you didn't like it when I wore this."

The first time he'd tied it on, Ildiko had stepped back, alarmed. "It makes you look vicious," she said with a scowl.

He still hadn't yet figured out how a mouth full of fangs or claw-tipped hands didn't bother her anymore, but a harmless eyepatch did. But he wished to please her and wore it only if they hosted guests or visited the villages and townships.

She shrugged. "This is your mother. She'll approve."

While Brishen had acceded to Ildiko's wishes of tearing the fortress apart and putting it back together again for the queen's visit, he refused to plan a greeting of great fanfare when she arrived. If he didn't think Secmis would try and take his other eye, he'd make her sleep in the stables. Instead, his soldiers lined up in two parallel rows and saluted the queen with their swords as she rode through the gates with a modest entourage.

Brishen waited at the end, Ildiko on one side of him, Anhuset on the other. His cousin spoke under her breath. "If you order a dance and command me to attend, I will gut you in your sleep."

Ildiko's muffled laughter lightened the moment, and Brishen quirked a smile at Anhuset. "No worries. If I didn't have to feed her, I wouldn't. Dancing would just invite her to stay longer."

The visit was as excruciating as Ildiko predicted, but his unflappable wife persevered under Secmis's contemptuous scrutiny and critical remarks. In fact, she mostly ignored the queen, except when spoken to or to ask if her accommodations were comfortable. Her focus centered on Brishen who counted the minutes until his mother finally left Saggara and left them in peace.

He didn't ask her if the Beladine had tried to negotiate his release with her by forcing an annulment of his marriage. And Secmis remained silent on the matter as well. Her curious gaze took in his altered features and the way he'd balance a pitcher of wine against his glass before pouring.

The loss of his eye was not without consequence. He was completely blind on his left side. No flickers of movement or changing shades of light. The first fortnight had been the most frustrating. He couldn't get out of the way of his own nose. It filled his vision, large as a crane's beak. That had faded over time, but he still struggled with a sense of depth.

Walking up stairs presented a challenge with the first step, but the angle of his shadow aided him in sensing the changing depth and height of the steps. Walking down was another matter. His shadow fell straight in front of him, and the steps were nothing more than a smooth, sloping descent to his compromised vision. He still kept one hand on the wall until he adjusted to the regularity of the treads' rise and fall.

He refused to be an invalid, and as soon as the healers pronounced him well enough to leave his bed, he'd donned light armor and joined Anhuset in the practice arena. His cousin treated his appearance as nothing out of the ordinary. Her patience was long and her sympathy non-existent as she helped him to relearn the skills of combat as a one-eyed fighter.

Brishen mentioned none of this to Secmis. He had no doubt she'd laughed when the Beladine had presented their threat to her. Her younger son's death was of little importance, his survival and recuperation even less so.

Patience finally worn away by Secmis's constant haranguing, Ildiko had excused herself well before dawn and fled for the sanctuary of their chamber. Brishen had let her go with a polite nod and cool bow. If Secmis even sensed his affection for Ildiko, she'd make things difficult for them.

Secmis tapped a claw on the rim of her goblet and watched Ildiko disappear into the stairwell. She turned to Brishen. "So, has she taken your Beladine neighbor as her lover yet?"

He had wondered how long it would take for her to fire the first volley. "No."

She arched a doubtful eyebrow. "Are you sure? I'm told he is handsome to human women and even to some of the Kai. And of course he has both of his eyes."

Second volley, this time dipped in malice. "I'm sure."

Secmis frowned at his lack of reaction to her insults. "You haven't yet asked me why I'm here."

Brishen shrugged. "Saggara is part of your kingdom. I'm its caretaker. I assume you're acting as the king's emissary." Whatever reason for the visit, it wasn't good. He just had to wait until she revealed her purpose and brace for whatever impact it had.

She stretched in her chair, reminding him of a great cat—lithe, hungry, and ready to disembowel anything that moved. "Maybe I just wish to visit my younger son."

He gulped down a swallow of wine to prevent breaking into guffaws.

Secmis continued their one-sided conversation. "Your claws are growing back. You don't seem any worse for your ordeal— other than the scar and being half blind." She spoke as if he'd taken a walk through the woods and stubbed his toe. "I bear strong children," she said.

When you're not snapping their necks, he thought but stayed silent.

Her self-satisfied smile changed, becoming something that sent a crawling chill down his back. It took everything within him not to shrink away or leap from his seat when she stroked his forearm in a slow caress. "It's a shame you're my son," she purred. "You would have made a magnificent consort."

A surge of bile burned up his throat. Brishen grabbed for the pitcher, braced it against his goblet and poured wine until it touched the brim. He emptied the cup in two swallows. "Why have you come, Your Majesty?" Never before had he struggled so hard not to reveal his loathing for the woman who bore him.

Her knowing gaze warned he might not be as stoic as he hoped. She reached into a pocket of her tunic and brought out a small decorative box. She placed it on the table and slid it toward him. He squelched the urge to push it back.

"I came to bring you this. It's yours." The queen gave a nonchalant shrug. "I have no idea why it was sent to me. It isn't as if I would do anything with it." She stood, and he scrambled to stand with her and bow. "You can wait to open it when your wife is with you."

She swept around the table and signaled to the two handmaidens who hovered nearby, ready to serve her every whim. "I'm not staying a second night," she announced. "Saggara lacks the most basic creature comforts. Uncomfortable beds, boring food and even duller company. No need to accompany me to the gates. I'll leave sooner without you and a dirty troop of soldiers following after me. I'll tell your father you send your regards."

Two hours later, Brishen breathed a sigh of relief as Secmis and company disappeared into the horizon. The journey would be hard-going for the riders. The queen would shelter in a wagon shielded from the sun by dark curtains. Her escort would have to ride hooded and squinting for several hours before they found relief. He didn't envy them.

He found Ildiko still dressed in her finery and standing at one of the windows in their room. She turned to greet him with a smile. "She chose not to stay? Thank the gods!" She literally skipped into his welcoming arms. "I will never believe you are that woman's son, bred and born."

Unfortunately he was, but he'd succeeded in his endeavor to be nothing like her when others expressed their disbelief that they were in any way related. His skin crawled again at the memory of her words. *"Too bad you're my son. You would have made a magnificent consort."*

"I've called for a bath," he said. "I need a good scrubbing. Will you join me?"

Ildiko nodded eagerly and spied the box he held. "What is that?"

"She said she came here to bring me this."

Ildiko backed away from him. "Maybe you should don your armor before you open it."

He had a notion of what might be inside. Secmis's idea of humor was usually someone else's idea of horror. "I'll open it later."

Unfortunately, his wife's curiosity couldn't be quelled. "Won't you let me see?"

He sighed. "I don't think it will be pleasant, Ildiko."

She frowned at him. "Then you should definitely not open it alone."

She had stood beside him through events far grimmer than opening a gift from Secmis and held her own. She'd do so again.

Ildiko did wobble when Brishen opened the lid to reveal the box's contents, and she clutched his arm. "That bitch," she breathed. "That vile, horrible bitch. She came all this way to sink a knife."

Brishen had guessed correctly and didn't flinch when he saw what lay inside Secmis's gift box. His eye, shriveled to a withered, ocherous orb, rolled back and forth inside the box like the carved pebble in a child's game of Heckle Stones. He put the lid back on the box and threw the entire thing into the fire built in the hearth. Flames devoured the container, shooting hungry sparks against the grate.

"She must have been bored in Haradis."

Ildiko scowled at him, her tone waspish. "How can you not be angry? I want to punch her in her smirking face." She fisted her left hand and smacked the palm of her right hand with a hard thwack.

Brishen turned her so that she fully faced him. The silk sleeves of her shirt rode smooth under his hands as he stroked her arms in a soothing gesture. "Because she's predictable. She has yet to do anything I didn't expect."

Tears turned Ildiko's eyes glossy, and she blinked hard. "She would have let you die. Perched on that throne like some great bloated spider and let them kill you!"

"Remember, wife. I'm the spare of no value."

She lunged for him and wrapped her arms around his waist. Her soft breasts pressed against his chest as she hugged him as hard as she could. "You are of great value to me," she said into his tunic. She raised her head, her eyes narrowed and still teary. "I wish I could kill them again, Brishen. I wish I could kill her."

He threaded her hair through his clawless fingers before bending to kiss her forehead. "I love you, my blood-thirsty hag."

Ildiko sniffed and offered him a watery smile. "That's a good thing, because you'll have to suffer through dinner later. I thought your mother would be here another night, so I ordered potatoes to be served."

Brishen threw back his head and laughed. He lifted Ildiko off her feet to spin her around.

She was breathless when he put her down and managed to wiggle out of his embrace with a dizzy stumble. "I have something for you as well," she said. "And it isn't a body part." She retrieved a velvet pouch from the chest at the end of their bed and handed it to him. "The jeweler from Halmatus township delivered it along with my necklace while you were healing. I'd forgotten about it until Sinhue and I were checking the wardrobes for hidden scarpatine."

Brishen opened the satchel and upended its contents into his palm. His breath caught at the sight of a cabochon half the size to the one Ildiko's mother had given her. This one was cut from citrine quartz and as bright as a Kai's gaze at midnight. A spark of deeper orange pulsed within the stone's depths. A recolligere. Ildiko had managed to find a memory jewel. He glanced at her. "How did he come by one of these?"

Ildiko shrugged. "He said they were rare."

"They are." If this stone held what he thought it did, he was going to revisit Halmatus township and the visit wouldn't be friendly. "Ildiko, the spell used to make these work is dangerous, unpredictable. You didn't..." She nodded, confirming his fear. "I'm going to kill that jeweler."

Ildiko huffed. "It was perfectly safe for me. Memory madness only affects the Kai, and I'm not Kai. Neither one of us thought the spell would work. I think he was as surprised as I was that it did."

Her fingers drifted over his, over the stone, hesitant, unsure. Her strange eyes pleaded with him to accept her gift. "If I die before you, I have no mortem light for you to carry to Emlek. That recolligere holds one of my memories. You can take that instead—a paler light."

She made him strong; she made him weak, and in that moment, she nearly put him on his knees. Brishen gathered her into his embrace, the recolligere clutched in his hand. He kissed her cheeks, her temples, the corners of her eyes wet with tears. When he reached her mouth, he paused. "Not a paler light," he said. "A radiant one, from a woman in whose presence I will never be blind."

"Love me," she whispered against his lips.

"Always."

EPILOGUE

In chambers far below the public rooms of the royal palace, Queen Secmis cut the heart out of her latest lover's dead body and dropped it into a pewter basin

Blood still pumped in sluggish streams from the severed arteries to half submerge the heart in a crimson pool. Secmis dipped her fingers into the bowl and sketched arcane symbols on the body stretched across the gore-soaked bed. She spoke words, neither bast-Kai nor Common, but ones that lacerated her tongue with every syllable uttered. The flavors of iron and salt filled her mouth and she spat between sentences so as not to choke on her own blood.

The Kai's butchered body twitched and began to flail while the exposed lungs did the impossible and bloated with air.

It was working. Her incantation was working! So many years, so many failed consecratives. Finally! She laughed, a gleeful sound as sweet as a child's, as mad as a demon's.

No longer would she just be queen of a fading race. She would rule all kingdoms, all people—Kai and human. And she would do so for thousands of years. Undying, never aging, all-powerful. A Night Queen instead of the weaker Shadow one.

The power she invoked had slept for longer than even the memories of the oldest mortem lights in Emlek. The spell to awaken it had killed more than its share of mages. It required blood and fear, memory and innocence. Secmis thought she held the final ingredient when she'd birthed a daughter—a child born, not made, deformed and pushed from her womb.

She growled even as she drew more bloody symbols on the thrashing body. Secmis never discovered who had taken the infant she'd marked for this ceremony, but she suspected.

Brishen had been a cheerful, congenial child. He did as he was told, never rebelled or shown any ambition to replace his brother as heir. Secmis had noted his character and promptly forgotten him. Only when he'd grown older had she caught hints of a hidden strength, an implacable will and a cold, reptilian hatred that flickered in his eyes any time she met his gaze.

His response to his new sister's unexpected death had been a shrug before he resumed his mock battle with Anhuset through the palace corridors. He'd given Secmis a wide, frightened stare when she'd raged about the infant's disappearance and yawned through the memorial they held for her.

Still, Secmis always wondered. Her younger son was far more layered, far more complex than she gave him credit for, and far more intelligent than the pliable heir apparent. He had cheerfully married that repulsive Gauri girl and gone about the business of settling her at Saggara without complaint. He hadn't confronted Secmis about the scarpatine in his wife's bedroom, preferring instead to pack up and leave. He'd outmaneuvered her by obtaining Djedor's permission first.

His was a quiet rebellion of strategy, manipulation and an unruffled demeanor. Only that glimmer of loathing in his gaze every time he looked at Secmis gave him away. When a Beladine messenger carrying demands for negotiation of his release handed her proof of his capture, she'd stared into that mangled eye and seen the expression stamped there in the flat, yellow gaze.

His torture had not broken him. She'd seen it herself. Scarred and half blind, Brishen still ruled Saggara with a firm hand and commanded both the respect and fierce loyalty of his followers. Secmis hadn't lied when she told him he would have made a magnificent consort. But only if they shared power, and Secmis was through with sharing power.

She completed the last of the spell. The dead Kai, a lesser ambassador of the royal court, stilled beneath her hands. His mouth was still warm as she pressed her lips to his and exhaled. Oily black smoke poured from her mouth into his before swirling out through his nostrils. His lungs expanded, contracted and repeated the process.

Secmis stepped away as the dead sat up. "Speak the words," she commanded.

The speech uttered was none ever spoken by the living and desecrated the dead who did. A wet coldness settled in the chamber as the dead man recited unintelligible words that tore jagged wounds into his skin and wrenched cracks in the walls and ceiling.

One crack widened to a gaping splice of darkness even thicker than what already existed in the chamber. It spilled out of the crack, thick as lamp oil and reeking of a charnel house. Secmis laughed and clapped her hands as the viscous black oozed up the walls and across the floor, spawning writhing silhouettes with crimson gazes. She'd done it! Rent the veil between worlds and brought forth an unconquerable legion bound to her commands.

"To me," she ordered, spreading her arms wide.

They came to her as she commanded but not as she hoped. One slippery shadow twined around her and struck with a gaping maw. Secmis yelped, suffocating in the thick sludge as the entity forced its way down her throat. She clawed the air and tried to scream. More of the sinuous shapes wrapped around her, seeking gaps in her clothing, every entrance to her body until she was nothing more than a choking, dancing puppet slammed one way and then another as the shadows shrieked and laughed and cavorted.

They fell silent for a moment, unfurling and creeping away from the grotesque jumble of bones and bloody flesh that had once been a queen renowned for her beauty and feared for her power. The shapes whispered among themselves, adding sibilant voices to the voice of the dead man with no heart who still incanted the words of a poisoned language.

The crack in the wall widened, spilling more of the demonic phantasms into the chamber. They eddied around the dead Kai, undulated across the floor and crawled around the door, seeping through the cracks between wall and frame.

The dead Kai spoke on, even when the first screams of the living resonated through the stones.

-End-

In a bid for more power, the Shadow Queen of Haradis has unleashed a malignant force into the world. Her son Brishen, younger prince of the Kai royal house, suddenly finds himself ruler of a kingdom blighted by a diseased darkness and on the brink of war. His human wife Ildiko must decide if she will give up the man she loves in order to secure his throne.

Three enemy kingdoms must unite to save each other, and a one-eyed, reluctant king must raise an army of the dead to defeat an army of the damned.

A tale of alliance and sacrifice.

EIDOLON

Coming Soon

ABOUT THE AUTHOR

Grace Draven is a fan of fantasy worlds, romance, and the anti-hero. Storytelling has been a long-standing passion of hers and a perfect excuse for not doing the laundry. She lives in Texas with her husband, three kids and big, doofus dog. You can check out her latest projects at http://gracedraven.com.